WICKED WEAVES

WICKED WEAVES

JOYCE AND JIM LAVENE

THORNDIKE
CHIVERS

This Large Print edition is published by Thorndike Press, Waterville, Maine, USA and by BBC Audiobooks Ltd, Bath, England.

Thorndike Press, a part of Gale, Cengage Learning.

A Renaissance Faire Mystery.

The text of this Large Print edition is unabridged.

Other aspects of the book may vary from the original edition.

Set in 16 pt. Plantin.

Printed on permanent paper.

LIBRARY OF CONGRESS CATALOGING-IN-PUBLICATION DATA

Lavene, Joyce.
    Wicked weaves / by Joyce and Jim Lavene. — Large print ed.
      p. cm. — (Thorndike Press large print mystery)
    (Renaissance Faire mystery series ; 1)
    Originally published: New York : Berkley, 2008.
    ISBN-13: 978-1-4104-1509-7 (alk. paper)
    ISBN-10: 1-4104-1509-0 (alk. paper)
    1. Craft festivals—Fiction. 2. Weaving—Fiction. 3. Myrtle
Beach (S.C.)—Fiction. 4. Large type books. I. Lavene, James.
II. Title.
PS3562.A8479W53 2009
813'.54—dc22
                                     2008056116

BRITISH LIBRARY CATALOGUING-IN-PUBLICATION DATA AVAILABLE

Published in 2009 in the U.S. by arrangement with The Berkley Publishing Group, a member of Penguin Group (USA) Inc.
Published in 2009 in the U.K. by arrangement with The Berkley Publishing Group, a member of Penguin Group (USA) Inc.
U.K. Hardcover: 978 1 408 44148 0 (Chivers Large Print)
U.K. Softcover: 978 1 408 44149 7 (Camden Large Print)

Printed in the United States of America
1 2 3 4 5 6 7 13 12 11 10 09

We would like to dedicate this book and the Renaissance Faire Mysteries to Sandy Harding, our editor at Berkley, who makes us laugh and is the best listener in the world, and to Jacky Sach, our agent, who is always encouraging, even when our ideas are crazy. It is a pleasure working with both of you. You guys are the best!

ONE

"We believe he is dead, faithful squire," Queen Olivia pronounced in grand, dramatic fashion. "The tournament belongs to our favorite, Sir Reginald."

"You are right as always, Your Majesty." The master-at-arms used one foot to push the black knight's head down when he tried to stand after being forced from his horse during the joust.

The crowd on Sir Reginald's side of the field roared its approval. The other side booed, of course. This *was* Renaissance Faire Village, after all, a faithful replica of an English Renaissance town where one could expect to find fairies flitting about, William Shakespeare creating odes, and strong knights competing in rugged jousts. Or so the flyers from the parent company, which owned three other villages, said.

"Sir Reginald," the queen trilled as the handsome knight kissed her hand, "you truly know the meaning of a good knight kiss."

The crowd laughed at the queen's double entendre. I waited impatiently at the side of the hay-covered dirt field, flipping a swath of sweaty brown hair from my forehead. Late June wasn't the best time to dress in Renaissance costumes, especially in Myrtle Beach, South Carolina, but that was part of the show.

No one in the crowd paid any attention as I bent down to help the black knight, aka my brother Tony, to his feet. They were all watching Sir Reginald depart the jousting field, accompanied by the queen and her court. Queen Olivia was in a flirtatious mood, bending close to her favorite and slapping her fan at one of her ladies-in-waiting when she came too near. Considering the king already knew about the queen's recent brief affair with Sir Reginald and the fact that the lady-in-question was actually the handsome knight's wife, I knew there were fireworks to come.

It wasn't unusual. Fortunately, it was difficult for the crowd to tell the difference between what was real and what was acting. They were generally dazzled by the actors, who came from high school and college drama departments across the state to keep up with crowds during the summer months when visitor traffic was at its height.

Last year, Queen Olivia punched King Harold so hard he fell off the royal dais. The crowd laughed, not realizing Livy had actually caught Harry fondling one of the flower ladies who walked through the Village selling her wares . . . of one kind or another.

"Looks like Harry and Livy are at it again," Tony said as he clanked toward the stables. "I don't know how they stay together. Or why, for that matter."

I fell in beside him. "That's easy. Where else would they find a sweet job like this?"

He laughed, causing his horse to snort. "Don't make it sound so great. If I ever get enough money together, I'm going to Vegas. This place gives me the creeps sometimes. It's unnatural to live stuck in the past, especially when it's not even *your* past."

"Then why are you still here, besides the fact that you owe me a hundred dollars?" I hoped he'd get the hint and give me my money. He'd owed it to me for more than a month, and it wasn't like I was rolling in cash. I'm just a thirty-something assistant professor who likes to spend her summers at Renaissance Faire Village. "You've been jousting here since you got out of college.

9

You could get on a bus tomorrow for $49.50 and try your luck at the slots you're always talking about. What's stopping you?"

The smile on Tony's face died. He took off his gauntlets. "You know, Jessie, you have an evil way with words. I have to change. I'll see you later."

As I looked at Tony, I realized how different we were. Despite being twins, Tony had managed to come out handsome, brown-eyed, and useless, like my dad. Fortunately, I looked more like my mother. At least I had her nose, her blue eyes, and her ambition. I wish I had her petite frame as well. She was medium height, while Tony and I towered over people at six feet. That's not a bad height for a man. It's not a bad height for a woman, if you're a supermodel. For an ordinary woman, it means no heels and a little slouching.

"Before you go, could you let me have that money?" I hated to sound heartless, but I didn't like living on crackers and Pepsi. The Village only paid once a month. And I wasn't going to break into my savings.

Tony gave me *the look*. That meant he couldn't believe I was asking him for money at a time when he was feeling sorry for himself.

Too bad. He always did this, and I always

gave in. I was going to stand my ground.

He took two dollars out of the pocket of his jeans and put it in my hand. This was accompanied by a lot of clanking as he reached beneath his armor. "I hope that helps you out. It's all I've got left."

I looked at the money, and I looked at my stupid brother. Then I gave him the money back. "I want that hundred dollars out of your next paycheck."

I love my brother, but I wish I'd never brought him to the Village. It was my sanctuary from the modern world. I'd spent every summer here since I was in college. But I wasn't going to let him push me into leaving, especially since I was in the midst of pursuing my Ph.D. at the University of South Carolina at Columbia.

I've learned a new skill at Renaissance Faire Village each year since I've finished college. I apprenticed with Master Archer Simmons last summer and even made my own bow and arrows. I won two of the three archery tournaments after spending all of my time immersed in the subject.

Simmons commended me for my effort and asked me to work with him this year. But I'd made my decision about the topic of my doctorate dissertation and needed to explore other crafts.

I'd titled it, "Proliferation Of Medieval Crafts In Modern Times." And what better place to do my research than Renaissance Faire Village?

About twenty of my students were also at the Village. I saw two of them working at the elephant and camel ride, helping kids on and off the nervous animals. It didn't look like much fun, and I was sure they wouldn't last long. Most were only there for a few weeks. Some might decide to stay for the summer. The pay wasn't great, but they got a free room from the Village and several credits for my history class when it was over.

As I came around the corner of the jousting bleachers, I saw Tony kissing one of the fairies. I knew my two dollars would go into buying her something. She was pretty and fragile looking. The type of woman Tony *always* chose. Last summer, he spent all his money on a volunteer student from Georgia State University who played a Rapunzel-type character whose bodice never stayed closed. This summer wasn't starting out any better.

I walked through the Village from the jousting field past shops, eateries, taverns and games. There were plenty of opportunities for apprenticeships with more than one hundred craftsmen in the Village. I probably wouldn't need to research all of them for my dissertation, but it gave me a wide range of crafts to choose from.

Beth Daniels at Stylish Frocks was an excellent seamstress who'd created all the costumes, including the dragon, for the Village. The costume shop was close to the castle, where a weekly feast was held by the king and queen. Livy liked to change clothes frequently, and it was easier for Beth to be close to her.

Master Archer Simmons waved to me from his shop, the Feathered Shaft. I smiled and waved back. I planned to include my time with him last summer in my dissertation. The clock maker's shop, the Hands of Time, was full of people. I walked around the customers who had spilled out into the street. Clock making was on my list, too.

Most of the Village was actually facade created to look old. It was built on what was left of the old air force base and studded with cobblestone streets. The heart of the Village was along both sides of the main runway with the jousting arena on one end. Shops and places to eat surrounded the castle, which was built around the old traffic control tower. It took up both sides of the King's Highway.

The jousting field blocked the street and

effectively ended the Village. Parking surrounded the wall that separated it from the rest of the world. The true purpose of the wall (never mind that most Renaissance towns had one) was to keep out people who didn't have tickets.

Sometimes it didn't work very well. There were too many people. Every day, the cobblestone King's Highway became a crowded thoroughfare with carriages, horses, the occasional cow, and thousands of pedestrians. It had to be difficult to keep track of all that, but I guessed they managed. The paychecks came at the end of each month.

No one wore watches, and I missed my cell phone almost as much as I missed my computer during the day while I was in character. Unfortunately, I didn't need any of those devices to tell me I was running late by the time I reached the basket shop, Wicked Weaves. I *always* ran late when I was with Tony.

"Where have you been?" Mary asked as she made change for another basket sale.

I was her apprentice this summer, which meant she could have me do almost anything. Most of the time, she had me taking care of the shop so she could weave.

"Sorry." I took the basket from her and

smiled at the customer.

"You been houndin' that boy again?" Mary laughed and shook her head, which was wrapped in a bright orange scarf. "You can't make him something he ain't."

"Wow." The petite woman in the purple fairy wings gazed at us in awe. "Did you learn that while you were weaving this basket?"

"That's right," Mary agreed. "That's why them baskets are so pricey. You get all of that with each one."

I finished the sale while Mary picked up her pipe and walked outside.

Mary Shift was a Gullah basket weaver from Mount Pleasant, near Charleston. Not strictly speaking a *Renaissance* basket weaver, although African baskets have been woven for much longer. She was a tiny, bird-like woman who made me feel like I should carry her around with me. I was sure she'd fit on one of my shoulders.

She could have been any age. She had an air of the ancient about her, but her skin was as smooth and dark as a mocha latte. There was a mystery about her past. I felt sure other people in the Village knew what it was, but they were busy protecting their own secrets.

A few more customers wandered into the

15

shop, picked up baskets of all shapes and sizes, then put most of them down again. Mary was right about them being pricey. But everything at the Village came with sticker shock. I supposed visitors were paying for the ambiance of walking through another time.

It was a little frustrating to me that I had to wait on customers. I'd spent months collecting information on basket weaving. I'd woven a dozen baskets since I'd gotten here, but that was on my own. I was supposed to sit beside Mary and learn the things books couldn't teach me. But there I was, a month into summer break, and I still hadn't learned any of Mary's techniques. The only thing I'd learned was how to make change from a hundred dollar bill and punch Visa card numbers really fast. I swallowed hard, waited until the shop was empty, and went to join Mary on the back steps, where she wove most of her work. I stopped before I went outside when I heard the sound of muffled voices.

Peeking around the corner of the door, I saw a black man with a grizzled gray head and a black suit that looked like it was made in the 1920s. He was bent close to Mary, talking fast in what I'd come to recognize as the Gullah language. Some of it I understood, since it sounded like pidgin English. Some of the words might as well have been Martian.

Mary shook her head and moved her hands furiously in and out of the basket she was working. I was surprised it didn't catch fire. The man was obviously making her uncomfortable.

I stepped out of the door and coughed loudly. Sometimes I have a tendency to butt in where I'm not necessarily welcome. It had gotten me in trouble before. It didn't seem to be something I could control, like biting my nails.

The man looked up and stared at me in a way as dismissive as if he'd actually said, *Get out of here.* He made a gesture to Mary, then stalked away. He was quickly lost in the sea of pedestrians.

"Who was that?" I tried to push my black linen skirt down to keep it from poufing up when I sat beside her.

"Who?" She exhaled smoke from her corncob pipe.

"The man who was just here." If she didn't want me to know who he was, she'd have to say so. I wasn't good at hints.

"He went away. Don't fool with him. Help me with this basket. My old eyes don't see so good."

I'd spent the last month with this woman. She could see a grain of salt on a sandy beach. Although I wanted to know what was going on, I did as she asked and focused on helping her.

Mary had the bottom of the coiled basket started with a big knot right in the middle. There were even lengths of the sweetgrass she went to harvest each week woven with pine needles, a nice rust-colored contrast to the yellow sweetgrass. I inhaled its unique smell, like vanilla and fresh air tinged with pine.

"You might have to wet the palm to sew it." She watched me as I started weaving the coil she'd begun around the knot at the bottom of the basket. "I think this one is for eggs. We'll make it not so tall and wider at the base."

"Have you collected eggs with a basket like this before?" I hoped to sidetrack her attention and then go back to the strange man's identity.

"Many times. They're good for collecting turtle eggs."

I stopped and stared at her. "You didn't *eat* turtle eggs, did you?"

She laughed, a thousand small lines fanning out from her eyes, telling of a thousand things she'd seen and done in her life. "Yes.

We ate what we found to eat. Sometimes there wasn't so much fish, or the crab basket was empty. You do what you have to do to survive."

I didn't want to go inside and get the basket I was working on. I was afraid it might spoil the moment, so I started a new one. I coiled one end of the sweetgrass into the smallest possible ring around the knot, holding the grass and pine together with one hand while I pushed the palm under and over with the bone.

I had been a little reluctant to use the bone when Mary first showed it to me.

She had laughed when she saw the look on my face, saying, "See? It's only an old spoon my great-grandmother found on the beach. See the little rose on the handle? She took off the bowl and used the end. You children today are too worried about everything."

Despite her explanation, even now I was a little reluctant to use the smooth tool polished by a century of weaving baskets. The whole "bone" thing really bothered me. Why call it a bone if it wasn't one?

This wasn't like weaving the other baskets I'd practiced before meeting Mary. The grass was more supple than reed and harder to hold in place, even though it was braided.

The palm leaf was stiff and held the grass well but also managed to cut my fingers a few times.

"There." Mary nodded and puffed smoke. "You're doin' fine. If you could only learn to keep better track of time and leave that boy alone, you'd be ready to sell your own baskets."

I put another stitch in, catching the beginning of a new bunch of grass and pulling it tight. "Who was that man, Mary? Why was he threatening you?"

"Let it go," she urged. "Look, you left out a piece of grass, and your hand is bleeding. Let me take that. You go and clean up. Fetch me more tobacco from the shelf and put a bandage on that hand."

Mary was the original whip-cracking boss. She might've been small and vulnerable in some ways, but she was as tough as that palm leaf. Those shiny black eyes that reminded me of dark diamonds saw everything. She didn't mind telling me, either.

There were two more customers in the shop. I cleaned my hand and bandaged it while they browsed. One of them, a heavy-set woman in a long, green velvet gown whose breasts were almost pushed out of her bodice, asked me about the weaving. "Is it true no two baskets are ever the same?"

"That's right. In fact, master basket weavers have distinct styles that are never duplicated by anyone outside the family or group of weavers. Some of them, like this one," I showed her a large, oval basket, "made by our master weaver, have a pattern handed down for hundreds of years."

The woman nodded, suitably impressed. "I've heard you can keep them outside, too."

"Because of the grasses and palm they're sewn with, they can get wet without any problem."

She was convinced and bought two $400 baskets. The skinny woman with her looked around but didn't buy anything.

"Jessie!" I didn't have time to turn around before I was lifted completely off my feet. Not a common occurrence for someone my size.

I'd been waiting a month to hear that voice. I stared into the familiar face, looking for any changes since last summer. "Chase! I was wondering where you were!"

"I was visiting my family in Arizona for a few weeks. Are you working at Wicked Weaves this year?"

Chase Manhattan looked as healthy and alive as always. He was six foot eight, 260 pounds of energy. He reminded me of a pirate with his long brown braid and one gold earring.

Chase had lived at the Village for the last five years. He told me once he'd played every sport imaginable in college but had a soft spot for history. I found out later, by snooping around, that he took unimaginable crap for not latching on to a pro team of some kind and buying a new Ferrari.

He was intelligent, well-spoken, handsome, and charismatic. He was also the bailiff for the Village, which meant he was kind of chief of security and circuit court judge rolled into one. He was appointed by the king and queen. Adventure Land, the owners of the Village, appointed Livy and Harry the same way. They'd been the company's top sales people.

Unfortunately, it meant Chase was as bad as my brother. He was content to live here and had no real ambition for his life. It was the only thing that kept me from throwing myself on him every time I saw him. Me, and half the other women in the Village. I wouldn't let myself be involved with someone like that.

Thinking about it was almost as good as taking a cold shower. "I'm working, Chase. Put me down."

"Sorry." He set me back on my feet and managed to look apologetic. "I just got back, and you were the first person I saw."

As though that explained everything.

A large group of visitors entered the shop. They were dressed in heavy medieval clothing made from leather and velvet, even though the Weather Channel said it would be in the nineties. These were the diehard medieval fantasy visitors. Not everyone gave up modern clothing to come here. A few of them carried real bows and swords. The only restriction on weapons in the Village was that they had to be something you could've owned in the 1500s. No visitor could carry a modern gun.

I let them look around as I talked to Chase. "I'm working as Mary Shift's apprentice making baskets."

"Excellent! I could use a basket at the dungeon. Maybe you could make one for me."

I took his remark in stride. Anyone who wears a size twelve shoe, even though it's a size twelve *narrow,* has to be realistic. Men who looked like Chase didn't date women who looked like me. Not that I *wanted* to date him. He was like my brother. I repeated the mantra over and over to protect myself.

"It's good to see you, Jessie. You should come visit more often during the year." He smiled at me, and his braid fell across his shoulder. "Meeting every summer like this is hard on my love life."

I laughed. I'm sure I was supposed to. Chase was a flirt. I told myself that to keep from being a slobbering mess around him. I've known him for so long, but I still don't know much about him. "What are *you* doing? Have you seen any thieves or scoundrels today?"

Chase looked down at his tight jeans and the T-shirt covering what I knew to be his washboard abs. "I'm looking for a costume right now. They seem to be in short supply this summer. I think we have extra workers."

I sighed and stared at the ceiling behind his head. "I hear the wizard has two apprentices this year." *That was brilliant, Jessie.*

The sound of trumpets, heralding the king or queen, or both, taking a royal turn through the Village, interrupted us. There was no way either one of us was going anywhere for a few minutes. A royal stroll came complete with either gentlemen or ladies-in-waiting and other courtiers, a minstrel or two and sometimes even a jester. That meant hundreds of people with cameras lined up to take their pictures. Both the king and queen loved being photographed and could pose for hours.

So I was stuck with Chase, who smiled at me and continued to make polite conversation. The visitors in the shop quit fondling the baskets and rushed to the big windows that faced the street to see what was going on. I glanced toward the back stairs, hoping Mary might decide to come in and watch the spectacle of the royal couple getting free lemonade from the shop next door. But I didn't see her at the back door. She was too smart and experienced for that.

"I think our queen, Livy, has put on a few pounds," Chase observed. "Either that or she needs a new royal corset tightener."

"I'm sure she'd be glad to let *you* have that position."

"I don't think so." He straightened my shawl. "I'm busy looking at baskets."

Before I could answer, a sharp screech came from beside Lolly's Lemonade Shoppe. I ran out the back door and saw Livy collapse to her knees. "We do believe this man is dead," she said. "Someone fetch our smelling salts."

Two

At first I thought it was part of the act. Like I said, it's hard to tell sometimes, and not just for the tourists, either. Half of the time, I'm not sure what's real and what's illusion. Of course, I have that problem even when I'm *not* at the Village.

Chaos broke out around the queen as all of her court rushed to her side and the visitors with cameras followed them. Shutters were clicking, but the sun was so bright there were no flashes.

There was only a small walkway between buildings in the Village. Most of the time, you could find the people who worked there sitting around eating lunch or smoking cigarettes in that space. One summer they kept the trash cans there, but the smell drove people away. So they put the trash cans against the back wall and left the space empty between buildings. Once in a while, we had a problem with kids hanging out there trying to get lost in the crowd in the evening so they could spend a night in the Village. Chase always caught them.

Anyone walking by could've seen this man. He was sitting against the wall on the ground, his head hanging forward, arms dangling at his sides. I stepped around the queen, who was still on the ground but at a safe distance from him. He looked dead. If he was breathing, I couldn't see it. Maybe Livy was right for once.

I hoped he was asleep. It had happened before. Sometimes older people got tired. The Village has a lot of walking. He was going to be embarrassed, if that were the case, but better embarrassed than dead.

I gritted my teeth and tugged at his leg, but he didn't move. Maybe that was a good sign. At that point, it was hard to say. I didn't want to touch him again, so I crouched close and pretended to be inspecting the area, hoping someone else would come and take charge.

"Let me take a look at him." I saw Chase come up behind me, and I moved to one side. He might not *really* be a police officer, but he seemed like the best person to deal with the situation.

"He's not dead," I assured him and myself. "Livy goes into hysterics regularly. You know that."

Chase agreed. "He might be sick."

"Maybe. Or he could be asleep. He's not dead. I don't see any blood."

"Good thing you're not a medical examiner. There are plenty of ways to be dead that don't make you lose any blood." Chase knelt down and put his hand against the man's throat. "There's no pulse."

It got very quiet around us, and I sneaked a glance back. No one was looking at Livy anymore. She'd even stopped pretending to swoon and was staring at the man with the rest of us. Everyone was waiting to see if he was going to wake up.

Chase moved back. The man fell toward me. I screeched and moved faster than I'd ever thought I could to get out of his way. He wasn't moving all *that* fast, but I didn't want to take any chances.

For another instant, there was complete silence. Then a general replica of my screech went through the crowd, and people ran in all directions. Livy lifted her heavy red velvet gown and took off after them, holding her crown in one hand and her scepter in the other.

Chase calmly reached across and laid the man's body down. "Well, that answers that question. Livy was right for once. He's dead."

Carefully (I didn't want to disturb the man on the ground), I moved farther away from him until my back was against the side wall of Wicked Weaves. "We need to call 911. I wouldn't want to lie here and have to take your word for it that I was dead."

"Relax," Chase said. "I've worked as a paramedic. This man is definitely dead. What's this around his throat?"

I looked. I didn't want to. I couldn't help it. I stepped close to Chase. There was something around the dead man's throat. It looked like basket weaving. The long lines of sweetgrass intertwined with pine. No way was I getting any closer to find out for sure.

There was something familiar about the man, too. He was dressed like the man who'd been with Mary earlier. His face was different — it was thinner and longer — but the distinct old-fashioned style of the suit was the same.

I glanced around and realized Mary still wasn't on the back step of the shop. I couldn't find her face in the small group of people who hadn't run away. She definitely wasn't there. I hadn't seen her come into the shop before Livy found the dead man. Where was she?

I looked up at Chase and started to mention it. Then I thought again. Whatever was going on might be a bad thing for Mary. It might not matter that she was gone. Just because the dead man *looked* like he was strangled by a piece of her particular basket weave didn't mean anything.

"Stand back!" Roger Trent, the glass blower, ran up from the street. "Don't touch anything. You should know better."

Chase shook his head. "Too late."

"What happened?" Roger took his past as a police officer very seriously and probably thought he should head up the investigation. He was an older man, still in good condition, whose shaved head was as sun-darkened as his face.

"He was sitting against the wall when we found him," Chase explained. "Then he fell over. He doesn't have a pulse, and he's cold. He's been dead for a while."

"Livy said he was dead when she ran by me toward the castle." Roger knelt beside the fallen man. "What did you see, Chase?"

"I didn't see anything until I got out here. I was in the shop with Jessie when Livy started screaming. We both ran out at the same time. Jessie got here first."

"It's true." I glanced at Chase, then at the wall, then at Roger. Anywhere not to look at the dead man. "You couldn't see anything from inside. There aren't windows facing this way."

Roger examined the wall behind me, then looked back at the dead man. "Does anyone recognize him? Have you seen him before, Jessie? Was he in the shop?"

"I don't recognize him." I kept it quiet that his suit looked familiar. I hoped it didn't make a difference. Anyone could wear a similar outfit. Especially here where so many people rented their clothes for the day. A black suit from the 1920s wouldn't really fit the Renaissance theme, but I've seen weirder.

Chase responded, "I just got in from Scottsdale. I haven't even had time to change. I can take a look at the video footage from the gate and find out how long he's been in the Village."

Roger leaned closer to the dead man without touching him. "Smells like he's been drinking. I think this man was strangled by this stuff around his throat. It's cutting into his skin. What is it?"

A shadow fell across the dead man's face. "It's my weave." Mary's voice was tight and flat.

"What do you mean?" Roger asked her. "Are you saying *you* strangled this man?"

31

"No," she denied. "I said it was *my* weave. I didn't say I know how it got there."

Roger got up and glanced around the area. "The police are on their way. I know you tell a pretty good story, Mary. I hope you have a good tale to tell *them.* They'll want to know how a piece of your weaving got around his throat if you didn't put it there."

"I got nothin' to say. I've been here weaving all day."

I knew she was lying. I liked her too well to call her on it, especially in front of Roger and Chase. It didn't make any sense to me, anyway. How could Mary strangle a man twice as big as her?

"The police will want to talk to both of you," Roger told Chase and me. "I wouldn't make any sudden moves or volunteer too much information."

"What happened?" Master Armorer Daisy Reynolds panted as she reached us. Her formidable breastplate, with the image of a phoenix engraved on it, shone in the sun. Her muscled arms bulged. "I heard the queen found a dead man."

Thankfully a few other craftsmen, some flower girls, and the Village dragon were all there by then. I was glad we weren't alone in that space between the buildings. No doubt the story would be recounted many times over. There was always plenty going on in the Village, but it didn't usually include death. At least not *real* death.

Briskly, Roger filled everyone in.

"The police." Daisy shuddered. "I didn't see anything. There's no reason for me to be here when they come."

"Me, either." Fred, the human voice from inside the large, red dragon, spoke. "I've got a few bad parking tickets. They might be looking for me."

"Don't be ridiculous," Roger said. "You know I'm an ex-cop. This will be a routine investigation. Nobody's going to wonder about your parking tickets, Fred. They'll want to know what happened to this man and who was here when it happened. Everyone needs to calm down."

"Livy actually found him, but I don't think that old rule of thumb applies this time," Chase volunteered. "As usual, her entourage was with her. I'm sure she's not involved."

Fred shrugged, not an easy thing in one of the heavy costumes. I was a giant for a whole summer one year. I wouldn't care to do it again, even with the air-conditioning in the costume.

Roger looked up at Chase and me. "So

the two of you were here in Wicked Weaves when they found him? You might be witnesses Mary will need."

I grabbed Chase's hand before he could answer. I couldn't tell him *not* to give Mary away. I stared hard at him and hoped he'd get it. It might've looked more like a sad puppy face, but it worked.

"That's right."

Chase squeezed my hand and continued to hold it.

"The three of us were in the shop talking when Livy came up to get lemonade." I dared Roger to question my lie.

He didn't. He stood up and began looking around the small alleyway again. I couldn't see anything unusual. But I'm not an ex-cop, and maybe they could see things I couldn't.

Mary didn't contradict us, even though she knew we were lying. She stood there as straight and tall as her five-foot-nothing frame would let her. Maybe she was there the whole time. Her tiny apartment was upstairs from the shop. Maybe she went up there, and I didn't see her.

Whatever it was, there was no point standing there talking about it. The nearest law enforcement was the police department on Oak Street. In the meantime, the paramedics, stationed at the entrance to the Village for emergencies, ran toward us from the street. "Step aside. Let us through."

Their equipment and modern blue uniforms looked strangely out of place, like Chase's jeans. I looked away from that sight quickly, once I'd realized I was staring. I didn't have any business looking at Chase's jeans.

Standing off of the King's Highway without the usual visitors in shorts and tank tops rubbing elbows with fairies and knights gave the whole incident a surreal quality, even more so than normal. It was like taking a real step back in history and finding there were time travelers in medical uniforms already there.

I've always had an active imagination. Sometimes it takes some quirky turns. This was definitely one of those times.

The two paramedics put on latex gloves and carefully checked the dead guy's pulse. One of them shook his head. "He's been dead a while. Why didn't you call us sooner?"

"We only found him a few minutes ago." Chase was still standing next to me. "If he was dead out here for long, I'm sure someone would've seen him. It looks like he might've been killed somewhere else, then moved here."

"I was a cop for most of my life," Roger said for the millionth time since I'd met him five years ago. "It looks like that to me, too. You should leave him alone before the crime scene is disturbed any more. We've probably done enough damage as it is."

"This is stupid." Daisy turned to leave. "I'm going back to the forge. Anyone needs to talk to me, they know where to find me."

Mary didn't say anything. She stood there, staring at the dead guy. The layer of basket weaving was very white against his black throat. The afternoon sunlight made it stand out even more. Maybe it was my imagination, but I was pretty sure Mary knew him.

The paramedics did what Roger told them to do, but they waited there with us for the police. It seemed odd that our little section of the Village suddenly got so quiet until I realized that gossip traveled quickly. In some ways, it surprised me even more that people weren't all over the area if they thought something interesting was going on.

One of the queen's pages ran up and announced that Queen Olivia was at her castle. She would receive anyone with questions there. She would not be back again until the untidy dead man was cleaned out of her kingdom.

After delivering her message, Debby, one of my students, stared at the dead man, then looked at me. "Who is that? He must not work here. He isn't wearing a costume."

As statements of undeniable fact go, it wasn't much. But she did have a point. He obviously didn't work here. I looked at his shoes for the first time. They were spats. I know that because a friend of mine wore them last year for a costume party.

They had mud on them. The trouser cuffs were muddy, too. There was sand around the Village property. The only place with this light-colored mud was around the privies. I wasn't sure what that meant except that he'd spent too much time walking around the privies.

"I'm going in b'dout you want me out here." Mary pulled her shawl closer around her thin form. "I got baskets to make that won't be making themselves."

Roger put his hand on her arm and told her he'd let her know when the police got there. "They'll want to talk to you."

She nodded but didn't speak, walking slowly into the shop. I thought she seemed smaller, less full of that vibrant energy I was used to. I guessed a dead man could do that to you.

"I'm going in, too." No one stopped me. I

guessed it was better to be ignored than considered a suspect. I wasn't worried about Chase. He could take care of himself. We both knew he wasn't involved in whatever happened to the dead guy.

I let go of his warm hand. That took some doing. I wanted to use my anxiety over seeing the dead guy as a justification to sleep with him. I mean, hold his hand. He was big and warm, and my logical brain got fuzzy around him. I repeated my mantra — Don't get involved with Chase; he doesn't want anything from life — but it wasn't helping. I wanted to stand as close to him as possible, but I made myself move away. No matter what happened, dead guy or not, I wasn't getting involved with Chase.

I found Mary inside the basket shop. She was staring out the front window at the cobblestone street that was strangely empty and quiet. Even the bakery shop across the way, the King's Tarts, was empty. And believe me, normally there are plenty of tarts, both varieties, inside. The three bountiful maidens on the sign looked overexposed and lonely.

"Are you okay?" I asked her. She was holding a small basket that almost defied the laws of basket weaving. It was so tiny and woven so tightly it could probably have held water. The colors woven into it were remarkable as well. There was a coral tint to whatever plant was woven with the sweet-grass. The whole thing couldn't have been more than an inch wide and an inch high with a tiny top.

"I'm fine." Her long, thin fingers rubbed against the grass grain in the weave. "I'm always *fine.*"

I sat on one of the stools that were topped with a strong weave. "I'm glad you're okay. I'm not. I haven't seen many dead people in my life, and that's fine with me. How about you?"

She didn't answer right away. I started to repeat myself as she looked up. There was something in her eyes that stopped me. I can't explain what it was. A terrible sorrow? Maybe the anger that makes you blind to everything else. I don't know.

"I've seen too many," Mary said. "I buried too many."

"I guess it's something you get used to." I was trying to keep the conversation going until I could ask her where she was when Livy found the dead man. Then I planned to go on to the suit the dead guy was wearing bearing a striking resemblance to her friend's suit.

"No." Her voice was glacial. "It's not

39

something you *ever* get used to."

I tried to think of something else to say. Something besides my questions and curiosity. I picked up one of the baskets and glanced at it, examining the cunning weave that had created it. Mary was more than a creative basket maker. She was gifted. I noticed how tight the weave was and wondered how she got it that way.

"Sometimes when you want them really tight," she responded as though reading my mind, "you can weave them wet. As they dry, they tighten up a little bit at a time. Sometimes they tighten dead tight."

"You mean like someone choked the dead guy with your weave?" I considered the terrible truth of how he'd died.

"That's right. I've seen it before."

A chill raced through me, even though it was the end of June and I was wearing twenty pounds of linen. I watched, hypnotized by the movements of her fingers against the basket she was holding. In a hundred years I might be able to weave something like that, but the chances were I'd never have that skill in my lifetime.

"What's that basket for?" My voice sounded like a bad car radio. I gulped after I'd said it and shivered.

"It's a ring basket." She held it out to me.

"It can hold any small trinket. I use it to hold my rings when my joints swell. Using your hands so much isn't good sometimes."

I took the basket from her and lifted the lid. Inside was a plain gold wedding band. "You didn't tell me you were married. Your husband isn't here with you?"

"No. I'm not married anymore."

Those steady, bright eyes stared at me, daring me to ask more. I could never resist temptation. "Where were you when Livy found the dead man?"

She tossed her head. "I was busy for a few minutes."

"And your husband?"

"He lies out yonder. I'm alone now."

THREE

It sounded crazy at that point, but my first instinct was to put Mary on a bus and help her escape. Clearly, she'd killed her husband. Maybe she had good reason. I speculated on all the motives that could have driven her to such an end.

I could've understood it better if the man I'd seen her with earlier had been her husband. *He* seemed to be threatening her. But the dead man outside was not the same man. Had the earlier visitor helped her kill her husband? When had she found time to strangle him? She'd been missing for a few minutes, but that didn't seem long enough to me.

Mary sat down on the stairs in back and started working again. The basket moved very slowly in her hands. I sat down beside her with the basket I'd started a few days ago. It had taken me almost a week to do what she could do in a few hours. My weave wasn't as tight or fine as hers. There were some stray bits of sweetgrass that stuck out like little hairs from the ponytail my mom used to make me before I went to school. The color was similar to Mary's, green and off white. The pine needles didn't want to stay in my weave. They poked out more than the grass.

"What kind of plant is that in the weave around his neck?" I asked like I was asking if there were raisins in the oatmeal.

"Bulrush," she answered without looking up from the basket. She didn't even appear surprised or pretend to question what I was talking about.

I used the bone she'd given me to push the palm leaf over and under the third coil in my basket. "You have to get out of here. The police will come, and you shouldn't be here."

She stopped weaving her basket, bone poised in midair. "Why? Why should I leave? I haven't done anything wrong."

I glanced around to make sure no one was listening. "You said the dead man is your husband. The weave around his neck is yours. I just got done explaining to that woman in the awful velvet dress that no two styles are exactly the same."

"What are you saying, Jessie? You think I

killed him?"

"No." I stuck the sharp end of the palm leaf in my hand, then put it up to my mouth to keep the blood from getting on the basket. God was punishing me for lying. "Okay, yes. I know you probably didn't mean to. I know it was probably an accident."

Mary made a noise somewhere between a cough and a grunt. "Don't be crazy. That weave was meant to kill. I've seen it before. Someone murdered my husband. But it wasn't me."

It seemed unlikely to me that it could be an accident. I mean, the man didn't fall into the weave and have it tighten around his neck. Someone had to choke him with it. There was little that seemed accidental about it. "How else could it happen?"

"Someone else did it."

"But that's *your* particular weave."

"Not just mine. *He* taught it to me. I was very young. It was important to me."

I heard the doubt and soft questioning in her voice, but the only thing that stuck with me was that *he'd* known how to do the same weave. "You're saying he killed himself? I don't think anyone's going to buy that. You have to think of something better, Mary. Don't you watch TV shows? They'll put you in jail. The *real* jail. Not the hokey dungeon."

"You know I don't watch them demmed things." She spat on the ground. "I don't have time for that foolishness."

"Well, let me tell you, the police won't fool around. They're going to ask hard questions. Who was he? Why was he here? Why did you split up? That kind of thing. And when they find out he was killed with something *you* wove, they might arrest you."

"That's crazy talking." But her fingers started moving faster up and under the coil in the basket she was weaving. "I didn't know he was here until Abraham told me."

"And that was the man with the same suit who was threatening you earlier?"

"Nah. He wasn't threatening me. He was telling me Joshua was here. He wanted me to send him home."

I took it all in while I nursed my finger and looked at the mess I'd made of my basket. There were holes between the places the coils were sewn and tiny bloodstains on two of the coils. "Your husband's name was Joshua?"

"It's a fine name where I come from."

"Why would Abraham want to keep you and Joshua apart?" This was beginning to sound more like Romeo and Juliet, the senior version, instead of *CSI*. "Is that why Joshua wasn't here with you? Because of Abraham?"

She waved her hand. "Lord, you ask so many questions it tires a body right out. And just look at your basket. You might as well throw it away. Nobody wants to buy a basket with blood on it."

I couldn't argue that point with her. I was about to press her for answers to my questions when Roger and Chase came around the corner with another man. Since he was wearing a suit and tie, I assumed he had to be a cop.

"Mary Shift?" The heavy folds of the man's chin vanished into his neck beneath his sweaty white shirt. "And you must be Jessie Morton?"

I didn't respond. He obviously knew who I was. I couldn't help but notice his shirt had some kind of stain where the food must have bounced off of his stomach on the way down from his mouth.

"I'm Mary. What do you want?"

"I'm Detective Almond. There's a dead man over there who looks like he was strangled with a piece of a basket." The detective looked at the basket I was holding. "Both of you make baskets?"

"I'm her teacher," Mary chastised him.

"She is doing what I tell her to do."

"Are you saying *you* made the basket that killed that man?" The detective opened a black leather wallet that had seen better days and read the ID inside. "Joshua Shift. Are you related?"

"In a manner of speaking." Mary looked up at him. "He was my husband."

I half expected to hear a loud, indrawn breath of surprise from Roger and Chase, who stood behind him. But he must've filled them in when he took the wallet from Joshua. They already knew he was related to Mary.

I glared at Chase. He couldn't take the guilt and looked away. It was bad enough we'd found a dead guy in the alleyway; now the police had to play games. Roger looked eager for blood or at least a full confession. It made me angry, and I always do stupid things when I get angry.

"Leave her alone. She was with me." That was stupid. I didn't have any idea where Mary was most of the time. But I couldn't stand all that leering and waiting. "We were weaving baskets together all day."

"Is that true, Miz Shift?" Detective Almond leaned a little closer. It had to be hard on his already tight pants. "Can anyone verify that?"

Chase and Roger glanced at one another. Fred the dragon peeked around the corner but didn't speak. No one but me seemed to be worried about Mary. Couldn't they see how bad this looked?

"No one needs to say anything. I know what happened." Mary stepped up with several accounts of past deaths attributed to people being killed with basket weave. She went into torturous detail about how Joshua had probably died. I could see the men wincing as she described the terrible death he may have endured.

"Are you saying you've done this before?" The detective scratched his head.

"No. I'm Gullah. My people have their ways." She tossed her head. "Someone stole a little piece of weave and choked him. I can't say more than that. Unless you want me to check him over for you."

"No thanks." Detective Almond's tone was brisk and sure. "We have up-to-date forensic facilities. There won't be any doubt about what happened to him by the time we get through. In the meantime, maybe the two of you should come with me to the office. We're going to need some answers to all this."

Chase stepped between me and Detective Almond. "Is that necessary? Surely you don't think *both* of them killed Mr. Shift."

"I don't know yet what happened here." He looked him up and down. "What the hell did you say your name was again?"

"Chase Manhattan. My parents were into banking. You know how it is."

I was flattered when Chase stood up for me. We'd been friends for a long time. He was a great guy. I could've easily read something into his words that wasn't happening. At least I didn't *think* it was happening. I'd been hot for him for so long, I didn't want to make a mistake.

I wasn't sure what I'd gotten myself into as the detective escorted Mary and me to his car and opened the back door. I knew I was lying about being with her all day. She knew I was lying. The chances were pretty good she'd killed Joshua. I didn't plan to tell the police my thoughts on that subject.

A white van with the words "Crime Scene" in plain black lettering on the side rolled up. A few goats ran out of the way, and the horse being ridden by the village version of Lady Godiva, Arlene, in a long blond wig and tan body suit, got a little skittish. It was a harsh reminder of the real world outside the wall.

"What can I do for you, Jessie?" Chase asked as we waited for the group of specialized technicians to check out Mary's husband. How many people had to look at the poor man?

"I'll be fine. Maybe you could close up the shop."

"I can do that."

"And don't steal the money," Mary added. "I know how many baskets are in the shop. If there's one gone, I expect to see the money for it, or I'll know the reason why."

Roger joined us. "I know this looks bad, but if you haven't done anything wrong, you have to believe in the system and trust the investigation will find that out."

I didn't find that comforting. "Do you know how many people are wrongly accused and sent to prison every year? Excuse me if I'd rather have a sharp lawyer."

"That's up to you." He glanced at Mary. "I've known you for ten years now. I don't believe you killed anyone. What was your husband doing up here, anyway? I thought you weren't supposed to have any contact with him."

That was news to me. Did he have some kind of restraining order against her? Of course, I barely knew her at all. She *seemed* like a good person, but how could I tell?

"I don't know why Joshua was here. I swear I hadn't seen him until I walked around the corner of the shop and he was lying there, looking like I killed him." Mary shuddered and drew her shawl closer despite the warm temperature. "I *knew* he was here. I *felt* it before Abraham came to tell me."

Roger put his arm around her shoulders. I was surprised by the move, but she seemed okay with it. "It'll sort itself out. You'll be fine."

He left us standing by the side of the car with Detective Almond while a dozen crime scene techs who looked like they were still in school stared at Joshua and finally zipped him into a black bag.

And that was it. That was the way it ended up. Someone strangled you with a piece of basket weave, and they put you in a rubber sack. I wanted time to think about twenty-first-century philosophies on life and death, but Detective Almond interrupted me.

"If you two ladies are ready to go, we'll head for the office. I'm sure everything will check out fine, as long as you've told the truth. One of my officers will have you back here later on today, so long as it all works out."

That sounded like a lot of supposition to me. Mary and I took our cue and slid across the seat. An officer closed the door behind us. I was scared. And not the upside down rollercoaster kind of scared. The whimpering, ready to do whatever the police asked kind.

I wasn't sure what to expect. I took out my cell phone and tried to call my brother, Tony. I wasn't sure what he could do. It didn't matter anyway, since he didn't answer his phone. He probably forgot to pay his bill again. I left a voice mail for him. No way was I going to disappear into the county jail without anyone knowing where I was.

I felt better. But I noticed my efforts didn't do a thing for Mary. She was huddled in the corner, staring out the window at the passing beach houses and hotels. "Can I call someone for you?"

She mumbled, "No one to call."

I glanced at the back of the detective's head. The man needed a haircut. The back of his neck was sweaty and dirty. It had stained his collar.

Leaning closer to Mary, I whispered, "I don't think he can hear us through that glass. Was Roger right about you and Joshua?"

"You ask too many questions."

"I was willing to say I was with you all day even though I *know* you disappeared for a while. I think I deserve a few answers."

That got her attention. The angry look

was back in her eyes. "You don't know me. If you think I murdered Joshua, you should'a spoken up. If not, you did what you thought was right. I'm grateful. But don't think I'm gonna tell you everything about my life because of it."

My feelings were a little hurt. Apparently she didn't feel the same way about me that I felt about her. She didn't trust me like she did Roger. He should have been the one in the car with her. He might have been if I hadn't lied.

I folded my hands on my lap and didn't say another word. If Mary didn't want my help, I wasn't going to push it on her. I knew when I wasn't wanted. *Sometimes.*

After a few minutes, she sighed and put her cool, slender fingers against mine. "Let me see your han'."

I held my hands out. They were covered in cuts and scratches from my efforts to learn the Gullah tradition of basket weaving.

She looked at them, then held her dark hands out to me. "You see? We all start out the same way. Lord knows how many times I cut myself on the palm leaf, that's how I got these ol' scars. But we're all the same, see?"

I looked at her hands and saw the marks

53

from her years of working on the baskets. It was simple and basic. Something men and women had done since the beginning of time. Humans saw a need and found a way to fill it. Mary worked with plants her ancestors had used a hundred years before she was born. That was what brought me to her and kept me going.

"Something bad happened. I lived with those people since I was born. Joshua and I were happy after we were married. I made baskets to sell, and Joshua caught crabs and fish to feed us. I never thought to leave."

"Then why did you?" I stared into her eyes, our hands touching, voices low. "What could've been so bad?"

"Sometimes, I picked roots and herbs to help out the sick. I never sold them. Just gave them away. One night a man brought his son to me. He was burning up with the fever. His father didn't want to take him to Charleston to the doctor. He asked me to help. I did what I could. The boy died."

There was a singsong quality in her voice that said there was so much detail Mary didn't have time to explain. It was like looking at one of her baskets and thinking I could go home and weave one exactly like it. The richness and fragrance of the sweetgrass would be there, but the years of experience wouldn't.

"What happened?"

She shrugged and pulled her arms close to her. "He said I killed his son. Our friends, the people I grew up with, were afraid of him. They couldn't stand up for me. I looked him in the eye. We both knew what happened that night. I was judged, and they told me to leave. Said I wasn't welcome in my own home. They said Joshua and I weren't married anymore. They told him if he left with me, he could never come back."

I was fascinated by the nuances and shadows in her voice. The story reminded me of something that could've happened in medieval times when being turned out of your village could mean a death sentence. You'd be looked on as a person who couldn't be trusted everywhere you went. "What did you do?"

"I left. Joshua's mother and father were old. He stayed to care for them. They needed him more than I did. I haven't seen him twenty years before today."

I'm not sure why I thought about it, but I asked, "Was Abraham the one who kicked you out?"

She nodded. "I couldn't believe it when I saw him. It was like seeing a stranger. But I'd know him anywhere."

"Did Abraham tell you how he knew Joshua was here or why he was here?"

"He didn't. He give me the warning: If I talked to Joshua, there was no going back for him either."

This was beginning to make an odd kind of sense. Maybe Mary didn't kill her husband after all. People have warned me about taking things at first glance. Maybe Abraham killed Joshua because he couldn't control him anymore. Maybe Joshua had finally come to his senses and realized what he'd lost. Abraham couldn't stand that because he wanted his revenge on Mary and instead, he killed her husband before they could be reunited.

Anyone (make that Abraham) could've picked up a piece of one of the baskets Mary was working on and strangled Joshua with it. He looked like a good suspect to me. He was there. He had motive. He'd probably found Joshua before he got in the Village, after picking up a piece of weaving from Mary. He'd strangled Joshua, then put him next to Wicked Weaves, knowing the police would suspect Mary.

As Detective Almond's car pulled into the parking lot of the Myrtle Beach police station, I decided my theory was correct. Abraham was there before he made his presence known to Mary. He snagged a piece of her weaving and used it to kill Joshua. That made sense.

Two officers helped Mary and me out of the car while Detective Almond waddled into the office. I could smell the donuts from there. But it didn't matter. I had my theory to protect me. I'd hoped to get a chance to tell Mary what I was thinking. If we both pushed the same idea, we were bound to be all right.

Unfortunately, my plan didn't go as smoothly as I'd hoped. My officer took me to a little room on the left of the building, and Mary's officer took her to a little room on the right. There wasn't any time to tell her what I was thinking.

I sat in my little room wishing I had something to weave to keep from biting my fingernails. I don't know how long I was in there, but it seemed like forever. I stared at the walls, trying to think what Tom Cruise would do in that situation. No doubt he'd find some way to climb up through the ventilation system and make his way to freedom, stopping to rescue Mary on the way. Then he'd go out and find Abraham, forcing him to confess to killing Joshua and declaring his undying love for Mary that had spurred him to such a heinous act.

Since I was wearing heavy, bulky linen and wouldn't fit through the ventilation shaft, I wasn't going to accomplish that feat. I sat there and ran my fingers over the names carved into the old table, thinking about all the people who were there in jail. Were they still there? Would I ever get out?

The door opened finally, and Chase walked in carrying a briefcase that had seen better days. "Are you ready to go home, Jessie?"

FOUR

Chase had shaved and put on a suit and tie that was a little wrinkled. But still he'd dressed up and come for me. I was amazed, shocked, and very pleased. I threw myself against him, and he fell back against an old table with me on top of him.

I didn't care about my mantra or the fact that he was never going to amount to anything. I locked my arms around him and kissed him until I had to come up for air. "We can never have a permanent relationship," I told him before I kissed him again.

He dropped his briefcase on the floor. "Okay. I can handle that. I thought we'd just be friends forever."

"I was worried about that, too." I couldn't believe he was saying this to me. "I didn't think you even noticed me. Not like *that,* anyway."

We kissed again, our arms struggling to hold each other tighter. Then we rolled off the table and hit the hard concrete floor. It was enough to bring me to my senses as well as make a few bruises. "How is this happening? Why are you here?"

"To get you out of here." He tried to kiss me again.

I moved my head. I couldn't believe I moved away, but the logical part of my brain, which hadn't turned to pudding like my body, refused to let it go. "I appreciate the effort. But unless you have *Legal Aid for Dummies* in your briefcase, I don't think we can walk out of here just because you got dressed up and shaved." I didn't mention how good he smelled or how hard it was not to kiss him again.

"Actually, I'm a lawyer." He smiled at me like he'd found the pot of gold at the end of the rainbow and had decided to share it.

"And a paramedic. And a ski instructor." I pushed myself off the floor before someone came in and found us there. "You've done a lot of things since I've known you, Chase. You can't *just* pretend to be a lawyer or you'll end up in here with me and Mary."

"No, I really am a lawyer." Chase got off the floor, too. "I took the bar and everything. I work as a consultant, mostly over the Internet. But I'm sure I can get you out of here. You didn't do anything. They know

60

that. They're just fishing."

I didn't know whether to believe him or not. He reminded me so much of Tony when he'd told me he was a certified pilot because he'd taken one lesson. "Do you have some kind of proof? They'll ask you for proof, you know. They won't just take your word for it."

He pushed at my forehead with his fingers. "You always get these cute little frown lines when you think. You might want to consider Botox before they become permanent indentations."

I wiggled my eyebrows up and down. I needed a mirror. "I suppose *you* could do that, too."

"Look, do you want to get out of here or not? I had to borrow this suit from Milton, and he needs it back for a date tonight." He checked himself out in what I thought was a two-way mirror. "It fits pretty well, too."

I felt my forehead furrowing and made myself stop frowning. "Who's Milton?"

"He's that new guy from the University of Minnesota. He's a knight. Livy already has her eye on him."

"And every other part of her, I'm sure." I looked at him, purposely not frowning. "Are you *really* a lawyer? You're not just saying that?"

"I'm really a lawyer. I don't have my license to practice with me, but I could run back and get it if it would make you feel any better."

"Then why aren't you out making the big bucks?" I pushed his shoulder. "Why are you still hanging out at Renaissance Faire Village?"

"I have my reasons. I'm not going to talk about them right now."

"I don't know if I trust you."

He picked up his briefcase. "That's fine. I'll get Mary out and leave you to rot in prison with a cell mate named Tiny Tina."

"I thought you said the police don't have anything, and I could go."

"You could, *if* you trust me." He smiled and took my hand. "These fingers deserve to be punctured by sharp-edged grass and needles again. I can make that happen."

My heart — and the rest of me — was melting. There was no going back from those kisses. I didn't know how Chase felt, but I wanted more. I wasn't likely to get more of anything with me in prison and him back in the Village, surrounded by pert little fairies and lonely ladies-in-waiting.

Besides, what was the worst that could happen? If Chase *wasn't* really a lawyer, he'd get in trouble, not me. I wouldn't be any worse for the opportunity. "Since you put it that way, get me out if you can."

He grinned, dark eyes making me wish we were somewhere more private. "I'll be back in a flash. You stay right here and try not to get in any more trouble."

"Ha-ha. I hope your legal skills are sharper than your sense of humor."

But before he could leave me, Detective Almond and a man in a blue suit, who introduced himself as the assistant district attorney, walked in and shut the door behind them. A woman with a tape recorder sat down in one corner of the room.

I hoped no one else was planning to join us. The room wasn't made for that many people and I was beginning to feel claustrophobic.

After introductions all around, we sat down at the little table Chase and I had recently occupied. The two men from the city stared at me intently. I could feel the frown lines coming back on my forehead.

"Miz Morton," Detective Almond began. "I'm sure you're trying to help your friend, Miz Shift. But the best thing you could do for her now is tell the truth. She may be sick. She may need help. She won't get it unless you tell us exactly what happened."

I started to open my mouth and tell them

I would never betray Mary, no matter what they did to me, but Chase spoke before I could get myself into more trouble. "My client has already told you everything she knows about what happened."

The ADA smiled in a slimy way that made me want to take a shower. "I'm sure your client wants to help us punish the one who did this terrible thing. We'd like to hear the story again from her."

"I don't see much point in that when you already know what she's going to say."

"We'd like to hear it anyway." The ADA nodded at Detective Almond, and they both looked at me.

I was ready to tell them everything I knew, starting with kindergarten and working up through college. There was no secret worth spending time alone with these two men. But before I could spill everything, Chase put his hand on mine. "I'll allow her to give you a short statement. Then we're leaving, unless you'd like to file charges against her."

"Nobody's talking about filing charges right now," Detective Almond said. "This is part of our preliminary investigation. We'll take a statement from her, and then she's free to go. We may need to speak with her later, depending on how our investigation proceeds."

Chase nodded. "She'll leave you her cell phone number where you can reach her."

"I'll need a permanent address, too," the ADA added.

"We can do that." Chase looked at me. "All right, Jessie. Tell him *briefly* what you know about Mr. Shift's death."

I could tell by the way he said *briefly* that I was supposed to keep it under one or two sentences; maybe 125 words. That's all. They didn't need any more.

But when I opened my mouth, it all came tumbling out: "My brother, Tony, owes me a hundred dollars, and I know I'm never going to see it. He's got some slutty fairy this year that's going to suck up all my money by the end of the summer. If that's not enough, I spent months getting ready to make baskets for the beginning of my dissertation on Renaissance crafts, only to find myself making change and conversation in Wicked Weaves when I'm not poking my hand with sharp grass and bleeding all over the baskets."

"Maybe that explains the dried blood we found on the basket weave." Detective Almond nodded to the ADA, and they both took notes. "Would you be willing to give us a sample of your blood?"

"Not without a court order," Chase answered.

"That won't be hard, Solicitor," Detective Almond promised. "Some cooperation would go a long way right now."

"Are you talking about a *real* blood test?" I asked. "Or a finger prick? I could do the prick but not the whole needle thing. I *really* hate needles. I think it's because I had so many shots when I was a kid. I was sick a lot, and we were always going to the doctor."

I saw the shocked, deer-in-the-headlights look on their faces. Even the clerk couldn't seem to write it all down. But I couldn't stop myself. "Now we have a dead guy. We weren't sure if he was dead at the Village, and Chase had to touch him. He almost fell on me, and I got out of the way in time. Then Mary says it's her weave that strangled him, but not her weave as in she didn't personally strangle him. And really I don't know how a little tiny woman like that could strangle that great big man or when she would've been able to do it."

I drew a breath to start again, but Chase stopped me. "That's fine, Jessie. I think they got all they need. In the interest of cooperation and because my client is innocent, she'll allow a blood sample."

"But only a finger prick," I reminded them. "If you show me the basket weave, I can probably tell you if it's mine."

For the next hour, they got a sample of my blood and brought the pathetic looking piece of basket weave in for me to inspect. It was definitely one of my failures. I guess that's why Mary never actually claimed it. But she must have known. Maybe she was trying to protect me. "This is mine. That's why it looks like Mary's, because I'm learning from her. But if you'd ever seen her work, you'd know the difference. You might want to take a look in the trash can outside Wicked Weaves. That's where this came from."

Another hour passed as they compared my blood to the blood on the basket weave. I glanced at Chase, who stayed with me through the ordeal and wished they'd left us alone for a while. But someone was with us the whole time.

Detective Almond finally came back in the room. "Looks like you're free to go, Miz Morton."

I was starting to get into the whole process. "Are you sure? There are a lot of really weird things going on out at the Village."

"I'm sure you're right. But those things will have to keep while we conduct this murder investigation. We appreciate your help."

I tried to say more, but Chase and Detective Almond hustled me out of the room. Before I knew what had happened, I was outside in the sunshine on the front steps of the police station. "You did it! You got me out!"

"I think you did it by yourself," Chase said. "I think they were afraid to keep you. Do you know the meaning of the word *brief*?"

"I don't care." I twirled around in my heavy linen. "I'm free! And I didn't incriminate Mary."

"Are you saying you did all that on purpose?"

I grinned. "I'm not stupid, you know."

"That makes me feel better. I wish it could stop my ears from bleeding. Next time, warn me, and I'll stuff cotton in them."

"What about Mary?"

"I'm going to get her out, too. You find someplace nearby and stay put. I'll find you when I'm done. This may take a little longer. I have a feeling she can't talk as fast as you."

"Thank you, Chase. I'm really glad you came for me."

"You're welcome. But next time, do what

your lawyer tells you."

"Okay. Go get Mary."

I watched him walk back into the police station before all the strength left my legs and I had to collapse on the green grass next to the stairs. A man with a poodle smiled at me in a strange way and said, "I'm sorry. Buzzy went right there, and you sat down before I could pick it up. Would you like a paper towel?"

I went inside and cleaned the poop off of my skirt. I couldn't do much about the smell, but at least it was clean. I knew the costume keepers wouldn't be thrilled when they saw a dog poop stain on the linen. As I was drying the skirt with a hand dryer in the bathroom, a woman smiled and asked me if I was at the police station for a historical event. "I visited Old Salem," she said with a ditzy smile. "Is that the same thing?"

I explained the difference between the Civil War and the Renaissance as I finished drying my skirt. "You should come out sometime. It's really nice out there at the Village."

The woman said she'd try to visit, and I started thinking about how the news of Joshua's murder was going to affect tourists. People expected fake things to happen at the Village, but real-life death was completely different. I hoped it wouldn't mean the end of Renaissance Faire Village.

I walked back out of the police station, hoping Chase would be out there with Mary, but no such luck. That's when I decided to sit down and practice my plaiting with some of the taller grass.

I didn't want to think how this event had altered my relationship with Chase. The logical side of my brain said that I was overwrought and emotional. That explained my jumping him when I saw him. The other part of my brain said it was about time. Of course, I had to worry about what Chase thought. He didn't seem to be resisting. He seemed to enjoy the experience as much as I did. But how could I know for sure?

The trick to basket weaving, which I was still trying to master, was holding everything together in your hands while you put it together with everything else. It sounds easy. It doesn't even look hard when you see someone else do it. But you almost need three hands to pull it off.

I pulled up some longer pieces of grass, made them equal lengths, then plaited them together like a braid. I made several braids, then worked at putting them together with other long pieces of grass. Of course I didn't have my bone and nothing to stitch with because the grass kept breaking. I guess that's why Gullah women never used fescue to make baskets.

I looked up and noticed that I'd attracted a crowd around me. There were murmurs of how interesting it was to watch me and what a good idea it was for the county to hire a historical reenactor to sit outside the courthouse. I smiled and chatted with them, explaining that I was from Renaissance Faire Village. Some of them threw some coins and dollar bills into the billowing folds of my skirt.

This was all right! I'd never thought about taking my show on the road. Maybe I could make some money on the outside of the Village.

Just as I had those thoughts, an officer stopped to see why everyone was standing around. "Have you got a vendor's permit?"

"No." My crowd began to disperse. So much for making some extra money.

"You need a permit to sit outside and solicit money."

"I wasn't soliciting, Officer. I was working on my basket weaving and people were watching me. I didn't realize they were throwing money."

"That's the worst excuse I've heard all day. Do you have a permit or not?"

I was about to tell him what I thought about his request when Chase came down the station stairs with Mary at his side. "Wait! There's my lawyer!"

The officer waited there until Chase saw me. He explained why I couldn't be there taking money from strangers under the guise of basket weaving. "If she's gonna dress like that, she's gonna raise a crowd. We can't have that around the police station."

"I understand, Officer. We've been looking for her all morning. Believe me, once we get her back to the hospital, she'll be adequately sedated." Chase looked at me significantly, and the officer looked, too.

"Okay. I understand. Keep a better eye on her next time. She'll have to turn in that money."

"That's fine. Come on, Jessie. Let's go home." Chase's voice was geared toward a two-year-old. He grabbed my arm, gave the cop the pitiful amount of money from my skirt, and hustled me out to where a silver car was parked.

As he opened the door, all I could think was, *You have a BMW?*

"Next time just paint a big target on your

skirt," he growled as he pulled out into traffic.

"Chase, do you have money? I know you don't work. Are you rich or something?" I knew I had more important things to think about, but I couldn't get over my surprise. Who would've guessed Chase had a car at all? And if he had, who'd expect it to be something nice and not some ratty 1982 Dodge or something? This was a sweet new BMW.

"Could we talk about this later?" He looked at me in the rearview mirror. Mary was in the front seat beside him. She was sniffling a little, and I realized she was crying.

Okay. So sometimes you have to hit me in the head with a battle-ax to get my attention. "I'm sorry, Mary. Are you all right?"

"If you don't mind someone threatening you and asking you why you murdered your husband, I'm fine."

Did everyone have to have an attitude? I sighed and tried again. "I'm glad you were able to get us out, Chase. Now what?"

"Nothing right now. Neither one of you was charged with anything. You might be called on to testify if they ever figure out what happened and take someone to court. Mary is their prime suspect. Or as they call it, their person of interest. She had motive and, according to them, opportunity, which is only being disputed by your statement that you were with her, Jessie."

"What does that mean, Chase?" Mary asked. "Will they come for me later?"

"It all depends. If they find something at the crime scene that points to you, they could bring you in and question you again."

"Well, we know they won't find her fingerprints on the basket weaving that killed Joshua. I think we established that it was my piece of crap weave that looked like hers."

"Of course my fingerprints weren't on that weave," Mary threw back at me. "But my spit might be, and maybe some sweat. I guess that makes us *both* killers."

"Take it easy, Mary." Chase put his hand on hers where it lay on the seat between them. "We know you didn't do it. We might have to come back a few times to get this settled. They'll get tired of seeing you after a while and start looking for the real killer. Right now you're just a convenient suspect."

"Maybe we should nudge them in the right direction," I added. "Maybe if we give them a few alternatives, they'll leave Mary alone."

"And how would we do that?" she asked.

"You can't accuse everyone in Renaissance Faire Village of killing my Joshua. No one knew him there. Why would anyone kill him?"

"Someone knew him and wanted him dead for some reason." The rationality of it hit me after I said it, but it was true. "What about Abraham?"

"Who's Abraham?" Chase turned on U.S. Highway 17 to go back out to the Village.

"He was there with Mary earlier today," I explained after telling him *briefly* about Mary's past.

She turned and glared at me. "That was told in confidence! You didn't ask my permission to tell him."

"Sorry. But I thought he should know, since he's your lawyer and everything." I was taking some serious grief over this whole thing, and I wasn't sure why. I'd done all I could to help Mary. It seemed to me she could be a little grateful.

She didn't apologize, and I didn't push the matter. Chase shook his head. "About me being your lawyer: it worked okay for today, but you guys may need real criminal lawyers. Probably public defenders, if you're actually accused of something."

I couldn't believe it. I had fantasized about Chase for so long and it was so close to being reality. Now my fantasy was turning into a big, hairy dust ball. "You mean you wouldn't defend us in court?"

"I'm a consultant patent attorney. I couldn't represent you in court. I'm not trained to do that."

I searched through everything I knew about lawyers, which took about fifteen seconds. "So what does a patent attorney do?"

"We research patents for wealthy clients who want to buy them."

"You're not a criminal lawyer?"

"That's what he said, child. You should learn to listen." Mary nodded as she looked out the window.

"But you acted like one. The police must've thought you were one."

"I watch TV. I loved Perry Mason when I was a kid." Chase grinned at me in the rear-view mirror. "But I was thinking of myself more like Matlock when I was in there today. You throw some legalese at someone, and they think you know what you're talking about."

"That's just fine." I vowed to use my brother Tony's lance on Chase when we got back to the Village. What was he thinking, posing as a criminal lawyer when he was really nothing more than some rich guy's flunky? Okay, it obviously paid well. And who knew Chase had a real job and a real profession of any kind. I was actually astounded. And totally excited.

FIVE

I realized I'd been a little too excited over finding out about Chase's hidden, respectable side when I woke up in his bed the next morning.

He was gone, but the indentation of his head on the pillow next to mine said it all. I didn't see a note, and I was embarrassed not to have woken up when he left. In my defense, it had been a hard day, and I sleep like the dead on a regular basis anyway.

But now it was morning. Chase lived in the dungeon located between the big tree swing and the Dutchman's Stage. It was two-story, with a mock jail on the ground floor and his living quarters in the top.

There wasn't time for me to pick up a new costume when we'd finally gotten back yesterday. Weeknights and Sunday, the Village closed at six p.m., staying open Friday and Saturday until ten. Except for the King's Feast after the Village closed on

Sundays. There was nothing open when we got back. Mary had walked back to Wicked Weaves, and I'd followed Chase to the dungeon. I think there was talk of him having a Corona or two sitting in his fridge, and I was incredibly thirsty.

I put my dirty costume back on, even though it made my skin crawl. It was early yet, according to the horse with the clock embedded in its side on Chase's dresser. I walked around the small rooms looking at his stuff. I'd known him for a long time, but I felt like I didn't really know him at all. Especially after last night.

He obviously liked horses. He had a collection of them scattered through his place. I looked at the suit he was wearing yesterday. It was still in a puddle of clothes I vaguely remembered taking off of him. Guess he forgot to take it back to Milton last night. I liked that idea. It meant he was focused on me.

My memory didn't stop there, and I was sure it showed in my face when he walked back through the door a few minutes later. "Coffee? Cinnamon roll?" He grinned as he said it. Apparently there were no misgivings on *his* part about last night.

"I should go. I have to turn in my costume, and I don't think Mary would be happy if I have to work with her as a strumpet or a fairy." I tried to stalk by him without looking up, but Chase is a big guy with broad shoulders. I think that's why they'd made him bailiff. He would've made a good bouncer.

"You promised me we weren't going to go through this." He put the cinnamon rolls and two cups of coffee on the dresser by the bed.

"Through what?" I tried my best to look completely unaffected by anything that had happened. I probably fell short, considering I couldn't find one of my shoes, and my blouse was stained. And why is it there's never a hairbrush when you need one? I'm not one of those pretty sleepers who can wake up looking like Miss America.

"Jessie, we both know this has been a long time coming." He smiled and took my hand. "I'm surprised you held out this long."

I snatched my hand back. "Held out how long?"

"*This* long. I mean, there's you and me, and what happened between us last night was incredible. We were perfect together."

I looked him over. "Would you say that's a ten on your scale?"

Something in my tone must have seeped into his incredibly thick head. "I know we're

80

not going to do this. I know we can have something special together."

"It was very special for last night, if you know what I mean." I held my head up and swept my filthy linen skirt around toward the door. "I don't know what I expected from you."

"Can't we talk about this?"

I grabbed a cup of coffee. "I have to get to work. Thanks for everything. I'm sure it was as wonderful for me as it was for you."

I walked regally out the door, down the stairs, and out into the cobblestone street. I felt confident he'd come after me, and we'd work everything out. It *had* been a special night. Why did morning always have to screw things up?

And I was right. Only a minute later, Chase came out after me, calling my name. "Jessie, stop!"

I stopped. It was good to be right. A few Village idiots (and I mean that literally) watched us as they practiced telling each other stupid stories that didn't make any sense and hitting each other in the head with rubber chickens.

"You forgot your shoes." The offending slippers dangled on two of his fingers.

So much for working things out. I stalked back to him to snatch my slippers. But when

I reached for them, he held them back. "What are you doing? Give me my shoes."

He laughed. "Take them. You're *so* bad."

I couldn't believe he was taunting me with my own shoes. "That's really mature. I can see why I was so attracted to you."

"You still have to come and get them." He held them up and jiggled them around. "What's the matter? Are you afraid to come get them?"

That was it. I launched myself at him, but he stepped out of the way, and I almost careened into one of the Lovely Laundry Ladies who washed clothes every day at the Village well. They laughed, and that made me angrier. "Chase, give me my shoes!"

"Come on, Jessie. Come get them."

I ran after him through the Village as merchants and tavern keepers threw open their wooden shutters to greet the day. Servants and varlets were sweeping the cobblestones, while delicious aromas of roasting turkey legs and corn filled the air. A few minstrels were practicing before the crowd at the Village Square, while jesters pranced, bells ringing, laughing at the slow moving Green Man.

Chase was tall and a good runner, but I was tall, too, and faster. When I could reach him, I gave him a hard push that landed him in a pile of fresh hay that was ready to be fed to the camels and elephants later that morning. Unfortunately, the move threw me off balance, and I landed in the hay with him. I tried to grab my shoes and run, but Chase grabbed me instead and kissed me. It was a poignant reminder of last night.

"What's up with you, Jessie?" His voice was breathless when he finally stopped kissing me.

"For one thing, you weigh a ton." I tried to throw him off of me, but he wasn't moving. "And you were gone when I woke up. In my experience, that's a bad thing."

He ran his fingers through my hair and took out a few pieces of straw. "I went for coffee. It's not like I left for years or something. You were in my bed. Where was I supposed to go?"

"I don't think that makes me feel any better."

"Look. Everything is good between us, right? This is something we've both wanted for a while. Let's not screw it up."

I didn't want to admit how long I'd wanted Chase. I vaguely remembered telling him about it last night when I'd gushed all manner of stupid things. "I'm not trying to screw anything up. It was a great night."

Chase's sweet brown eyes looked into

mine. "I thought so."

I wasn't sure where that meant we should go from here. Now that we'd finally done the deed, I knew I really cared for him. That was too scary for words. But with him sitting on top of me, his handsome face inches from mine, I couldn't deny what I felt. "Me, too."

He kissed me again and started both of us rolling through the hay until the animal keeper came up and told us to leave the stuff alone. "You think these poor animals want to eat that after you've cavorted all over it?"

We laughed like little kids and got out of the hay. I grabbed my shoes, finally, and we walked together through the early morning. Okay. Maybe it wasn't a match made in heaven, but it was pretty good. And who knew where it might go?

It was nine before I got to the costume shop. I had to wait in line with fifty college and high school drama students who left with costumes for everything imaginable. Ten of the young, giggling girls were going to be belly dancers in the new section of the Village that was becoming the Caravan Stage. A dozen other men and women became wandering scribes or musicians. One of the

Village astrologers had a tear in his purple robe and had to trade it for a blue one. Fairies flitted with their new costumes, checking their wings, and another dozen people became knaves and squires.

By the time I'd reached Portia, she was a frazzled costume keeper who kept yelling back to her varlets and servants in the back to speed it up. She took one glance at my dirty costume and let go a stream of modern day cuss words. "What've you done? Beth is going to have a fit! Do you think we can just clean that up? Linen isn't good at releasing soil. And what's that stain on the back of your skirt?"

I wasn't about to tell her I'd sat in dog poop, although the smell that lingered seemed to be evidence enough. I made up a story about sitting on a bench and not noticing a piece of fudge left behind by some careless eater. "I'm sorry, but I'm running late. Do you have something apprentice-like for me?"

"You're a craft apprentice, right?" Portia started looking through her catalog of costumes. "Beth is working on some new stuff, but it isn't ready yet. It's been busy all morning, Jessie. You're gonna have to take what you can get and come back tomorrow."

"All right. As long as it's not a fairy costume, anything'll do."

Portia passed me a troubadour costume; some green and gold satin tunic with green tights. "I heard about what happened to Mary's ex-husband yesterday. That was awful."

I was still staring at the costume, knowing Mary was going to have my head. "Yeah. It was bad."

"I wonder what he was doing here. I don't think she's ever seen him since she's been here. Do you know why the police questioned her?"

"Not really." I knew Portia was just looking for gossip. "Are you *sure* you don't have something else?"

"That's all there is, Jessie. Sorry." She leaned closer through the opening cut in the wall above the countertop. "You know, they say Mary killed someone, and that was why they ran her out of her home. Maybe it's true. People like that don't just stop killing after they get a taste of human blood."

"That's really disgusting!" I stared at her, wondering what else her little mind could come up with. "And I think you might be talking about dogs or chickens. I don't think Mary killed anybody. And no one tasted anyone's blood."

She shrugged and waved her hands. "That's just what I heard. Of course, Ham the blacksmith knows more about it. He's Mary's cousin or something. They came here together, you know."

I didn't know that, but I didn't tell her. I thanked her for my costume and rushed off to Wicked Weaves. The Village was opening at ten, and I only had a few minutes to take a shower and change clothes before Mary would need me in the shop.

I made a mental note to talk to Ham later about what had happened to Joshua. Portia was mostly useless, but she knew her gossip. Maybe there was something Ham knew that could help Mary.

Every year I stayed someplace different in the Village. Last year, I had a nice little apartment above the stables that I'd shared with a minstrel. It had been her job to walk around the Village and make up songs. Tourists paid her five dollars to make and sing a song about whatever they'd wanted to hear. She'd left at the end of the summer, going back to the University of Iowa with a sweet nest egg. If I didn't sound like a screech owl when I tried to sing, I might've considered that. Of course, that wouldn't happen now, since I'd decided to go after my Ph.D. in history.

This year, I was staying by myself in a room barely big enough for a twin bed and a bathroom. It looked like the inside of one of those tiny little campers. There were no windows, and the electricity was skittish. Sometimes there was air-conditioning and sometimes there wasn't.

I didn't stop to notice that this was one of those times when there was no air-conditioning. I took a quick shower, the only kind you can take with no hot water, and got dressed. I twisted my hair up on my head and secured it with a large clip. It was naturally thick, so it stayed where I put it. I didn't bother with makeup. It was too hot.

Thankfully, I didn't have any idea how bad I looked in the gold and green troubadour's getup until I reached Wicked Weaves. Mary took one look at me and burst out laughing. "Oh *that's* nice."

I shook my head, and all the little bells on my tunic jingled. *Thank God I didn't wear the crazy hat.* "I do the best I can to be here for you, and you make fun of me."

She didn't stop laughing until tears ran down her dark face. "Thank you, child. I needed a good laugh. What is it you're supposed to be? You're too tall to be an elf."

"Elves were very tall and slender, actually.

That's why they were so good with the long bow. You're thinking of dwarfs."

"Whatever you are, you're funnier than anything. I think we'll have good sales today with people wanting to look at you."

"They were out of peasant apprentice outfits." I moved a few baskets around on the display table. One of them, my favorite, had a circle base of about nine inches and sides two and a half inches high. The inside contained the most intricate weaving, with six twirl circles of woven sweetgrass. It was meant to hold iced tea glasses. There was a band left open on each side that formed a handle. It sold for $500. A little pricey for me. Maybe I could make one for myself someday.

"You'll do. It's not us that sells the baskets anyway." Mary lit up her pipe. "The baskets sell themselves. How 'bout you even off some sweetgrass?"

I'd almost rather pluck a chicken down at the butcher shop. It sounds easy: take a bunch of grass, hold it together, and cut the ends so they all match. Piece of cake, right? Think again. The grass won't keep still, and as you're cutting one side, the other side gets uneven, though it was even just a minute before. It's an exercise in patience and handling high levels of frustration without running away screaming. A little like teaching a freshman history class.

Mary settled down on the back step to start weaving for the day. We still had a few minutes before the gates opened. I grabbed a bunch of sweetgrass and sat beside her in the still, cool morning air. If I was going to have to do this slightly disgusting task, I was at least going to pick her brain. "I hope you're okay after yesterday."

"Why wouldn't I be?" The smoke from her pipe circled her head before it moved off.

"Well, your husband's dead. That's kind of traumatic. Even if you didn't kill him, you could still be upset after all of that stuff with the police."

"I'm not saying Joshua didn't mean nothin' to me," she corrected with careful words. "At one time, I lived and breathed for that man. But that was a while ago. It was hard seeing him there, but that's where we'll all be one day. From the dust to the grave. That's the journey all of us is taking."

I let some sweetgrass drop when I looked up at her. I'd learned the first day she didn't like swearing so I cursed inwardly. I was sorry I'd brought the incident up. Now I'd be depressed for the rest of the day thinking about what she'd said.

But I pushed forward anyway. In my vision of the world, there's rarely a time I shouldn't be talking. "So, what do you think happened? Do you think Abraham sneaked in here, stole a piece of basket weaving, and choked Joshua with it outside?"

Mary's black eyes narrowed. "You've got way too much imagination, Jessie. What makes you think Abraham would kill Joshua? They were brothers."

"Brothers? You didn't say that. But it wouldn't be the first time one brother killed another."

"Don't be foolish, Jessie, and watch the ends of that sweetgrass!" She took her pipe out of her mouth and studied the twisted branches of the small tree, the only thing that grew behind Wicked Weaves. "Abraham would never hurt Joshua. Don't you know nothin' about family? Sometimes even if they grow all twisted like this old, gnarly plum tree, it all comes right. Sometimes you think the fruit is bad, but there'll be a plum or two in there."

I was sure there was a lesson to learn from her words, but I was totally confused. I gave up on the metaphor of the plum tree and concentrated on what I was really trying to get at. "If you don't think Abraham murdered Joshua, who did? He didn't strangle himself."

"And now you don't think I did it?"

"I never said —"

"You didn't have to. I'm not deaf and blind, Jessie. You were trying to protect me yesterday because you thought I'd killed my Joshua." She took a puff from her pipe. "While I 'preciate the help, I didn't murder nobody. I ain't running."

I didn't want to get caught up in protesting that the idea didn't cross my mind. "Where were you when Chase and I went outside to find Joshua?"

"What difference does it make? The police told me Joshua died earlier. That's really the only reason he let me go. He has to try to figure out how I moved Joshua's body after I strangled him."

I hadn't thought of that. I was still on the idea of how Mary could forcibly strangle such a large man. I didn't think she was strong enough. "You must have some idea of what happened. If you don't think Abraham killed his brother, who else would do it? It had to be someone who knew he was here and had something against him. Did anyone know Joshua besides you?"

She shook her head. "There's only me."

"Then don't you think it's odd Abraham was here, too, for the first time in twenty years? And Joshua just happened to die?" I felt a little like one of those shows about lawyers on TV. I didn't know any lawyers personally, except for Chase, of course, and that was too new to tell if he ever really talked like that.

Mary stood up. "Mind that grass and your tongue. You don't know what you're saying. Too much can be a bad thing said."

"And what about Ham?" I pulled the question out of my brain like a magician pulls a rabbit out of his hat. "I know about your cousin, Mary. Are you trying to protect him?"

"Ham is my brother. I've had enough, Jessie. Go tend to that customer in the shop and leave me be."

She walked off with her pipe, leaving her half-finished basket on the steps. I felt bad because I could see she was upset. On the other hand, she was obviously protecting someone, even if it meant her own life would be ruined because of it. I wasn't going to let that happen.

Six

Two hours later, I was sitting in Sir Latte's Beanery next to the tart shop across from Wicked Weaves. Between the TV and newspaper reporters and the crime scene people, they had all but closed the basket shop down. The yellow lines of crime scene tape blocked off the alley and extended to both sides of the area where we'd found Joshua.

Chase was taking a break with me over a couple of iced mochas when Debby decided to join us. I didn't mind so much. She was my best history student and always a big help in class. Chase and I were having conversational problems. Most of what we had to say revolved around what had happened to Mary rather than what had happened to us.

Debby grabbed a cup of coffee, and the three of us sat at the window, watching the police and media circus that had come to Renaissance Faire Village. "What do you think they're looking for?"

I shrugged. "I don't know. I gave up watching detective shows a long time ago. I could never figure out who did it."

"They're looking for pieces of material, hair and skin samples, anything that might've been overlooked yesterday. Something they can use to make a case against Mary." Chase took a sip of his drink, never taking his eyes off the scene in the street.

"I'm surprised they didn't make all of them dress like us." Debby pointed at one of the blond reporters whose short skirt and sexy blouse was hardly something you'd find during the Renaissance.

"They were out of costumes this morning," I observed. "Besides, I'm sure the strain of outfitting that many extra people would've popped Beth's buttons."

Chase laughed and looked across the table at me for the first time (at least it seemed that way to me). "You're probably right. I don't think the police officers would've gone for it anyway. Can you imagine them in tunics and tights?"

Tony, minus his armor but still attached to the pretty fairy, entered the coffee shop and glanced around until he saw me. He and the fairy made a quick dash through the long line waiting for coffee. "There you are! I've been looking all over for you."

I was surprised and moved by his show of brotherly love. It never occurred to me to tell him what had happened yesterday. I didn't think he'd care. "I'm okay, thanks. It's been crazy, but I think I'm in the clear anyway. The police said I might have to testify, but they know I'm innocent, even if it was *my* weave that killed Mary's husband."

His clear brown eyes looked startled at first then confused. He drew up a chair and the fairy perched on his lap. "What are you talking about?"

"I thought you heard about Mary and the dead guy."

"What dead guy?"

I drew a deep, ragged breath. "Why were you looking for me?"

"It's kind of complicated, Jess, but I was wondering if you could loan me a few dollars until payday." He smiled and nodded at Chase and Debby, checking Debby out with the fairy sitting right there.

This was one of many times I wished I was adopted. That way I wouldn't have to claim Tony as my brother. It makes it much worse that he's my *twin* brother. You know all that stuff they say about twins thinking alike and finishing each other's sentences?

That's never happened with us. I can only assume it's because when the egg split, he got all the good looks and I got all the brains.

"I can't believe you." I sipped my iced mocha and turned my head. "Everything that's happened and *you* want twenty bucks to make it through the week."

Tony smiled, while Debby and Chase looked the other way, probably pretending they didn't know us. "Actually, I need more like forty, Jess. I have a few necessary expenses." He put his hand on the fairy's glittery thigh, and she giggled.

"I don't have any money. Except for that hundred you already owe me. If you have *necessary* expenses, I suggest you get a second job. A *real* job." I knew it sounded harsh, but I had to draw the line somewhere.

"Jessie, you're embarrassing me here." Tony smiled at the fairy and nodded at Chase and Debby.

"Too bad. Find someone else with money." I wondered how the fairy he didn't even bother to introduce felt about my loser brother. "Maybe your friend has some in her costume."

Tony shot to his feet. Chase joined him. He took some money out of his pocket and gave it to my brother. "Maybe that'll hold you."

Tony grinned and pocketed the money. "Thanks! I voted for you for bailiff, by the way. It's nice Jessie has made some friends. She's never been very good at that."

Chase didn't blink. "Don't ask her for money again, or you might find yourself in the dungeon for the night."

"I don't think you have that authority." Tony laughed, and the fairy joined him. "Don't worry about it anyway. We'll get paid soon, and then Tammy and I are off to Vegas. We're gonna score big and never come back to this dump. Well, we might visit and buy a few pretzels or something."

I didn't say anything until Tony and Tammy the fairy were gone. I appreciated what Chase had done, but I was really embarrassed by it, too. We were about to have our first fight.

Debby, maybe sensing the hostility in the air, despite the smell of mocha and cinnamon, took her coffee and said she'd see me later.

Being an assistant professor, I was used to bottling up my frustration and anger without showing a thing on the outside. "Let's walk for a while, Chase." My voice was a model of calm and control. I was very good at not showing emotion. You could ask any of my old boyfriends.

"Come on, Jessie, you can't really be angry that I warned off your brother, the leech."

"I didn't say anything about that." *Not yet anyway.* I was waiting for the right time and place, definitely not in here where everyone was listening.

"I know you're mad," he continued. "Just say it, and we can talk about it."

"I'm not going to be mad on *your* schedule," I ground out through clenched teeth. "Will you *please* step outside?"

He smiled. Chase has this really cute way of smiling where he kind of tilts his head a little and his braid falls to one side. I can't really describe how it makes me feel, but this wasn't the time or place for it, either. I was mad, and no cute smile or hair trick was going to make me feel better.

"I just wanted to help you." He took my hand. "I've known you for a while, remember? Tony has been like this since I met you. He needs to grow up. It's not gonna happen as long as you baby him. The guy needs to stand on his own for a while."

I opened my mouth, but nothing came out. Even worse, while Chase was holding my hand, he started playing with my fingers, and it didn't take long before I wasn't thinking about Tony anymore. That really cheesed me.

"You can't solve my problems for me." I wanted to snatch my hand back, but I wasn't up to that. Instead, I glared at him, and we stood there like idiots looking at each other.

"Okay. I won't ever try to solve any of your problems again." He grinned and brought his head close to mine. "Want to go back to the dungeon for a while? I've still got some time, and from the look of that crowd out there, you do, too."

I couldn't even say how much I wanted to go back to the dungeon at that moment. I wasn't even sure my legs would hold me up getting back there. Chase might have had to carry me. That made things even worse. "I forgive you. Maybe we could go back to the dungeon for a while."

But before I could throw my cup away, Detective Almond ducked his head into the coffee shop pretty much the way Tony did and spotted us. "I was looking for you two."

Everyone in the coffee shop stopped what they were doing to look at us. I dropped my cup in the trash; the urge to go to the dungeon left me. "I don't know what else I can tell you. I think we went through it all yesterday."

"That was yesterday, Miz Morton." He smiled in a way that made me wish I could follow my cup into the trash bin and hide out there for a while. "I think we might have a *little* something more to talk about today."

Chase and I followed him across the street to the crime scene. Photographers snapped our pictures, wondering who we were, and TV reporters hailed Detective Almond, trying to get some answers.

I looked around for Mary but didn't see her. Queen Olivia was there with Roger Trent and Fred the Red Dragon. They were recounting their stories about what they'd seen before Livy found Joshua.

I wasn't sure what else I could say that would make any difference. I still wasn't motivated to tell him things about Mary that could be bad for her. I looked up at Chase, and he shook his head. I felt like we were on the same wavelength. He wouldn't say anything either.

Detective Almond finally led us behind the privies and stopped at an area enclosed by yellow crime scene tape. "We think this is where Mr. Shift was killed. There were traces of the chemical used in the toilets on his clothes and this mud on his shoes and trousers. We found some seepage back here.

If you look close, you can see where there was a struggle."

I looked, but I couldn't see anything except a lot of footprints that looked like everywhere else in the Village that wasn't grassy or cobblestoned. Maybe it took a trained eye to see something more. "I'm not sure why you brought me here, Detective. This doesn't look any different than the muddy area by the stocks."

Chase nodded. "Except there wouldn't be chemical over there."

"Exactly, Mr. Manhattan." Detective Almond leaned down the best he could in his tight pants (why didn't the man go up a size?). "We found some other things out here I'm not ready to divulge as yet. Suffice it to say, it could be enough to implicate someone for this crime."

"Could be doesn't get it," Chase reminded him. "What is it you want from us?"

"I want to give you both a chance to recant your statement that you were with Ms. Shift the whole day. See, I kind of figure she was alone long enough to kill her husband."

"You know, that theory is a *little* stupid." I ignored Chase's warning look. "Have you *really* looked at Mary and at her husband? How in the world would she be able to hold him by the throat with some basket weaving until he was dead? I'm not a cop, but common sense dictates that she's half his size. Wouldn't he have fought back?"

He chuckled. I didn't like the sound. It told me he knew something I didn't know. I don't really like anyone to know things I don't know. Especially when it has something to do with something I should know.

"That's a mighty good point, Miz Morton. I'm glad you brought it up." He snorted hard, obviously congested. He adjusted his pants and narrowed his eyes. "I'm gonna go out on a limb right now and tell you something I shouldn't. I'm doing this so you can understand the error of lying for your friend."

Besides being disgusted by his hygiene habits, I didn't think there was anything he could tell me that would change my mind about lying for Mary, including him knowing I was lying. He'd have to prove it, right?

"We both need to get back to work." Chase spared me a glance that pointedly reminded me to be quiet. "Can you get to the point?"

"I sure can, Mr. Manhattan." Detective Almond chuckled again. "Say, is that Manhattan like New York City or Manhattan like Kansas?"

"I'm sure you have more important things to do than discuss my lineage," Chase said. "So do I."

"Settle down, young fella. Just making a little small talk. No harm done."

I was about to jump in and demand he quit dragging out everything like a bad soap opera, when he continued.

"Okay. I'll level with you." He looked around like Suzy Snow from the cable news channel was listening. "What if I told you a *kid* could've strangled Mr. Shift?"

I tapped my foot. If he was waiting for an indrawn breath or a loud *dun-dun* like in some horror movie, he wasn't getting it from me. "What does that mean?"

"It means Mr. Shift was inebriated. His blood alcohol was almost enough to kill him. He wouldn't have been too steady on his feet. Anybody, including your little friend, could've taken him. We don't think he did this on his own either. There was evidence of blunt force trauma to the back of his head, and we think he was force-fed the alcohol from the marks on his mouth, but we don't know how yet."

Detective Almond stared at Chase and me, waiting for some revelation from his announcement. Chase looked at me. I looked down at my feet, wondering if I was ever going to be able to get that chemical smell off my sandals.

"That doesn't change anything for me," Chase finally said. "I'm sticking to my story."

"What about you, Miz Morton?"

"Ditto." I meant to leave it there. I mean, that said it all. I just couldn't stop myself from adding, "Just because Joshua was drunk doesn't make Mary a killer."

"But it evens the odds in that supposition you made," he said. "How was it possible some little woman could kill a man twice her size? Get him stinking drunk first."

I felt like we were wasting our time. "If that's all you have, Detective, I need to go."

"That's it." He held up his hands. "I just don't want you to come crying back to me that you never had a chance to make it right. I'm sure your lawyer friend here can tell you what the penalty for withholding information or outright perjury is in this state."

"I'll do that, Detective." Chase took my hand. "Thanks for the information."

We double-timed it out of the crime scene area. Chase walked around the throng of people in the alley, not stopping until we were on the other side of Wicked Weaves by the Pope's Pot, a nice pottery shop I

105

was considering apprenticing to at some time.

"That was lame." I was the first to say it. Visitors were already cramming into the streets, leaving the pottery shop with their purchases. "I mean, really, what did he expect us to say?"

Chase drew me down to a bench beneath one of the few large trees in the Village. Because this had once been an Air Force base, most of the trees were put in as an afterthought. "Seriously, Jessie, were you *really* with Mary all day? They said Joshua was killed about two hours before we found him. Were you with her that early yesterday morning?"

"No! But I didn't have to be with her to know she didn't kill Joshua."

"How? You barely know her. She's been here a while, but she's not like Trent or Daisy, where everyone knows all about them. Mary has always kept to herself. Are you really sure, like *jail time sure,* she wouldn't kill anyone?"

I didn't like the way the conversation was going. Out of the corner of my eye, I saw people leaving the Three Chocolatiers. I wanted some chocolate so much it made my eyes water. It had been a stressful day. The mocha at Sir Latte's wasn't enough. I needed the real thing, preferably in dark bar form.

"I'm sorry." Chase apparently misunderstood my chocolate craving for a deeper emotion due to his guilt over questioning my loyalty to Mary (I minored in psychology). "I didn't mean to badger you over your statement. If you stand by it, I'll stand by you."

This worked for me in more than one way. As he spoke, Chase swept me into his arms and pushed my nose into his chest. He smelled really good, like clean linen and fresh air. My chocolate craving was replaced by other feelings. Spending time with Chase was better than chocolate, and it didn't make my face break out.

"Thanks." I leaned closer to him and hoped he was feeling the same way. It wasn't far to the dungeon. We could probably make it there and back in a few minutes. Okay, an hour with the time spent there. "Chase, I was thinking about what you said about going back to the dungeon."

One of the few devices not from the Renaissance allowed on the streets of the Village by the people who worked there was a two-way radio issued to the bailiff, paramedics, and other emergency personnel. Chase's radio went off at that moment. It was Jeff, the kid who was managing the stocks that summer. It seemed someone got a little too excited throwing fruit and vegetables at the poor sinner in the stocks.

"I'll be right there." Chase's eyes said it all. He wanted to go to the dungeon with me. It was almost as good as going. *Almost.* "I'm sorry, Jessie. I have to go. I'm on duty again in ten minutes anyway. Rain check?"

Disappointment almost overwhelmed me. I hadn't felt that bad about not getting to do something since Terry Tyler didn't invite me to her birthday party when I was in fourth grade.

He raised his left eyebrow. It was a quirk of his that I found particularly attractive. I expected him to say something, but instead he leaned closer and kissed me. "I'll see you later."

I wanted to tell him he couldn't just get cute with me, and everything would be all right. The best I could manage as he was walking away was, "Yeah. That's what I was thinking." It was lame; I knew it. But in my own defense, I was quite smitten with him, as we say in Renaissance Faire Village.

I trudged back to Wicked Weaves. The shop was empty, which was not surprising, considering all the police officers outside combing through the garbage and the privies. Mary was sitting on the back step, still working on the basket she'd started yesterday. If nothing else, I could tell she was upset by how long it was taking her to finish the basket. She normally would've had that one done already.

"There you are." She glanced up at me. "I was wondering where you'd got off to. Not that it really matters, since no one is coming in the shop."

"Detective Almond talked to me and Chase again. He found where he thinks Joshua was killed. He says Joshua was drunk and anyone, even *you,* could've killed him."

"He does, does he?" Mary pulled the sweetgrass tight and started the next coil in her basket. "He doesn't know much then. Joshua never took a drop of alcohol in his life. Whatever that detective says, he's wrong."

I picked up my basket and made a stitch to start a new coil. "Maybe you should tell him. If the autopsy showed Joshua was drunk, he was probably drunk. But maybe someone forced him to drink liquor."

Mary spared a quick glance at me as she started quickly stitching her coils of sweetgrass on top of each other. "And you think I did it?"

"No. I didn't say anything like that. Detective Almond just wants an easy arrest. I don't think you killed your husband."

"And why not? You think I couldn't hate him enough after he cast me out? You think I couldn't be angry enough after all these years alone?"

I hadn't thought about it that way. I used my bone to guide a second strand of palm through the tightly wrapped sweetgrass. I was surprised when I didn't poke my finger and bleed all over the basket. "I don't know you all that well. But from what I know of you, I don't think you'd kill anyone."

"No? Not even if my husband kept me from my child all these years?"

SEVEN

I was shocked and horrified. And curious to know how something like that could happen. I didn't want to sound nosy, but she did mention it. "That's terrible. How did it happen?"

Mary kept her face close to her busy hands as the coarse black rush was added to the inside of her basket for strength. I knew she didn't have to be that close to the weave and thought she might be crying.

"Joshua lied to me. I left our boy Jah with him. I was supposed to get to see Jah every so often. A few months after I left home, Joshua told me he died from the same thing that killed Abraham's son. I grieved, but I went on. I never went back to see Joshua again."

"Did Joshua tell you your son was still alive?"

"No. He didn't say a word to me about Jah. All these years he let me think he was dead. He cut me off from my child. For that, I'd have words with him now if he wasn't already dead. He had no right."

My brain started racing along with my hands, weaving the sweetgrass and palmetto leaves back and forth with the strong vanilla smell of the grass surrounding me. "I wouldn't say that too loud." I looked around like the police were hiding behind the privies. "How do you know Jah is alive if you didn't talk to Joshua?"

Mary took a balled-up piece of paper from her pocket. "Joshua left me a note. He told me about Jah and said he'd bring him to see me."

I took the note from her and read the thick, coarse writing. "Where did you get this?"

"It was on the door the day Joshua died. I found it before Abraham got here."

"Do you think Jah is here somewhere?"

"I asked Abraham about him." She yanked the black rush through the basket with a rough hand. "He told me my boy was dead and that Joshua lied to me."

"But you don't believe him?"

"No. Joshua died to tell me my son was alive. How can I doubt his word?"

I sat back on the stairs in the sunshine, the little bells on my costume jingling to remind me that I wasn't really on a coastal island living in another century. This was real and now. History was one thing; real life was much harder to understand. I wrote a 300-page paper once on Napoleon's valet. At the time it seemed very real to me. I could immerse myself in other people's lives and forget about my own. Right after that, my parents had died. Even history couldn't get me through that without breaking down.

"What are you going to do?"

Mary shook her head. "I daren't go anywhere until they find who killed Joshua or they will be sure it was me. But when I can, I'm going to find my son."

"Do you think Joshua lied to him and told him *you* were dead, too?"

"I don't know. But I want to see Jah so bad it aches inside of me. He was only a boy when I left. Now he's a man. He had his father's eyes and my mother's disposition. He was all that was good in life. It was the hardest thing to leave him."

"I don't understand why you left. You could've sued for custody if you had to. You didn't have to give up visitation."

"You don't understand our ways, Jessie." She held out the basket she was working on so I could see it. "This is our heritage. Every year, some of it slips away. Someday it will all be lost. I don't want to be part of that. I obeyed our laws when I left. But now I know I was cheated out of seeing my boy grow up."

"You think Abraham had something to do with this?" I touched the bulrush that was a rich, tawny color in the sunlight. "You think that's why Joshua came to tell you Jah was still alive?"

"Abraham adopted my son in place of his own who was lost. Joshua let him do this to make peace between the members of the family who believed I killed Abraham's son. That's why Joshua lied to me. He knew I wouldn't let that happen."

For a few moments, I could only stare at the intricate craftwork in the basket Mary held. It seemed poetic to me that I heard this tale sitting on the steps in Renaissance Faire Village. It was like a myth or folklore. It didn't seem possible something of this sort could happen in the last twenty years.

I didn't know what to say. If the police found out about Jah and about Joshua's decision to let Abraham adopt him, that might be the motive that pushed the investigation forward, but in the wrong direction. I felt like I was the only thing keeping Mary out of prison. She might have motive, but the police couldn't place her at the crime scene at the time Joshua was killed.

"Excuse me, ladies." An officer came around the corner of the shop. "Mrs. Shift, Detective Almond would like a few words with you."

Mary got to her feet and handed me the basket she was weaving. "Study that for a while. The most likely place for a basket to break is where it's sewed together. Even though that black rush is strong, years and weather can make it soft."

I knew there was a parable of some sort in her words. I worked at my basket for a few minutes longer, glancing at hers on the step beside me from time to time. Was she trying to tell me she was like the black rush; worn down by life but staying together by the strength of her will until she heard about her son still being alive? Or was she telling me she was soft compared to what she used to be?

I wasn't sure, and it bothered me. She had abundant reasons to hate and kill Joshua, as far as I was concerned. I was also sure a jury would agree with me. If the police ever found out I wasn't with her when Joshua was killed, they'd arrest her.

With that thought, I jabbed a sharp palmetto leaf into my finger. By grabbing a Sir Latte's napkin I'd put in my pocket, I barely kept it from bleeding on my basket. I took both baskets inside the shop and washed the cut on my finger. Looking around for a bandage, I realized I'd used them all. Since there was still no one in the shop, I decided to close down for a while and go get some bandages from the first aid station in the back of Merlin's Apothecary.

It was midday now, and that was the busiest time on the weekends. Thousands of people, knights, ladies, and sorcerers were roaming the streets of Renaissance Faire Village. The smells of baking bread, cinnamon rolls, turkey legs, and coffee all blended together to make even the most weight conscious person hungry.

I realized coffee with Chase had been a while before, and I was hungry, too. My Village cup was attached to my belt like everyone else who worked here. It meant you could get free drinks at the various pubs and cafés. Food was another matter. You either had to bring your own or pay for what you got.

Some of the eateries gave us discounts or even free day-old bread or pastries. But it was amazing how tired you could get of eating cinnamon rolls every day because they were twenty cents.

But, since my finger was bleeding through

the napkin, Merlin's Apothecary was first on my list. The guy who played Merlin was really named Merlin. I don't know if he had a name change, but it was his legal name as well as his Village name. He was a crazy old dude who I think really believed he was a wizard. He was always casting spells on rude tourists or lazy Village workers.

He had the whole wizard look going on with a full white beard and long, straggly white hair. His pointy purple hat was etched with symbols of power. At least that's what I thought they were. He wore a long purple robe that matched his hat. Some of the flower girls and fairies swore there was nothing under that robe. There had been rumors of him flashing a few unsuspecting females. But Chase had never caught him at it, and the girls had refused to press charges.

I liked the apothecary shop with its hundreds of colored bottles and powders. There were herbs in bulk form as well as drying from the rafters. The shop also sold candles, rubbing oil, some magic tricks, and a few wands. The smell of the drying herbs was always incredible when you first walked in. Then you had to face Horace, and that almost ruined everything.

Horace was a bull moose; or what was left of a bull moose. It was primarily a giant moose head that was situated right in front of the door. You had to walk around it to get in the apothecary. Tourists didn't seem to mind. They actually had their pictures taken with the mangy old head. It kind of scared me. It was creepy; even creepier than Merlin.

Still, I went in that way when I could've gone into the first aid unit attached to the shop in back. I didn't like looking at Horace's lifeless glass eyes, but I liked the rest of the shop. I wished there was some craft that went on in the shop so I could apprentice there. But if there was a craft, I was probably better off not knowing about it.

"Come in, Jessie!" Merlin wasn't swamped with visitors and saw me right away. "Let me guess; you sliced your finger on some kind of basket grass. Am I right?"

"You got it. We ran out of bandages."

"No wonder! It must've taken a few to put on that poor man's throat you found over there. Having one's throat cut is a bad and messy affair."

"Actually, he was strangled. His throat wasn't cut. We didn't need any bandages for him. He was already dead when we found him."

Merlin nodded and swept around the

shop. "I have a potion for that. It can bring the dead back to life. At least temporarily. It was used by King Arthur to find out who killed one of his knights from the Round Table. It was deemed too dangerous to use after that and hidden away until I found it."

"Thanks." I was beginning to regret coming in here after all. "I think we may be too late for that. It was a good idea, but the police have the body, and there's already been an autopsy."

He rubbed his hands together, mindful of his wand. "And what did they find?"

I shrugged. "That he was strangled to death."

"Is that all?"

"No. They also found out he was drunk."

Merlin laughed and swished his robe around. I hoped I wasn't about to be a victim of flashing. "Now *that's* another story. Around here, *not* being drunk would be unusual."

"Except that he never drank alcohol."

"Let me think about that. You go get your bandages and come back. Although to stay in character, you should just tie a rag around the cut. I suppose in your case, you wouldn't be able to move your hands for all the rags on them. Oh well."

I walked past the stuffed, dead birds, trying not to touch them. The jars full of bugs and worms only creeped me out, but the dead birds could've had diseases. The shop was a compendium of everything weird; exactly what you'd expect from a wizard's apothecary. I guess that's why I liked it and hated it at the same time.

The first aid station was manned by Wanda LeFay, the nurse. In all the years I'd known her, she'd never told anyone where she was from or anything about her past life. I wasn't sure how she got to be a nurse, since she didn't enjoy human contact. No one went to her first aid station unless they had no choice, like me running out of bandages.

Wanda was patching up Rafe, the pirate, who looked like he'd had a run-in with a canon. The pirates, including the pirate queen, did a show twice a day and an extra one during the King's Feast. They were a rowdy group who seemed to have a good time as they pillaged and plundered, even though they could never take over the castle.

"Sit down," Wanda said when she saw me. "I'll get to you as soon as I can."

"Oww!" Rafe protested her ungentle ministrations. "You don't have to pull that so tight. I won't have any circulation to the rest of my arm."

"Better that than your arm falling off." She made the bandage even tighter. "You all better take it easy up there. You're the third pirate I've seen today. I'd hate to have to report you for being too careless. This *is* a job site, you know."

Rafe laughed, showing fake gold teeth. He pushed back his long, black wig and moved his arm away from Wanda. "I'd like to see OSHA come in here and try to deal with everything that goes on. They'd go crazy the first day."

Wanda jerked Rafe's arm back and finished her bandage. "Maybe so, but if I were you, I'd pass the word along. No more than one pirate per day at this first-aid station. That's the rule."

"I'll pass that on." He stood up, adjusted his scabbard and doublet and swaggered my way. "Hey there, Jessie! Heard you found some dead guy. I hope you covered your tracks, my lovely."

"It's not a joke." I wasn't in the mood to be amused by his playacting. "He was really Mary's husband."

He smiled and curled his mustache. "Is that Mary, Mary Quite Contrary or Mary Had a Little Lamb?"

"Go away. Go plunder something."

He growled at me. The pirates take themselves *way* too seriously. "I'd love to plunder *your* castle sometime, sweetie."

"Like *that's* going to happen." I got up and walked past him toward Wanda, and he barked at me. I ignored him. Rafe and I had a thing once. It didn't even last the whole summer. The guy was a whack job. I think he really thought he was a pirate.

Wanda who, by the way, had a lovely, *real* British accent, one of the few in the Village, changed her sterile gloves, then lit up a cigarette. I wasn't sure if my lungs or my finger felt more assaulted by her lack of hygiene. "So, what's wrong with you this morning, ducks?"

"I just need a bandage." I wanted to tell her she didn't need to touch me, but I knew better. Blanket statements like that drove Wanda into a doctorlike frenzy. I didn't feel like having brain surgery that day.

"I'm the nurse. I'll be the judge of what you need. Let me see that hand."

Wanda looked at me with her cold blue eyes that reminded me of fish eyes. They weren't on either side of her head, but there was something creepy and fishlike about them. She put out her hand for mine, and I started to give it to her. Then she blew a puff of smoke in my face, and I changed my mind.

"You know, the surgeon general thinks those things are bad for you." I wondered if I could reach the box of bandages sitting on the shelf without her crippling or harming me in some way. "I really only need a little bandage, Wanda. *Really*. I just cut my finger on some palm, like usual. A bandage will keep the blood off my basket. We don't have to make a major production over this."

That was a mistake. Wanda grabbed my hand. I sat down in the chair; it was either that or fall on the floor. "I think I see a piece of foreign matter in this cut. We should explore it."

"I'd rather have leeches put on me. Thanks anyway. May I *please* have a bandage?"

Wanda wasn't budging. Obviously she was bored. Her cold fish eyes stared at me, and I shivered. It was either get a bandage myself or die trying. The last time she'd decided to explore one of my cuts, I had to have three stitches at the hospital the next day. No way was I going through that again.

I acted like I was going to give her my hand, then made the dive for the bandages. Wanda tried to stop me, but her block came an instant too late. I grabbed the box; a handful of bandages came out and scattered around us like brown butterflies.

The look on Wanda's face was terrible.

She yelled, "No!" and dropped to catch them before they could hit the wood floor. I doubted that she cared if they got dirty. It was probably more that she'd have to buy more bandages.

In the meantime, I'd grabbed at least ten bandages and stuffed them into the pocket of my troubadour's outfit, the bells jingling as I moved. I looked back at her with a feeling of triumph. I knew I'd pay for it some other day, but today I was victorious. That was enough for me.

"Jessie, I heard about Mary's husband." Wanda's voice was bordering on the maniacal. Or at least it seemed that way to me. "Ask her about Lord Simon. This isn't the first time a man in Mary's life has died mysteriously."

I didn't waste any time getting out of there. You know how the good guy always goes back to check and see if the bad guy is really dead? That's when the bad guy always jumps up and pounds the good guy a few more times before he dies. That's what I was afraid of with Wanda. If I hesitated, I would lose. I just got the heck out of there. Whatever crazy stuff she had to say about Mary didn't matter to me.

I was kind of pleased with myself; the bandages were in my pocket, and Wanda's cursing was at my back. It was a successful trip to the first aid station. Hopefully it wouldn't happen again anytime soon.

Merlin jumped out in front of me, purple robe flying. I closed my eyes, hoping I wouldn't see anything that might put me off men for the rest of my life. This might be what the fairies were talking about. It wasn't so much that Merlin purposely flashed them as that someone needed to make the old wizard wear boxers.

"I know what I was going to tell you before you went back there with Nurse LeFay." He whirled around a few more times and waved his wand.

I'd had about enough crazy stuff for that hour. I was ready to go back to Wicked Weaves and stick my hand with a palm leaf a few more times. Mary was obscure, and sometimes she worked me too hard, but at least she wasn't completely insane. Some people in the Village, like Merlin and Wanda, got a little worse every year.

"All right. Tell me. I have to get back to Wicked Weaves."

"A funnel." He pulled a brown funnel out of the air like, well, like magic. "During the Inquisition, it was a common torture to use a funnel to drown someone by pouring water down their throat."

"Lovely." I located the door behind him and wondered if I could dash around him without touching any of the dead birds.

"You see?" He held the funnel up near his mouth. "Anyone could use something like this to force someone to take in alcohol or any other liquid. They'd have to be subdued, of course."

"Of course." I didn't want to know where he was going with this.

"Mary purchased one of my finest leather funnels several months ago. It was February." His feathery white brows knit together. "Or was it March? It was definitely before May."

"I'm sure she had a good reason to buy a funnel."

"I'm sure she did." He did a little jig of some sort. I'm not totally clear on what a jig actually is, but it's the best way to describe the dance he did. "Amazing that she would have opportunity to use the funnel, eh?"

I thanked him for telling me about the funnel, then ran out of the Apothecary and smack into Chase. "Hey! I've been looking all over for you," he said.

"Merlin thinks Mary used an Inquisition funnel to murder Joshua." I couldn't help it. The weirdness took me over and forced me to say these things. "He and Wanda both think Mary killed Joshua. And who is Lord Simon?"

EIGHT

"Slow down and tell me what you're talking about," Chase encouraged.

I took a deep breath and repeated everything Wanda and Merlin had said to me. "That means Merlin thinks Mary used the funnel she got from him to pour liquor into Joshua, and Wanda says it's happened before with some guy called Lord Simon. Do you know anything about that?"

"It must've been before my time as bailiff. Back when I was jousting and chasing elephants, I didn't know much that went on around here."

I laughed when I remembered that time Chase was herding goats around the Village. "No wonder! It was all you could do to keep up with the animals."

"Especially the large ones. That time the camel stepped on my foot, I thought I was going to lose my toes."

We'd gotten off track for a minute, but I

felt less tense. "Everything is going against her, Chase. If the police talk to Merlin or Wanda or anyone except you and me, she could end up going to prison. We both know she's not guilty. She's a little weird and bossy, but you should see the look in her eyes when she talks about Joshua. And did you know they had a son together?"

"No. I've never heard that. Did Mary tell you?"

"Yeah. She hasn't seen him in twenty years. He could be here in the Village right now, and she wouldn't know him. Life has pushed her around a lot. We can't let it push her any more."

"That's poetic, Jessie, but do you have any idea on how we start proving Mary is innocent?"

"I think I do. We have to see Ham the blacksmith. I think he may have some answers."

"I've got about an hour until my next court appearance and tour of the dungeon. Maybe we could squeeze it in now."

I hugged him, and he kissed me. We were almost sidetracked again. An hour is plenty of time for a *lot* of things. But we decided to put those off and talk to Ham.

The blacksmith shop was wedged between the jousting arena, the privies, and the

Caravan Stage, where the new belly dancers were. It made sense to have him near the field and the stables. I'm not sure why the belly dancers were so close. It seemed like it would've been better to have the archery board or the hatchet throwing close by. But nothing made sense all the time. I suppose Renaissance Faire Village did the best it could, especially with its otherworldly atmosphere.

We walked past William Shakespeare, who was composing a sonnet on the color of one of the fairy's wings. Mother Goose was telling nursery rhymes as she stroked the pure white feathers on her bird. Galileo was showing his experiments to a group of campers from a day school. There was always something going on.

Shakespeare called out to Chase as we went by. "Bailiff, where goest thou?"

"To the blacksmith," Chase answered. "What doest thou, Sir Shakespeare?"

"I believe I am attempting to woo yon fairy, Sir Bailiff." Shakespeare, aka Pat Snyder, grinned almost as wide as the starched white ruff around his neck.

"Carry on, Sir Shakespeare." Chase waved to the rutting playwright.

"What is it about those fairies?" I kept walking fast, trying to ignore both men looking at the pretty fairy's almost-transparent dress. "I think they should make them wear velvet or linen or maybe a nice wool like the rest of us."

Chase caught up with me and casually draped his arm around my shoulders. "Methinks thou dost not appreciate the female fairies."

"Think you?" I shrugged off his arm. "I canst imagine why."

He stopped and pulled me off my feet. "Thinkest thou I do enjoy fairies more than you, my fine troubadour?" He jiggled me a little until the bells on my costume were ringing.

"Put me down, knavish oaf!"

"Methinks you should make reparations for impugning my honor, wench."

"Put me down, and I will impugn you no longer, sir."

It was only then I realized we'd drawn a crowd. Cameras started flashing, and children started asking their parents what we were talking about. Queen Olivia went by with her procession of ladies-in-waiting. Her look said we'd better cut it out. No one was allowed to interrupt Livy and her adoring crowd during her hourly stroll through the Village.

Chase put me down, put his arm around

me, and we walked away.

"Forsooth," Shakespeare exclaimed behind us, "the troubadour and the bailiff make an unusual couple. What say you, beautiful fairy?"

Thankfully, I didn't have to hear what the fairy said. I forgave Chase. After all, if there were any boy fairies, and they wore next to nothing, I'd be looking at them, too. I suppose there's some rhyme in that reason.

We reached the blacksmith's forge a few minutes later. Little Bo Peep was chasing her sheep, but the Big Bad Wolf had stepped in to help her. They were on the outs right now, so it was good of the wolf. He and Bo Peep had been together for a while. I hated that they broke up. Maybe the lost sheep would get them back together.

Chase called out for Ham, which was short for Hammer; no one seemed to know his real name. We didn't see him at his usual spot by the forge. His tools were there, along with a horseshoe he was working on. "It's me, Ham. I need to talk to you."

"I don't see him." I looked around the small smithy. There was no sign of Ham, which was unusual, because the hot coals were ready to soften the iron. "He doesn't just leave like this."

Chase looked back where the horses were

kept when they were waiting to be shod. "He's not back here, either. Ham? Where are you?"

I heard a groaning sound and moved some hay out of the way. Ham was underneath it, nursing a bump on the head.

We dragged him out of the smithy, and Chase called the paramedics. I sat with Ham, who seemed disoriented but otherwise okay.

"What happened?" I asked him. "Did you fall?"

"No. Someone sneaked up behind me and hit me in the head." He turned so I could examine his scalp beneath the thin black fuzz on his head. "I didn't see who it was, but whoever is gonna be sorry when I catch up with him."

Inspired, I ventured, "Could it have been Abraham?"

"Abraham?" Ham stared at me. "I don't know anyone named Abraham except for the piper's son who keeps stealing that stupid pig."

"No. I mean Abraham, Joshua's brother."

"Is he here?" Ham looked around. "Does Mary know?"

"Yes. He's here. He talked to her before we found Joshua. He was threatening her, I think. He told her Jah is still alive."

He shook his head and groaned. "I ain't seen Abraham, Joshua, nor Jah for so long, I'm not sure I'd know them to see them. What's this about Mary killing Joshua?"

"It's not true. That's why we're here. We thought you might be able to help us."

"She never tells me anything. I wouldn't know if she killed all three of them and hid them in the back of that shop. That's the way she is. That woman wouldn't open her mouth to tell her secrets if death was standing in front of her wanting to know."

This was getting me nowhere. Ham was almost as bad as Merlin and Wanda. Of course, someone *had* hit him in the head. Could it be the same person who killed Joshua? Maybe this time, he wasn't able to finish the job for some reason. Maybe he was about to pour liquor down Ham's throat, then strangle him.

I looked around the smithy for any sign of what had happened. "Where were you when you were attacked?"

"I was standing at the forge, like always. I bent over to pick up a horseshoe, and something came down hard on my head. Next thing I know, you and Chase were dragging me out of the hay."

Chase and the paramedics stopped my interrogation. They took Ham away to have his head X-rayed. I kept looking through the straw while they hooked Ham up to an IV and called the ambulance.

"What are you looking for?" Chase asked when the paramedics were gone. A small crowd had gathered around the smithy, waiting for any other excitement that might happen.

"I'm looking for clues. Who do you think did this?" I glanced at the curious onlookers. "You're the bailiff. Shouldn't you do crowd control?"

He went to shoo away the people and keep the foot traffic moving. I continued to search through the hay, hoping Ham's attacker might have left something behind. I started sneezing and finally had to give up, sitting back against the wall and blowing my nose.

"They don't call it hay fever for nothing." He sat beside me. "Any luck?"

"No. I guess it was too much to hope for." I told him my theory about Ham. "We might've saved his life by coming to look for him."

"Why would someone want to kill Ham?"

"Maybe for the same reason they killed Joshua."

"You two interested in what happened to the blacksmith?"

We looked up and saw one of Robin Hood's Merry Men. He was totally dressed in forest green from his slippers and tights to his tunic and mantle. He wore a pointy hat and had a bow slung across his shoulder.

"Is that you, Alex?" I got to my feet and dusted off my costume.

"Jessie? I didn't recognize you in that getup. I didn't know if you were here this summer."

I walked toward him at the same time he came toward me. I put up my arms to hug him, and he unexpectedly kissed me. Alex and I had a history. It was only one summer when I was just a kid. But he was still a good kisser.

Chase cleared his throat. I stepped back, and Alex grinned. "Same old Jessie. It's good to see you."

I did the introductions quickly. Chase kind of knew Alex anyway. He wasn't looking very friendly, and they didn't shake hands.

"What can you tell me about what happened to Ham?" Despite the sudden tension in the smithy, I still wanted answers.

"I saw some guy in here a little while ago when I was going by to see my wife. She's one of the belly dancers."

"Really? I didn't know you were married."

"Who'd guess?" Chase mumbled.

"Yeah. Her name is Sally. She's an English professor at Auburn. She loves to come out here for the summer." Alex smiled without looking like he felt guilty at all for kissing me, despite the fact that he was married.

"So what exactly did you see, Alex?" Chase kept the conversation going away from the personal stuff.

"There was a tall dude here." Alex looked at me. "He was wearing one of those hooded monk costumes. I don't know if he was from the bakery or what."

I should explain that the name of the baked goods shop is the Monastery Bakery, and all the people who work there dress like monks. They even made a CD of their chanting a few years ago. "And you saw him here with Ham?"

"Not exactly. Ham was working at the forge, and the monk dude was behind him. I didn't think anything about it until I heard Ham got hit in the head. Now I think the monk might've done it."

"Okay. Thanks for your input." Chase was using his crowd control voice. "We'll send a page if we need you. Now move along."

"Maybe we could have some coffee or dinner." Alex smiled at me and ignored Chase.

"What did you say your *wife's* name was again?" I smiled back, but there was no way

I was going to do anything with Alex, even if I hadn't already been mostly committed to Chase. At least for the summer.

"I think we need to go now." Chase took my arm and nodded to Alex. "See you around."

"Don't be so jealous," I whispered as he hustled me away from Alex.

"I should be happy you kissed him like a long-lost lover?"

"He is kind of a long-lost lover. I didn't know he was married."

"That makes all the difference. In the meantime, during the ten-minute lip-lock, here's good old Chase watching and waiting."

"It wasn't like that."

"What was it like then? I was there, but it kind of left me in the cold."

I stopped, grabbed him by his handsome but incredibly thick head, and kissed him. "It was in the past. That's what it was like. Now can we focus on helping Mary?"

He put his arms around me and kissed me again. "You mean by finding the monk, finding the missing guy who might've killed the dead guy, and maybe the son that no one knew about?"

"That's exactly it."

He kissed me again, this time longer and

with more feeling. "I only have about thirty minutes before Bailiff's Court. I don't know if we have time to do all that. But the dungeon is only a two-minute walk. We could go there instead."

I was tempted. That last kiss had me tingling all over. But I was resolute, and Chase's radio went off again. It was a conspiracy to keep us apart.

"I have to go." He kissed me again. "This may take a while, and I'll have to clean up the vegetables after court. Do you want to have dinner tonight?"

"You know I do."

"I'll pick you up a little after five." He smiled at me and tucked a stray strand of hair behind my ear.

"I'll be waiting." He started to walk away, and I grabbed his hand. "You know Alex doesn't hold a candle to you, right?"

"I know. Just wondering if *you* knew. See you later."

I wasn't sure how Chase could be jealous of anyone, but I'm sure even someone who looks like him can have inferiority issues. I managed to walk all the way back to Wicked Weaves before I realized I'd meant to swing by the Monastery Bakery. I guess that's what they call having your head in the clouds.

Mary was back, and the shop was open. The police were gone, but a few reporters were still hanging out. Customers were jammed in the shop, wanting to buy baskets and gossip. I put on my apron and helped Mary sell some baskets.

By the time the rush of customers was over, I was sweating and thirsty. I grabbed a bottle of water from the mini fridge hidden behind a panel in the wall. Every shop had places they hid their modern conveniences, except for the cash registers. They kept those out front. They were merchants, after all.

"I was beginning to wonder if you were ever coming back," Mary scolded, a bead of perspiration on her upper lip. "Were you out chasing that boy again? I tell you to leave him alone. You ain't his mama."

"No, I was doing a different kind of chasing." I smiled, thinking about Chase.

Mary laughed. "I know that smile. You found a *real* man to spend some time with, didn't you? That's good. A girl your age should be with a young man. Did I ever tell you about the first boy I ever kissed?"

Have I mentioned that Mary's second passion after basket weaving is storytelling? I read online that Gullahs are master storytellers. They weren't kidding.

Mary lit up her pipe and grabbed the basket she'd been working on, and we went out to sit on the back steps and weave. "Mind that knot. It won't hold if it's sagging. You have to make it strong. Don't forget, everything rests on each coil of the basket supporting the next coil."

I listened to her talk about a young boy who'd taken her fishing and managed to share her first kiss. I watched her hands for a while before I started on my own weaving. Her voice continued, singsong, in the background of my thoughts while I threaded the old end of the palm through the next coil and cut the leftover grass. I coiled and stitched and added until I had the sides of my basket several inches tall. I tied a new slipknot and got ready to start the next coil.

"Why, Jessie, child, you got the hang of it! Look at you! Not even a drop of blood, either. You gonna be weaving baskets for sale soon enough."

I was pleased with her praise. I admit it; I'm an overachiever. I like it when people tell me I've done a good job and I can see I'm working at an above-average level. We were actually bonding for a change instead of arguing.

I thought this might be a good time to

tackle Mary for more information. I couldn't help her if she didn't tell me everything I needed to know. "Did you hear what happened to Ham today?"

"Ham?" She turned her head, and her fast, brown fingers stopped flying through her basket. "Oh, you mean my brother, Mvuluki."

"Is that his real name? No wonder he never uses it."

"It means *rememberer* in our language. It's a beautiful name."

I didn't want to comment on a name I wasn't sure I could pronounce. "I was going to talk to him about Joshua, but someone attacked him while he was working on a horseshoe."

"No! Who would hurt Ham? He's a gentle soul. And why were you mixing up in my business? I didn't ask you to talk to no one about me and Joshua."

I stopped moving the palm leaf and bone in my hand. "Someone has to do it! You're so busy denying there's a problem, you'll be in prison before you realize what's happening. Didn't you ever hear that old song about the lights going out in Georgia? They hung that poor man, actually the woman's brother, before she could say the tracks were hers."

She stared at me like I was crazy. "What are you talking about, Jessie? You children ain't got a lick of sense between you. Who cares what some old song says?"

"I think the thing you should focus on here is that Joshua was killed, and your brother was attacked. The two of them are both from your home in Mount Pleasant. Abraham is probably here somewhere and maybe your son, too. Someone might have it in for all of you. Or Abraham wants to get rid of you, Joshua, and your brother so Jah will turn to him."

"That's crazy talk." She started working on her basket again. The coils of grass had to be fed constantly to maintain the foundation of uniform thickness. That was one of the first things I'd learned. Mary's basket was losing uniform thickness, so I knew she was upset.

"It's not crazy. Joshua is dead. Ham was attacked. Merlin told me you bought a leather funnel from him that could've been used to force-feed Joshua alcohol."

"I bought it to put tobacco into the pouch," Mary defended. "Why would Merlin even think I would use it on Joshua?"

"Maybe because Wanda thinks you killed Joshua."

"That's even crazier. And who cares what

Wanda thinks, anyway? This whole place is nothing but gossips and crazy people. I don't know why I stay here."

"Because it's your home now. Like you told me, you're not running away again." I covered her busy hand with mine. "I can help you, if you let me. We can't let the police add up two and two and get five. That would mean you'd go to jail."

"If I had one idea of what you were talking about, Jessie, maybe I could help. But what you're saying don't make no sense. How can two and two make five?"

"It doesn't matter. But what might matter is Lord Simon. What happened to him?"

Mary groaned, then took a puff from her pipe and gazed off in the distance. I could hear the sound of children singing in front of the store and horses going by on the cobblestones. The day was beginning to cool down, even a small breeze fluttering through the flags that waved in the Village.

"Lord Simon." She puffed on her pipe again. "Well, I guess there's some truth behind all that crazy talk. He died, almost right here where we're sitting. But I didn't kill him, either."

NINE

I kept my hand steady as I heard Mary speak. Was I wrong about her? Was she some kind of super murderess? She was sitting here telling me another man had died on these steps, but she didn't have anything to do with that, either. Did the police know about it?

"You know I was always afraid of them snakes when we went out in the swamps to pull sweetgrass." Mary paused and smoked her pipe, gazing away as though she could still see her younger days. "I put turpentine on my shoes to scare those snakes away. Sometimes it worked, and sometimes I think it just made them mad, and they ran back after me."

I wasn't sure what that story had to do with Lord Simon, but it was her way of imparting information. I kept moving my bone over, under, and through, pulling the stitches tight. My basket was actually starting to look like a basket. I wasn't sure if it was going to be even on the sides, but I began to feel I was getting the hang of it.

"Lord Simon was one of them fancy-pants boys who lived up at the castle with Livy and Harry. He thought he was so fine. I didn't have no time for him. If I couldn't be with Joshua and Jah, I sure wasn't gonna be with no fancy pants."

"And you told him you didn't want anything to do with him?"

"Too many times to count." She looked at me and poked me with her bone. "Mind that stitch, child. Pull too tight, and it will be uneven. Relax. Your hand has to be guided by the Lord to do the right thing. He won't let you do wrong if you trust in him."

"And he kept coming back." I tried to keep the story moving along with the new rhythm my hands seemed to be developing. I took a deep breath and shook my hands to relax them.

"Every day. I couldn't make it no plainer. He just wouldn't listen."

"So you killed him."

"Jessie! How can you say those things? I should take you inside and scrub your mouth with soap. Didn't your mama teach you manners?"

"I was just asking."

"Like I'd kill someone! Like I have time to kill someone." She humphed at me and started working on her basket again. "I think they said he had a heart attack. Some folks blamed that on me. They said I made him work too hard. But when you don't have love in your heart for a man, it don't matter what they do or don't do."

"So you didn't kill him! How is that like what happened to Joshua?"

She smacked me in the back of the head. "What did I just tell you? Now you're saying I killed Joshua."

I rubbed my head and wondered if it was worth all this torture. "I didn't say you killed anyone, Mary. All I'm saying is what other people are saying. I don't think you killed Joshua, and it sounds like Lord Simon had a personal problem."

"And that's the right of it."

"But you have to admit, two men dying sounds a little suspicious. And if the police find out . . ."

"What? What can they do? They're not gonna find anything that says I killed Joshua like they couldn't find anything that said I killed Lord Simon. You got to have faith, Jessie. You're too young to be so harsh on the world."

I picked up a new handful of sweetgrass, inhaling the wonderful fragrance. Maybe she was right. Maybe I was too harsh on Tony and Chase. Maybe I should've just let things happen and not worry about them so much.

Maybe my hair should turn blue, and a big diamond stud would appear in my nose. That had as much chance of happening. I worry. That's who I am. "Mary, you have to help me. Give me something I can use to help find out what happened to Joshua."

"Leave it be, Jessie. Everything will work out just fine. I'm not bothered by it." To show me how not bothered she was, Mary continued puffing and weaving, her nimble fingers racing around the edges of her work. The coils of sweetgrass interlaced with the pine needles to create the wonderful rust color that contrasted with the yellow of the grass. The coarser, thicker black rush was tawny and strong with the delicate strands of grass.

I wasn't so easily placated. It's not enough to say everything will be fine. How will it be fine, and when will that happen? Those are the important issues. "I can help with this if you'll let me. Someone attacked Ham. You could be next."

Mary made a noise in her throat somewhere between a pshaw and a groan. "Now why would someone want to hurt me?"

"Maybe they want to keep you from making baskets," I suggested, even though it sounded crazy to me. "After all, you and Joshua were the only two who could weave baskets like this."

"Ham can weave some, too."

Great! I wasn't serious about the whole someone wanting to stop the basket weaving. I was about to shift the conversation to something more serious and sinister, like Abraham wanting to keep Jah to himself. That moment was gone like a puff of her pipe smoke. Instead, I was left grappling with the stupid idea of Mary, Joshua, and Ham being in danger from some basket-weaving pervert.

"I didn't really mean it that way." I tried to get the conversation back on track.

"Oh? How did you mean it then?"

"I really think Abraham killed Joshua, even though he was his brother. I think he might be after you and Ham, too. Maybe he wants to keep Jah for himself, and if he kills all of his real family, that would take care of the problem."

She laughed and slapped her knee. "You know, you must be part Gullah, Jessie, 'cause you can tell some stories! I declare you can!"

So much for that. Not only did she think it was funny, it was slap-your-knee funny. And I was being serious, too. So much for the nice approach. "You know, if you don't help me, the police will be sitting here asking these questions."

"I hope they can make a basket faster and quieter than you."

"Fine. I give up. You don't want me to help. I won't help."

I was following through on a downstroke when Mary grabbed my hand. "It's not that I don't appreciate what you're trying to do for me, child. You don't know how much it does this old heart good to have someone like you here right now. But you can't help me, Jessie. Only the Lord can take care of this mess. Then I can go and find Jah."

There was nothing I could say to that. I was in serious danger of crying on my basket, adding to the bloodstains with my tears. Maybe no one would want to buy this basket, but no one could say I didn't put everything into it.

We kept on stitching the coils together as the sun set and the visitors to the Village walked wearily to their cars and went home. The noise level didn't change at first, since everything had to be put back in place every

night when we closed. The minstrels continued playing as they walked back to wherever
they spent the night. Horses' hooves hit the
cobblestones as their trainers took them
back to the stables after another long day's
performance.

Then slowly, as the night cooled, the
smells drifted away, and the storefronts
closed. The tired giants, knights, flower
girls, and even the fairies, huddled around
tables eating dinner and finally turned in
for the night.

Mary and I closed up Wicked Weaves,
counting the money and re-sorting and
stocking the baskets. "Not a bad day," she
said. "With all those TV and police people,
I expected worse."

"If that's it, I'm heading out."

"Not going to see that new beau?"

"Does everyone know everything around
here?"

She looked out the window. "Not hard to
guess. I think he's waiting for you."

I followed her look and saw Chase. He
waved and smiled. My heart pounded and I
forgot what I was saying. I said good night
to Mary and floated out the door.

We ended up eating with everyone at the
Pleasant Pheasant. Every night the rotis-

serie and alehouse offered whatever it had left over from the day to the characters that made up the Village. Since it was free, almost everyone ended up there. There wasn't always as much to eat, but I don't think many people went home hungry.

It was a rowdy group, as usual, that night. I saw Tony, sans fairy, with some of his friends. Seeing him made me think about Mary and her brother. I wished Tony and I were closer. People always made a big deal about us being twins and both working at Renaissance Faire Village. But it was a bigger deal to them than it was to us. It was almost like a default position that we were both there.

I wished I knew some way to change that. We were all we had left of family in the world, yet sometimes it didn't seem like we were family at all, much less two halves of the same egg.

"Halfpence for them." Chase tossed a coin on the table.

"They aren't worth that much."

"What's up, Jessie? Still brooding about Mary?"

"Yes and no. She won't help and told me to lay off. I guess that's pretty clear. I was thinking more about me and Tony. Do you have a brother or sister?"

"Nope. I was lucky. My parents knew they were blessed when I was born. Why try to improve on perfection?"

I looked at his big, stupid grin and was more depressed. "I'm going home now. I'll see you tomorrow."

"I thought we were going back to the dungeon. There's no point in you staying in that little hut they gave you this year. You can stay with me the rest of the summer."

I was tempted. I wanted to stay with him. Then that part of me that worries took over. "I don't think that would be a good idea, Chase. I think we should each keep our own place."

He laughed. "Please tell me you're joking. This isn't an apartment or a house. It's just for the summer."

That made me even more depressed. I stood up. "I don't think so. Thanks anyway."

He walked outside with me. Tony didn't even look up. I knew I was in for a terrible night. The appeal of going back to my little hut, as he'd called it, was rapidly diminishing.

"If you don't want to live with me at the dungeon, at least come up for a beer. You can do that, can't you?"

The ale hadn't flowed freely that night, since it doesn't spoil, and Sam, the owner of the Pleasant Pheasant, didn't seem to be feeling especially pleasant. It didn't take much for Chase to convince me to come up for a beer. In all fairness, I wanted to be convinced. Being alone didn't sound really interesting. And he'd promised peanuts with the beer. That was enough to make me walk with him to the dungeon.

It was strangely quiet on the King's Highway. Nighttime was like this. People sort of became normal, modern versions of themselves after all the visitors went home.

The Green Man, a stilted vision of a mythical being that looked like a tree with a face, was still up and around. He, who was really a she, seemed to be practicing walking in circles on the cobblestones.

"Hey Kelly!" Chase greeted her. "How's the leg?"

"Could be better," she said from behind the mask. "That kid really walloped the heck out of me."

"Kelly was posing with a kid, maybe nine or ten years old," Chase explained to me. "All of a sudden, he went crazy and kicked her in the leg."

"Of course it wasn't my leg," Kelly went on, "and he broke my stilt. I crashed down on the ground, and about a hundred cameras flashed, taking my picture. This is a stupid, mixed-up world."

"Were you hurt?" I asked, agreeing with her. I think it happened every year, because every year, there was a new Green Man. The idea was good, but it was a tricky job.

"I almost broke my *real* leg," Kelly explained. "I'm bruised all over. It's hard getting back up here again knowing you could be killed by some evil eight-year-old."

"Keep working on it," Chase encouraged. "Maybe next time, you shouldn't let them get so close."

"Or maybe next time, I'll hit the little runt with some pepper spray." Kelly, as the Green Man, spun around one more time, leaves and branches moving slowly with her.

"I guess it's just one of the problems with dressing up like a tree." I shrugged as Chase and I walked by.

"At least they don't let dogs in here." He laughed, enjoying his joke.

I was too depressed to appreciate it. I was hoping the beer would help. I didn't think it would. If anything, I'd probably be more depressed. But at least I'd be with Chase, although in some ways, that was depressing, too.

"What's wrong?" He noticed my lack of response and put his arm around me. "Still brooding about Mary?"

"And the rest of the world."

"Maybe we can find something else for you to think about."

"If that were the case, I would've done it years ago. I just get melancholy sometimes."

"I have just the cure for you." Chase smiled and took my hand.

What was it with guys, anyway? Why did they think sex was the answer for everything?

I started to tell him that another trip to his dungeon bedroom wouldn't make much difference to my mood. Instead, before I could open my mouth, he'd picked me up and put me on the tree swing that was anchored in the large old oak beside the dungeon.

"When was the last time you swung?"

I wasn't sure, and his nonsexual overture took me by surprise. "I — I don't know. I — I think I was ten or so."

"Sorry." He got behind me and put his hands on my hips. "It was actually a rhetorical question, Jessie. It doesn't really matter. But I'll bet it makes a difference."

I would've told him it wouldn't matter, but it was too late. He was already pulling the swing back with me on it. He let it go, and I soared up into the evening sky. On the first rush of air, I tried to choke back a smile and failed. What was this wondrous magic? How simple would life be if all you had to do was swing?

On the return trip down, I dangled my feet. Chase gave me another hearty push and a small *yipe* escaped from my lips.

"See? I told you. Swinging is good for you."

I could hear him talking, but I couldn't see him. The night was closing in on the Village, casting shadows from the wide umbrella created by the huge oak. The stars were dancing in the sky around me. It was amazing! It seemed like I was up there with them, and there was no way to worry about anything. I couldn't believe I hadn't tried it before.

I didn't even feel silly when Portia walked by with Sir Reginald, the queen's favorite. It crossed my mind that their relationship was doomed, since Livy was already having an affair with him and he was mostly married. They huddled in their cloaks, and I pretended not to see them. I guess Chase was doing the same thing, since he didn't call out to them.

Just when I was about to forget about Mary and Tony and everything that was weighing down on me, I came down, and

Chase stopped the swing. It was an abrupt kind of thing. I would've fallen off the wide wood plank, except he put his arm around my waist.

I laughed up into his face. The starlight blended with the lights of the Village around us, creating a magical halo around his head. I looked into his eyes and twined my fingers in his braid that slid across his shoulder as he held me. I was sure at that moment that I was in love.

"Jessie," he whispered.

"Yes?" I waited breathlessly to hear him say that he loved me, too. For once, I hoped the guy would say it before me. That way I'd know it was really from him and not just an echo of what I said.

"We're not alone."

I wasn't sure what he was talking about. At first, I wasn't even sure what he'd said. Then I saw them out of the corner of my eye.

There were at least ten monks in full robes surrounding us. I mean that literally. They were in a circle around us and the old tree. Maybe no one had told them the day was over and they could go back to wearing jeans and listening to their iPods.

"What do they want?" I whispered back to Chase, not taking my eyes off the monks.

"I don't know. I was hoping they were here because you'd asked them."

"Not me."

Chase cleared his throat and stood up straight as I got to my feet. "Hey guys. What's up? Is there some monk orientation I wasn't told about?"

One of the monks slowly raised his arm to point down the King's Highway. All of them slowly turned to look that way.

"What's up with that?" I muttered to Chase. They were starting to scare me. It was like suddenly waking up in some monk horror movie.

"Okay," Chase tried again. "Jessie and I are going to the dungeon now. I know we don't technically have a curfew in the Village, but the day starts early, and you might want to get some beauty sleep, even if you do wear robes."

As a speech, it wasn't terribly inspired. Chase and I linked arms and started to walk through one of the open spaces between the monks. Instantly, they closed ranks and kept us in the circle.

"This whole monk thing is cool; don't get me wrong." I tried my hand at reasoning with the robed men. "But we have to get to bed, even if you don't. I have baskets to weave, and Chase has bad guys to put away.

Good night."

We started through the open space again, and the monks moved together again. This was seriously creeping me out. I didn't know if they'd been inhaling yeast fumes or drinking too much ale, but whatever it was, I didn't like it. "What do you think we should do?" I asked Chase.

"I'm not sure. I've never seen them this way."

"Why aren't they talking?"

"They take a vow of silence at sundown," he explained. "I hope they have a health insurance policy, because I'm about to start my own version of monk bowling."

But before Chase could knock over any of the monk pins for his new game, the monks made a corridor, and all pointed silently in one direction. "I think they want us to go this way."

"You think?" I wasn't crazy about the idea of passing through the monk gauntlet, but I didn't see any way around it. "I think they want us to go to the bakery with them."

"It looks that way to me." Chase took my hand. "I don't know what's up, but we both know all of these guys. I don't think they mean any harm. Maybe they have a new sourdough starter or something they want us to try. I'm game if you are."

I squeezed his hand. "I hope they have some jelly to go with that bread."

TEN

We walked between the two columns of monks to the bakery. It felt more like a forced march with them as soldiers holding us hostage. Only they were soldiers in robes who smelled like bread. It wouldn't have been as intimidating during the day. It was kind of weird and spooky at night. The dark Village windows reflected back at us. No one else seemed to be out. No one stopped us to ask what was going on.

"Oh yeah," Chase whispered as we reached the Monastery Bakery. "Did I tell you Detective Almond came in to investigate what happened to Ham? We took a look at the video footage from the front gate. Not really much to talk about. Your buddy Alex gave him the whole story about the monk attacking Ham."

"What do you mean my *buddy* Alex? I told you it's over between us."

"That's not the way it looked to me. I'm

surprised Detective Almond didn't come and talk to you."

"*Now* you tell me."

"Silence!" The head monk obviously was able to break his vow of silence after sunset. I wasn't sure which brother he was. They changed positions from time to time.

He seemed taller than the rest of the monks, or he was standing on something in the front of the bakery. All the chairs and tables had been cleared out of the way for the event. It felt like a bad movie about the Inquisition. I didn't look around me in case they'd moved the thumbscrews in after closing the bakery for the day.

I still held Chase's hand. I squeezed it and looked at him in the dim candlelight. Apparently the monks had forgotten they had electricity, too. There were hundreds of candles in the room, but I couldn't see my feet.

Chase squeezed my hand in return and whispered, "Don't worry. It'll be okay."

"You have been brought here because of falsehoods told against my brother monks in the matter of an attack on the blacksmith."

Part of me was laughing irreverently at this point. Obviously, the monks had illusions of grandeur. I knew they were creepy

163

and weird. I didn't know the state had empowered them to hold court in Renaissance Faire Village.

The other part of me, the one who told the amused part to shut up, was scared. We were out here with a dozen or so crazy guys dressed up like killer monks from hell, and they thought we'd wronged them. Detective Almond was probably home by now tucked into his cozy bed with his cell phone turned off. His officers were half an hour away probably playing cards and eating donuts. They might find our cold, lifeless bodies in the next batch of pumpernickel bread.

"No one told any falsehoods about the monks to the police, Carl. Alex told Detective Almond he saw one of your monks in the smithy before Ham was attacked."

"That is a falsehood." The head monk's voice rang out in the quiet room. "And don't call me Carl, Chase. You know I'm Lead Brother of the Sheaf."

Chase laughed, even though I squeezed his hand and kicked him in the leg. "You know it seems to me, Brother Sheaf, that you should have Alex here instead of us."

Brother Sheaf clapped his hands, and two monks brought in a struggling man with a hood over his head. When they removed the hood, it was Alex. "Chase! Jessie! Get me

164

out of here."

It sounds stupid, but the first thing I noticed was that Alex's hair was messed up. Even when we'd slept together, his hair never got messed up. Of course, I hadn't thought of covering his head with a hood. It seemed appropriate somehow.

"This is deeper and weirder than I ever imagined," Chase muttered. "I'm gonna have to break these guys up."

"Do you think it's the total dichotomy of having a Renaissance town that's in a permanent, year-round location as opposed to the other festivals that move around?"

"Jessie, I don't know what that means, and I don't think this is the time or the place to speculate on why these guys are crazy."

"Silence!"

Brother Sheaf gained our attention again. "There is a conspiracy among the people of this Village to destroy our monastery. We will *not* allow this to happen as long as there is bread in our ovens."

The urge to laugh overpowered me. I laughed long and hard, then moved up close to Brother Sheaf. "You guys have lost it. I mean, come on, 'as long as there is bread in our ovens'? What kind of code is that? I get the whole monk/druid concept; although the druids would've been too early for a

Renaissance Faire Village. Couldn't you come up with anything better?"

One of the monks at my right side stepped forward. "The woman is right, Brother Sheaf. Many of us have long believed our code needs to be tweaked."

"Tweaked?" Brother Sheaf roared. "How dare you challenge the code of the Brotherhood?"

Another monk stepped out into the opening where we stood. "Brother John is correct, Brother Sheaf. There are many of us who question a code of belief that ends with loaves in the oven. Surely there is something more befitting to our order than that."

"Okay." Chase stepped forward. "I've had about enough of all the wheat and bread stuff. I'm tired, and the three of us non-monks are leaving now. But let me remind you guys that I'm the law here in the Village. Keep this stuff up, and you'll be in the dungeon."

The monks broke into unmonklike talking and disagreeing. Chase grabbed Alex, and the three of us went outside.

"What was that all about?" Alex stood still, while Chase untied his hands. "Those guys are crazy. You need to call the police and have them arrested."

"*You* call the police and have them arrested." Chase finished the job and took my hand again. "These guys may seem crazy sometimes, but they were a big help last month when that little girl was lost in the Village. There are all kinds of bands and factions here. I think you know that, since Robin and his Merry Men do their little thing all the time."

"We didn't think you knew about it." Alex looked around like he was violating some oath by admitting it.

"I know *everything* that goes on in the Village," Chase assured him. "If we call the police about the monks, we'll have to call them about the other hundred or so factions. I don't think any of the long term residents would like that, including Robin. Everyone has their place here. It all works."

"Except for tonight," Alex reminded him. "They kidnapped me from Sherwood Forest and held me against my will."

Chase shrugged. "I'm the bailiff. If you want to press charges, come to court. Right now, I'm going home. See you later."

"I don't think you're taking this seriously enough, Chase," Alex yelled. "I'm going to tell Robin about what happened."

"I don't know which is scarier; men in tights or men in robes." I looked up as one of the monks followed us outside. Alex was already on his way toward the forest. A waxing gibbous moon was beginning to rise over the Village, outlining the shapes of the houses and the towers on the castle close to where we stood.

"Chase." The monk called his name.

"Brother Sheaf." Chase folded his arms across his broad chest.

"You can call me Carl." The monk shrugged and removed his hood, revealing a middle-aged, balding head. "Sorry about the craziness. But we've been maligned here, man. It wasn't one of us at the smithy today. I don't know who it was, but he must've taken a robe from the bakery and impersonated one of us."

"Or he rented a monk's robe from the costume shop." I shook my head. "It happens, Carl. This is a tourist attraction, and we have tourists who dress up like monks."

"Those aren't the same as *our* robes. But I think we should put a stop to that practice anyway. Our Brotherhood is sacred. They shouldn't rent out monk's robes."

"But then the dragons would demand the same treatment," I argued. "Then it would be the fairies and the knights. Where would it end?"

He half smiled, then turned to Chase, effectively dissing me. "Seriously, man, it

168

wasn't one of us. I think someone should tell the police. It wasn't fair to blame what happened to Ham on our order."

"I'll be sure to mention that to Detective Almond the next time I see him," Chase promised. "But I'm serious about this kind of stuff going on in the Village, too, Carl. No more kidnappings or anything else weird. I know you don't want Robin attacking the monastery. I know *I* don't want that."

"No. You're right. We'll write something up and tack it to a tree over there," Carl said. "That's the best way to get a message to them unless you happen to run into Maid Marion."

"Okay. I'll leave it alone for right now. But don't let it happen again," Chase warned. "Even Marion couldn't save you from Robin if he gets mad."

Carl thanked him and shook my hand before vanishing into the dark monastery/ bakery again.

"Well, that was too strange." I looked up at the moon and the mostly sleeping Village. "This place gets weirder every year."

"That's what I like about it. A person could live anywhere and never encounter problems like these. Sometimes it's *really* like living in a Renaissance Faire Village with plumbing and electricity."

"I know." I nudged him. "It's what I like about it, too. I'm at the college the rest of the year, and it's so normal and boring. Not a dragon or a knight in sight."

"I guess that's what your brother likes about it, too."

"I don't think so. Tony's just a slacker, and this is another in a long list of ways to waste his life. The next seems to be gambling it away in Las Vegas."

We had started walking, our footsteps leading us past Squire's Lane, where three manor houses stood. The Honey and Herb Shoppe still had a light on inside where someone was probably making candles or bottling herbs. Peter's Pub and Harriet's Hat House were quiet and dark. In other words, we were headed back toward the dungeon.

I felt like I needed to go back to my own little hut, but I didn't know how to tell Chase. We walked past the Village Square, where a group of wise women were doing some kind of moon magic ritual. They were all dressed in white, thank goodness. The Village had outlawed naked rituals a few years back.

"I'm really tired. I think I'll just head home." We were coming up to a path that led between houses and shops. It cut off some time getting back to where I was staying.

"I'll walk you back." Chase didn't argue.

I wasn't trying to be flirty or anything, but I wished he would've at least tried to persuade me to go with him to the dungeon. I know it seems contrary, but a woman likes to know she's wanted. Maybe he didn't really want me that much. Maybe it was better to find out at that moment. Our friendship was important to me, too. I didn't want to lose that because we didn't make it as a couple.

I told myself that over and over as we cut through alleyways and sidestepped horse droppings the Village Drudges had missed. The Village Drunk — it's an official cast position every year — was walking with one of the Village Fools. Chase and I talked a little, keeping our voices down as though we didn't want anyone to hear us.

We finally reached my hut, and I was a little embarrassed, even though I had no choice in its selection. "Well, here we are. Thanks for walking with me."

"This place used to be where they stored the push brooms and other cleanup stuff," he remarked. "They must've been desperate to find housing for everyone. They need to open up some of the spaces above the shops. Harry was talking about that last week. The Village is growing in population if not in size."

That was mundane enough to allow me to say, "I'll see you tomorrow, Chase."

He looked down at me for a minute, then said, "Aren't you going to show me what you've done with the place?"

"I don't think so." I took a deep breath as I prepared for my we're-better-off-friends speech. "Chase —"

"Jessie, don't even think about it."

"What? You don't even know what I was going to say. I don't even know what I was going to say. This whole thing is crazy. I know it can't work out. We'd be better off —"

I would've finished; I swear I would've. But at that moment he kissed me, and the next thing I knew, we were going inside. Sometimes things work out despite my help.

The next morning was Sunday, a quiet day in the Village until noon when it opened. I left Chase sleeping in my bed, hogging up most of the room. I smiled at the way his shoulders and feet stuck out from under the sheet. I kept on smiling as I walked to Wicked Weaves. I didn't know what it was about Chase that made me smile, and I

172

didn't have time to reflect on it. I was filled with renewed determination to find Joshua's killer. I figured Sunday was as good a day as any to bring him or her to justice.

Sunday night was always the King's Feast. It was a huge affair at the castle that usually hosted dinner for a few hundred people who sat around the inside jousting ring and ate those little chickens, potatoes, and plum pudding for dessert. At least it was the Village version of plum pudding.

The castle cook and I have a long-term disagreement on what makes up plum pudding. He seems to think it's like bread pudding with plums in it. Of course, that's not true. They called it plum pudding, but it was short for plump pudding. It described the round shape of the boiled pudding that was made from suet, bread crumbs, raisins, some kind of liquor, and spices. Any history buff knows that.

But the enthusiastic guests don't seem to care. They eat everything in sight and swill hundreds of gallons of ale while they watch the best knights compete. The guests have also learned to throw their chicken bones at the knights they don't like.

There are also fools, knaves, jugglers, and musicians, who fill the castle with activities. Everyone from the Village staff is required to participate in one way or another. One year I got stuck serving the little chickens and the next wiping the sweat from a knight's brow. One year, I was stuck feeding grapes to the king on the throne. I'd rather wipe sweat or serve food. Royalty gets on my nerves.

I stopped at Sir Latte's Beanery for a mocha and a muffin. As usual this time on Sunday morning, there were only a few residents lounging around and enjoying the quiet. I didn't have to wait in line and was ready to go across the street to Wicked Weaves when I heard someone *psst* from the kitchen area.

I wasn't sure at first if they were *pssting* me. I glanced through the doorway and saw Lonnie, Debby's brother, beckoning me. I thought maybe he was talking to someone else, but I was the only one there. I took my muffin and my mocha, then went into the kitchen.

"I heard you've been asking questions about that dead guy." Lonnie looked around the area where we were standing, but there was only us and the supply closet.

"Yeah. I want to know what happened."

"I have something for you." His little rat-like features screwed up and were more pronounced.

"Okay." I've never been crazy about Lonnie. He kind of creeps me out. "What've you got?"

"I saw what happened." He looked around again, and I swear, I expected him to twitch his whiskers. "It was a monk. He was over there by the privies with that dead guy. Only it was before he was dead."

"A monk?"

"Yeah. They're a strange group of guys, you know. I wouldn't put anything past them."

"I'm beginning to realize that. Did you actually *see* the monk kill Joshua?"

"Who?"

"The dead guy. His name was Joshua."

Lonnie has this terrible snorty laugh that wasn't meant to be heard by other humans. He also rubs his paws together — I mean hands. It's really awful, and I thought it might keep me from eating my muffin that morning. "What a weird name!"

"Yeah, well, never mind his name. Did you actually see the monk kill him?"

"No. But I saw him talking to him. It was earlier that morning before you tripped over the dead guy."

"I didn't trip over him. I got out of the way so he didn't fall on me."

"Whatever. I saw what I saw. Take it or

leave it."

I thanked him and got out of the kitchen. I wanted to run back to the hut and take a shower, but there wasn't time. I needed a notebook to keep up with everything that was going on. Somehow the monks seemed to be involved in Joshua's death and Ham's attack. Or someone who was dressed like a monk was involved. I knew there was a fine line between the two. The monks knew what it was, but they were the only ones.

It was a relief to get to Wicked Weaves and find Mary weaving her basket on the back steps. It was wide and flat; I couldn't see where it would hold anything. "This is one of the first baskets slaves ever made when they brought them to America," she explained. "It's called a fanning basket, and slaves used it to harvest rice on the plantations. Slaves who could make baskets were very valuable back then. It meant the master didn't have to pay for baskets. Mostly those slaves didn't have to work as hard, either."

I sat down beside her in the morning sun, the smell of her pipe tobacco and sweetgrass filling the air around us. It was peaceful there; no worries about monks killing people or what would happen next. "So making baskets was handed down to you?"

"That's right. My great-great-grandmother was brought to this country as a slave from her home in Africa. She made beautiful baskets. The master kept her in the house and didn't require her to do nothin' except make baskets. He was afraid she might hurt her hands and not be able to make baskets anymore."

"What was her name? What happened to her?"

"The name they give her was Sarah. But she had what we call a basket name that was the secret name she went by with her own people. That name has been lost down through the years. But we know she cut her hand one day slicing up a peach to eat. The master sold her because he was afraid her baskets wouldn't be as good after that. She never made baskets again, at least not for the new master. They set her to picking cotton and tending the animals. She had two daughters she taught to make baskets before they were sold at seven and nine years old. She never saw them again after that."

I couldn't imagine what that must've been like. I could empathize but not really understand. I worked on my basket, thinking about Sarah and her daughters as they might have sat like we were, making fanning baskets for rice.

"You seem happy today," Mary observed.

"Somethin' going good for you?"

"Maybe." I grinned. "It's Chase. He makes me smile."

"Don't let him go then. Those men are few between. Look! He even helps you make better baskets. I swear it looks like you're gonna finish that one. I didn't know if that would happen."

I looked at my almost completed basket. I was willing to give Chase the credit for my smile but not for my basket. "I started feeling the rhythm yesterday. I think I'm getting it."

"You keep those stitches tight and mind the grass stays the same length. Don't let that coil stick out longer than your finger."

I listened to her as I continued using the bone and coiling the sweetgrass; over, under and through. I heard the bell ring on the front door in the shop. It was too early for customers, but could be a resident. "I'll get it."

Mary nodded and puffed at her pipe as her fingers flew through the coils of sweetgrass with her bone.

I left my basket on the back stair and went inside. A tall, thin black man was looking at the baskets. He looked familiar; something about the eyes, but I was sure I hadn't seen him around the Village. And he was dressed like a visitor in khaki pants and a tan T-shirt. "Can I help you?"

"I'm looking for someone. She makes baskets, and I was told she might be here."

Mary came in through the back door and dropped her basket on the floor. "Jah!"

ELEVEN

Jah looked like he was in his early twenties. He had broad, thin shoulders and long arms. His shirtsleeves looked too short for him. His face was narrow and angular. He had his mother's dark eyes, sensitive but sharp, and his mouth looked as though it rarely smiled.

"Mother?" His eyes narrowed as he took in the red scarf covering her head and the patterned red dress she wore.

"My son!" Mary rushed to him, apparently not feeling the doubt I saw in Jah's eyes. "I thought I would never see you again. But here you are, a man. Of all the gifts I have received in this life, this is the best one."

She hugged him with one of those full-body hugs. I could see him holding back, not wrapping those long arms around her. He didn't seem prepared to meet Mary, even though he was looking for her. She, on

the other hand, might not have been prepared but was willing to put everything
aside to be with him.

Mary wiped tears from her eyes as she
asked him a hundred questions every
mother wants to know: Are you well? Are
you happy? Is there someone special in your
life?

Jah didn't answer. He stood there looking
awkward and uneasy, taking in the baskets
and the layout of the shop around him.
Mary tugged at his sleeve and introduced
him to me. I could tell that made even less
of an impression on him.

"How did you find me?" she asked. "Did
your father tell you where I was?"

"My father told me you were dead," he
shot back. "Another man, a man who
claimed to be my real father, told me where
to find you."

She stared at him. "Abraham Shift is *not*
your real father. He forced me out of our
home and demanded your father give you
to him to raise. Joshua told you the truth."

His nostrils flared. I know it sounds silly,
but that's what it looked like to me. He
didn't have a large nose, either. I guess it
was the angle of his head. I think he was
looking down at us in more ways than one.

"The truth? That my birth mother left me

with my father, who chose not to raise me and gave me to another man. That's a hard truth to learn. I've known where you were for a year. I couldn't bring myself to come and face you."

Mary looked crushed. It was as if the weight of all the bad things she'd endured in her life suddenly came down on her. She folded her arms protectively across her chest and raised her chin. "You don't understand. I never thought I'd have to explain to you. Your father told me you'd died after they made me leave. I believed him. I didn't learn until a few days ago that you were alive and living with his brother. If I'd known, no power on earth could've stopped me from seeing you."

"Yet you left and didn't take me with you. That tells a different story."

"Your father — your *real* father — and I had an arrangement that he would meet me with you every few weeks. There was no way for me to know what really happened."

"My *father.*" Jah said the word like it was poison on his tongue. "I have no father. I have no mother. I'm alone in the world."

The silence after his words was enough to keep me from jumping in and pointing out that Mary had done the best she could and that times had changed. Jah might've been good to look at, but he had a lot to learn about life.

"Why did you come here?" Mary demanded. "Why did you seek me out if you felt this way?"

"I wanted to see what the face of deception looked like. I wanted to know what kind of woman leaves her son to come to a place like this and make baskets for *tourists*."

"And what do you see?"

"What I expected." He stared hard at her, then looked around the shop again. "A woman who has lost her dignity and is no longer welcome with her own people."

Mary had been getting feisty at the end, but hearing those words, she wrapped her shawl around her and walked out the back door.

I looked at the big dumb oaf who was her son. My God, how stupid could one man be? He turned to walk out of the shop as well, but I wasn't stunned into silence anymore. "And that's it? You came all this way to insult your mother, a woman who has more dignity and grace in her little finger than most people have in their whole bodies? You aren't as smart as you look."

He faced me with rage burning in his eyes. "You don't know. Stay out of this. It's a family matter."

"Maybe. But I still get to say what I think. As far as I know, Harry is the only king in Renaissance Faire Village. You're just a big bully. I deal with students like you every morning before breakfast and six times a day after lunch. You don't scare me."

"No?" He started walking toward me with a murderous expression on his dark chocolate face. "You look scared to me. If you're not, you should be. You may not be as smart as you think."

The front door burst open, and Chase entered with a wide grin. "Donuts, anyone? They're fresh out of the cooker."

Jah gave me one last furious look, then stalked out the door, brushing by Chase as he went. I sort of collapsed back on a basket table, surprised and pleased that it didn't collapse under me.

"Who's the thundercloud?" Chase watched as Jah strode away from Wicked Weaves. "Hey! Are you okay?"

"Yes. It was just very . . . intense." I filled him in about Jah while I wolfed down both donuts he was holding. "I may have to rethink my investigation into Joshua's death. It's very possible Jah murdered him instead of Abraham. That boy is super angry with life."

"Don't say that!" Mary yelled as she came back into the shop. "Jah has every right to be angry, but that doesn't make him a killer. Where did he go, Jessie? I have to talk to him."

"He went that way." Chase pointed down the street toward Baron's Beer and Brats.

"Tend to the shop," she told me. "I'll be back after I find my son."

The door closed quickly behind her. I looked at Chase. "You should go after her. Otherwise, he might kill her, too."

"Aren't you being a little paranoid? Just because the guy is angry doesn't make him a killer. Mary's right."

"Mary doesn't think anyone killed Joshua. She thinks he died of natural causes that just seem to include almost having alcohol poisoning and being strangled. She's not a good judge of what's going on."

"And *you* are?"

"What's that supposed to mean?"

"It means she might know best. You have to leave this to the police, Jessie. Someone could get hurt."

This wasn't the time or the place to talk about it as two visitors dressed as ladies-in-waiting with high hennins and long veils came into the shop, laughing. I dragged Chase into a corner. "I don't have time to argue with you right now. I think Mary could be in danger, and you're the only one who can do something about it, since she'd kill me if I left the shop while she's gone."

I pulled him close and kissed him hard. "You have to take care of this for me. Even if we got the police involved, it could be too late.

"Is that it?" He raised that left brow at me. "Is that all you've got? Because it's really hot out there, and following Mary and her son could be a long, hard job."

"What else do you want?" I eyed the customers warily, but they were too busy exclaiming over baskets to notice us. "We're in a public place with people watching us. I'm not —"

Chase lifted me off the floor. It's a bad habit I wished he'd stop. He finally put me down and put his hands in my hair and kissed me, slowly and thoroughly for a few minutes. "Okay. Now I can go." He walked out the door, whistling.

Now the two ladies were interested. "Was that playacting?" one asked.

"Yes." My heart was pounding hard, and my lips could barely form coherent sentences.

Both women giggled and asked how they could get summer jobs there. I couldn't answer, since my brain still felt like it was filled with cotton candy. The women each bought a small basket and left Wicked Weaves.

I took my basket outside on the back steps and thought about lighting up Mary's pipe. But that was going too far. Instead, I stared off and thought about Mary and the life she'd led. I thought Tony and I had a hard life without our folks. At least we knew who they were and that they were dead, not just hiding out in an old village somewhere.

It was three, and there was still no sign of Mary or Chase. I wished I had my cell phone and that Chase had a cell phone, too. Or we could both have two-way radios. Anything so that I'd know what was going on.

The Village closed early on Sunday for the King's Feast. At this rate, I was going to have to close up and head over to the castle without knowing what was going on. I wasn't crazy about that idea. Chase was right; I was paranoid. I kept picturing all kinds of terrible things happening to him and Mary — like Mary was dead and Jah killed Chase when he'd found her, and it was all my fault because I'd sent him after them.

I'd sold a few baskets. The crowd was light. It might've been a race weekend again. I couldn't keep up with what was going on at the speedway. At least I couldn't imagine Chase being killed by a car in the Village. A fast-moving camel, maybe, but not a car.

I'd waited as long as I could before locking the front door and counting up receipts. I stashed everything in Mary's rooms upstairs. There was no protocol for closing up without her. I guess she never thought it would happen.

I took the opportunity to look around her apartment. I knew it wasn't polite or nice to look through someone else's things. I wouldn't have liked it if someone looked through my stuff. I told myself it was okay because I needed some clues to what was going on, but really I was just curious.

The three rooms on top of Wicked Weaves were sparse like my room in the hut. You'd never guess Mary had lived there for ten years. There were small, personal touches, but mostly it was very plain.

I looked at the tiny, carved wooden animals she collected. There was an owl, a horse and a chicken. There was no sign of baskets or sweetgrass up here. I guessed she got enough of that downstairs.

Her clothes in the tiny closet were brightly colored and almost the same; dresses and matching scarves and shawls. Everything was made of cotton. She seemed to have two pairs of sandals: the one she was wearing and the other in her closet. They were exactly the same.

In all, I had no feeling for the woman who lived here. If I hadn't known Mary already, I wouldn't have learned anything about her besides the fact that she liked carved animals. Everything else was something you might find in a hotel.

I took a brief peek at her bed. Now there was something that gave her away. Mary might not have any elegant clothes or room decor, but she had expensive sheets. They were at least a thousand threads per square inch. Premium. I smiled, thinking about that indulgence.

I heard a noise downstairs and hurried out of her room. I didn't want her to come back and catch me snooping around. Especially since I hadn't learned anything of value doing it.

But it was only my brother Tony. "How did you get in here?" I asked him. I knew I'd locked the doors.

He shrugged. "I don't know. I have a key that opened the door."

"Let's see." We went outside and locked the front door. Tony used his key and got back inside. "Where did you get that?"

"Remember when I was working at the pub for a while? Brewster gave it to me to open early so he wouldn't have to come in." Tony frowned. "What? Why are you looking at me like that?"

"So one key opens the whole Village?"

"I don't know. I haven't tried it. One key seems to open Brewster's and Wicked Weaves. Why all the questions?"

"In case you haven't noticed, weird things have been happening here the last few days. Give me the key."

"Weird things *always* happen here, Jessie." He laughed and handed me the key. "We're in the middle of a village built on an old airstrip and set up to look like it's in the Middle Ages."

I totally lost it with that statement. "This is *not* the Middle Ages. The Middle Ages were between 1000 and 1450. The Renaissance came *after* the Middle Ages. I can't believe you don't know that!"

"I can't believe you bothered *telling* me. They all look the same to me. If you see one group of peasants riding horses, you've seen them all."

"Tony, peasants don't ride horses. Haven't

you learned anything being here?"

"That my sister is a crazy history person? Yeah, I've learned that."

We stood facing each other, and I thought again about how different we were. I'm not sure the doctor knew what he was talking about when he said we were twins. How could that be possible when we're so different?

"Why are you here, anyway?" I stopped staring at him and started straightening up the baskets around the room.

"I'm getting ready to leave with Tammy. I wanted to say good-bye."

"You're *really* leaving?"

He smiled and grabbed my hand. "Come with us. There's more to the world than this place, Jess. We can have some fun."

"You forget; I come here for fun every summer. I have a job the rest of the year. This *is* a fun time for me."

"Okay. I'll call when I can. We're taking Tammy's car to Vegas. Maybe you can come out sometime and visit." He hugged me, and I closed my eyes. I couldn't pretend I wouldn't miss him, even though he was always a problem.

"Be careful out there. They do mean stuff to cheaters."

He pushed away from me. "What are

you saying?"

"I don't know. You've always cheated at Monopoly. I thought you might cheat at cards. They're experts out there at catching card cheaters."

"Thanks for spoiling the nostalgic mood, Sis. I guess I've always known what you think of me. Don't worry. I can take care of myself."

I watched him slam out of the shop, sorry I'd said anything. He was right. I'd spoiled one of the few bonding moments we'd ever had. I don't know why we aren't closer, since we're the only family we've got, but that's the way it seems to be. People at the Village thought we were close. The truth was, we might be closer with him in Las Vegas.

With that depressing thought, I closed and locked both doors into Wicked Weaves and walked toward the castle, hoping to see Chase and Mary. The tide of people was flooding that way down the cobblestone street. Jack Be Nimble was hopping that way but took the time to stop and ask how I was doing. He was another summer love affair. But that was a long time ago.

Mother Goose was hurrying toward the castle with her bird. I asked her if she'd seen Chase or Mary. She said she hadn't seen either one of them but would tell them I was looking for them if she did.

I would've scurried along with her to the castle, but I wanted to stop and test Tony's theory. I figured the Three Pigs Barbecue would be as good a place as any. It looked like it was closed already; probably taking barbecue to the castle.

I glanced around, and no one seemed to be looking my way. Everyone was intent on what they were doing. I took the key Tony had given me out of my pocket and tried to open the Three Pigs' door.

Just as I got the key in, one of the pigs came out with a surprised look on his pudgy face. These guys weren't cast; they owned the place. All the brothers had a distinctly porcine look to their faces. "What are you doing?"

"I was wondering if you were gone already." I tried to laugh it off. "I've had a craving for barbecue all day."

He glanced at me. "You'll have to get it at the castle. We're closed."

I thanked him, wishing I could remember any of their names or tell them apart. I hurried away, embarrassed to be caught trying to break into the diner. But I'd found out Tony was right. There *was* a master key. Who else knew that? I was going to have to ask Chase about it, if I ever saw him again.

The closer I got to the castle, the more congested the King's Highway became. There were hundreds of visitors waiting in line to get inside and hundreds of vendors from the Village waiting in line to take their stuff inside. It was total chaos, even though Roger Trent was trying to organize everyone with a list on a scroll.

"My jerkin for a Palm Pilot," the glass blower growled as I came closer. "This gets worse every year. We might have to do it more often or not at all."

"Can I help?" I don't know exactly what made me volunteer. I guess I felt sorry for him, and I knew I wanted to apprentice with him in the future.

"If you could organize the rabble, I can deal with the visitors."

He handed me a list and a quill pen, then pointed me toward the vendors who I assumed must be the rabble. I got to the front of the line and started crossing off names. "The Feathered Shaft; the Hands of Time; the King's Tarts; Lady Godiva; Merlin and his apprentice; Honey and Herb Shoppe; Harriet's Hat House."

It read like a Who's Who of the Village. Most of the people I knew. They'd been there since the Village had opened. Some were new. Businesses closed and opened every few years. Maybe not so much here as in the real world. Most of the people who came here stayed because they fit into their strange surroundings.

The Three Pigs checked in with the head pig, the one who'd greeted me at the door, growling as he went by. The barbecue they carried in a white wheelbarrow smelled good. I smiled and passed them through.

Little Bo Peep came through with one fake sheep. It was actually a puppet, since they'd banned her real sheep from the castle after an accident a couple of years back. Now the only real animals allowed in the castle were the horses used for jousting.

A troupe of minstrels bowed to me as I checked them in. They were resplendent in gold and blue silk. I hoped they knew what they were doing. There was an ancient rule about out-dressing the king, queen, or any of the court that was established here as well. Anyone dressed grander than their betters could be asked to wear a flour sack the rest of the evening. It hadn't happened to me, but I'd seen it happen to others. There was a protocol, crazy as it was. It had to be observed.

I looked up from my thoughts to check in the next person, dragon, or fairy, and stared into Abraham's dark face. He was wearing a monk's robe.

TWELVE

Abraham broke into a sprint when he recognized me. I dropped my scroll and ran after him. "Someone with a radio, call Chase!"

"Get back here, Jessie! I need you." Roger didn't understand why I was leaving my post. I didn't have time to explain.

For a semi-old guy, Abraham could really move. A professional football team could have used him. It had to be all that healthy living. He probably ate right and walked ten miles a day.

I kept sight of him through the crowd. The stream of people pushing into the castle was the only thing in my favor. If he wouldn't have had to keep stopping for them, he would've lost me right away.

There was only one entrance into the castle. There were several exits, but that was because Harry and Livy were worried about people getting inside without paying for tickets. They probably wouldn't have had any exits at all if the fire department hadn't made them. But even Renaissance Faire Village wasn't above the law.

There were several large turrets added on both sides of the castle last year. They flanked the great hall, which made up most of the castle space. Extensive work was done there each year to accommodate the growing numbers of visitors to the Village. There was balcony seating around the arena where the horses and knights competed.

It made the whole thing a little ungainly once you got inside. It didn't look anything like a real castle in England or France. But the outside facade was enough for the visitors. Besides, they wanted someplace to eat their little chickens while they watched the bloodless show.

But back to getting into the castle. People were ushered into a long hall that divided at the end to allow for seating on both sides of the arena. At one end, like the head of the table, was where Livy and Harry held court. The other end was the massive kitchen where the food was prepared.

I skirted around the crowds of people jammed in, waiting to be seated. There was no sign of Abraham or his monk's robe. There were no other monks in the crowd, which wasn't unusual. Most people wanted to dress up for the occasion, and the event became a sea of lace, satin, and velvet. Of course there weren't as many colors back in the days of the Renaissance, but historical accuracy can only go so far. I wouldn't want to be the one to tell any of them their outfits didn't fit in.

I caught sight of one of the handful of security guards who were specially hired for the feast. I tried to make him understand, but he blew me off. Probably thought I was a crazed troubadour. The bells were about to drive me crazy. They were bad enough when I wasn't running.

I wished I could find Chase, but there was no sign of him. The chances were he wasn't even at the castle yet. He always came to the feast late so he could make sure the Village was empty during that time.

I climbed up on a cask and surveyed the crowd. Not a brown monk's hood among them. The security guard made me climb down when he saw me, even though I showed him my Village pass. There was nothing more I could do.

It was embarrassing to admit Abraham had eluded me. Maybe I wouldn't say anything. On the other hand, he was wearing a robe. That strengthened my theory that it was him who attacked Ham. What were the odds he'd be wearing a stolen monk's robe and our only witness said a monk was in the smithy with Ham?

My antics caught Livy's attention, and she beckoned me to follow her courtiers. She'd changed her velvet for lighter evening apparel. Her dress was made of silver silk and embroidered with little blue butterflies. Her bright red hair was pushed way up on her head and had huge, fake silver clips in it. The effect wasn't good on her overall. She looked like a big bug of some kind. Not the most flattering thing you can say about someone.

I nudged aside a few ladies-in-waiting to reach her and tell her what was happening. She needed to know why I couldn't indulge her every whim this evening. Otherwise, I'd be there all night entertaining her. "Livy! I think I found the man who murdered the guy you found by the privy."

She looked down at me. "Are you speaking to us, Troubadour?"

"Yes, Your Majesty." I bowed my head both to her and her position, even if it was only queen of sales. "I am speaking to you. You must release me from your entourage so that I may still find the murderous monk."

She waved her hand at me as three ladies adjusted her gown so she could sit on her throne. "Troubadour, we are not amused by your actions. Sing us a pleasant song. Where is your lute?"

"Majesty, I do not play the lute."

"A lute!" she called out. "This troubadour needs a lute."

Several of them were shoved in my face. No doubt, all the lute-carrying members of the queen's court were glad to let me have the honor. "I apologize, Your Majesty," I tried again. What was wrong with this woman, anyway? "I cannot sing nor play the lute."

Livy deigned to look at me again. It wasn't a good thing. "How can you be a troubadour if you cannot sing or play the lute? Thou must be a false troubadour. Forsooth, we think you are a knave in troubadour's clothing. Guard, take the knave away to the kitchen where she might serve dinner and learn her lesson."

I'm as much into character as the next resident of the Village. But this was taking it too far. I knew Harry and Livy were absolute monarchs at the feast. If they said go to the kitchen, you went to the kitchen. I needed an opportunity to look around. The kitchen wasn't going to allow me that freedom.

I grabbed the closest lute and started singing. I had no idea how to play the instrument, but I figured it couldn't be much different than the guitar. I'd learned to play the guitar in high school along with half of my sophomore class. There was no better instrument for teenage angst than the guitar.

I hopped around a little and tried to be entertaining. Livy looked the other way, but Harry seemed to be amused.

Not one to miss an opportunity, I worked on entertaining him. Anything was better than the kitchen. Serving food to a few hundred half drunk lords and ladies was not my idea of a good time. Every plate was the same: one little chicken, one baked potato, one roll, and a boiled egg. That was as close as they could come to a Renaissance feast. Dessert was *plum* pudding with plums. Like I'd said, imperfect history.

King Harry was highly amused with my singing and dancing. I made sure to shake enough of my body to ring my bells. "Thou art entertaining, Troubadour. Come join our court."

This didn't sit well with Livy. "The troubadour is ours, sir. She will remain with us or be taken to the kitchen."

Harry chuckled. "You forget yourself, my royal wife. We are king here. We say the troubadour stays."

I felt like one of the little chickens. No one really wanted me, but I was cheap and fit on the plate without too much trouble. I didn't dare say anything that might interrupt their royal argument.

The other courtiers stood around buffing their nails or playing with their hair — and those were the men. The women looked bored, except for those who were worried about their breasts tumbling out of their low-cut gowns. You could always tell them because they kept their arms folded across their chests.

I tried to back away as the argument ensued. Livy saw me and had her royal guard hold me until their highnesses could make a decision.

"We shall settle this on the field of honor," she finally decided. "My champion, Sir Reginald, will face your champion, the Black Knight, for the fate of this troubadour."

The king agreed. "An admirable solution, my dear. Where is my Black Knight?"

I hated to be the bearer of bad news, but Tony was gone, and there probably hadn't been enough time to hire a new Black

Knight. I kept my mouth shut as our visitors began to eat and the noise level in the great hall increased.

Jugglers, singers, belly dancers, and other performers wove their way through the crowd while Harry decided what to do about his lost Black Knight. The smell of roasting chicken mingled with the smell of horses as Sir Reginald presented his red and gold standard to the queen in hope of her favor.

"You do please us so, Sir Reginald." Livy giggled and presented him with her scarf. Sir Reginald bowed low, then took the silver scarf from the end of his lance. He wrapped it around his neck, then bowed again.

"This cannot be a contest without our Black Knight," Harry complained. "Which of our brave courtiers will take the field against the queen's champion?"

Not surprisingly, no one volunteered. It was different being up on the dais with the king and queen than it was being down in the sawdust with the horses. I wouldn't have volunteered, either.

"Is there no one, no brave knight, who will pit himself against Sir Reginald?" Harry yelled out over the sound of the crowd.

Hardly anyone heard him. The trumpeters had started, not realizing the Black Knight had gone to Las Vegas with a fairy. They were set for the tournament just like any other feast night. There were knight replacements in the Village, but either they didn't want to step forward, or they were playing hooky from the feast.

The courtiers parted amid the sound of starched ruffles and sequins. Chase bowed low to the king and queen. "Your Majesties, I am here on Village business to question yon troubadour on a matter of urgency."

The queen smiled at Chase. "Sir Bailiff! Thou art always a welcome sight!"

Harry growled. "Perhaps your loyal bailiff will joust as the Black Knight this evening."

"I would love nothing more," Chase lied. "But I would be forced to fight against my queen's champion."

"Never fear, dear boy." Livy smoothed her hand down his deep blue dress tunic. "We shall discharge Sir Reginald for the king's use this evening. You shall represent us in the troubling matter of this troubadour."

I could see Chase had run out of ideas. He'd started at the Village as a knight, the Black Knight, until someone else got the job. He couldn't deny that he knew how to joust. This was a valuable commodity during the feast or if they ran out of knights for the jousting tournaments during the day.

He looked at me and shrugged. He knew the rule of absolute monarchy at the feast as well as I did. He didn't have much choice. He bowed low to the queen. "I would be honored to represent you, Your Majesty."

Livy giggled again and leaned forward dangerously from her throne. "Sir Reginald!" she sang out in her high-pitched voice. "Give Sir Bailiff my standard."

Sir Reginald didn't look too happy about that. "I ride for the queen. I am *not* the King's Black Knight."

Livy stood up and put her hand on Chase's arm. She was getting uncomfortably familiar with my boyfriend. "Posh! You will do as we say, sir, or you will suffer the consequences. The kitchen is still short-handed."

The visitors, sensing a confrontation, put their half-eaten chickens down long enough to see what was going to happen.

But Sir Reginald knew the rule of absolute monarchy as well. He bowed his head to Queen Olivia's decision. "I will represent the king, but only because you command it, Your Majesty. And I will rip yon knight to pieces before your eyes!"

I had worked as a squire many times, and

Livy had granted my request to aid her knight. I noticed the silver armor was heavy as I helped Chase buckle it on in one of the staging rooms off of the arena. It wasn't real, but it felt real. "Are you sure about this?"

Chase paused in putting on his helmet to kiss me. "Absolutely. Tell me again what happened with Abraham. Did you lose him completely?"

"He and I got separated in the crowd." I adjusted his breastplate. That was the part that would take the full brunt of the lance. The lances were rigged to fall apart on impact, but I'd seen my share of knights who were bruised anyway. "I don't know where he went. But I think we've found our killer."

"Whoa! Just because he was wearing a monk's robe doesn't make him a killer."

"It makes him responsible for what happened to Ham. We've got a witness to that event."

"Jessie, I hope you never become a cop. Alex saw a man in a monk's robe standing *near* Ham. He didn't see him hit him or anything else. He said he couldn't identify the man. How does that make Abraham the killer?"

"It stands to reason."

"Just like Jah's bad temper makes him the killer, right?"

"I didn't say that." I helped him put on his gauntlets. "But you have to admit he was mean to Mary. I think that's a little suspicious."

"But where was his monk's robe?" Chase wiggled his fingers in his heavy gloves. "I think we have to give these men the benefit of the doubt. They're innocent until proven guilty."

"I can tell you've worked as a pretend defense attorney." I held the midnight-black horse that would carry Chase onto the field of honor, the red and gold livery identifying the queen's champion. "I'd be a prosecutor, if I was bent enough to be a lawyer."

He laughed as he stepped up on the block to climb on the horse. "I think you would. Just be careful, huh? Somebody really killed Joshua, and that person might or might not be involved with the attack on Ham. They might come after you if you ask too many questions. Or chase them through the castle."

I looked up at him from the sawdust-strewn floor. He was gorgeous: tall, broad-shouldered, everything a knight should be. No wonder Livy wanted him. He brought to mind all the books I'd read on King Arthur and the days of chivalry. It was what had first inspired me to study history. The Renaissance was still my favorite time. "Be careful out there. I think Reggie might think there's something going on between you and Livy."

Chase made a face. "You didn't have to put that picture in my mind before I went out to fight."

"Don't worry. I was about to slam her if she didn't quit rubbing her hands all over you up there. Maybe I could take the throne. What do you think about Queen Jessie?"

"I think you better get the lances and let's get this over with." He put down his visor and rode out into the center of the arena.

While we'd been getting ready for the joust, the rabble rousers, or cheerleaders in tunics and tights as I preferred to think of them, were egging on the crowd. Sir Reginald's side of the arena booed heartily as they saw Chase. Little chicken bones flew across the sawdust at the horse's feet.

The same thing happened from the queen's side of the arena when they saw Sir Reginald, his shining silver armor now exchanged for black. The booing was long and loud, and one of the chicken bones bounced off his shoulder.

Both sides cheered when the two knights faced each other with the master of ceremonies, Lord Dunstable, telling them and the audience the rules. Dunstable was the queen's second favorite. "If either man is unseated, his loss is immediate on that round. There will be three rounds where each knight will be tested for strength, courage, and agility. Whichever knight is victorious for two of the three rounds will be the winner. If there is a tie, the princess Isabel will make the final decision by giving her favor to one or the other of the knights."

Chase's horse seemed a little hard to control. The big Percheron wanted to dance around the arena instead of waiting for the joust. I had to move quickly to avoid being stepped on by the huge hooves. "He's kind of feisty." I handed Chase his first lance.

"I know. He probably wasn't ridden much today. I seem to be the only one who likes the big horses."

"That's because you know the little horses wouldn't be able to hold you up, especially in armor."

"Remind me to laugh when I get back." He pushed down his face protector and advanced onto the field.

Sir Reginald, in the meantime, was chasing his squire around, threatening to beat the boy, much to the amusement of the crowd. It seemed the young squire had given the knight the wrong lance. Sir Reginald became all business when he saw Chase riding toward him.

"Okay, you two," Lord Dunstable said into the microphone, a modern device but one necessary to be heard over the crowd. "We want a clean fight this evening. No cheating. Especially from you, Black Knight."

The crowd alternately booed and applauded, depending on the sign their rabble rouser held up. Historically, the Black Knight was the bad guy and the cheat who'd do anything to win the joust. Sir Reginald, despite normally being the queen's favorite, was perfect for the role, especially with Livy's attention on the line. He might flirt with the fairies, but Reggie wanted to be with Livy. It was a complicated situation.

Both knights cantered their horses to the end of the arena to ask for favor from the queen and king. Livy gave Chase her necklace. Harry hung his coin purse on the end of Sir Reginald's lance.

Each man went to his own corner. They paused, then rode sharply at each other. Lances went down toward the other knight's chest. I closed my eyes and waited for the sound of wood hitting steel.

Chase's horse neighed loudly, and I opened my eyes to see his lance splinter on Sir Reginald's chest. It didn't unseat the other knight, unfortunately. Sir Reginald's lance glanced off the side of Chase's arm. The crowd booed on the Black Knight's side as Chase was awarded the points for the first joust.

The next joust was a test of skill. Each knight had to catch colored rings on their lance. It was up to the squires to throw the rings into the air.

The queen decided to change the rules. "I believe we should allow the troubadour, who plays at being yon knight's squire, to stand in the middle and throw the rings for both men. What say you, Your Majesty?"

King Harold waved his hand, too absorbed in one of the courtiers' cleavage to care one way or the other. "As you wish, my dear."

I took the colored rings from our side, and Sir Reginald's squire gave me his rings. "Better you than me," he muttered. "They don't pay enough for this job. I never knew horses smelled so bad."

I climbed up on the barrel in the middle of the arena and got ready to throw the rings into the air. I didn't think much about it. I'd done it plenty of times in the outside jousting area when one of the squires didn't show up. It wasn't like I was the target.

I tossed the red ring up first for each knight. Each man caught the ring on his lance. I tossed the green ring for each knight. Each man caught the green ring, although Sir Reginald barely made the catch. He gave me a sour look. Like I had anything to do with it. I wasn't a baseball pitcher.

It was time for the last ring when Livy's voice rang out over the microphone. "We weary of this sport. We are looking for more excitement. What say you, citizens? Are you looking for more excitement as well?"

Both sides of the arena roared and stomped their feet while they threw chicken bones all over the arena. I raked one out of my hair and tried to stand behind the two knights.

"We believe both knights to be equally matched. We require them now to show their bravery and skill by catching the last ring blindfolded." Livy smiled and held up her scepter that Daisy had made for her.

The crowd yelled, "Huzzah!" until it sounded like the rafters would fall in. *Blindfolded?* I looked at Chase, who shrugged and came closer as the young squire for Sir

Reginald retrieved the blindfolds from the king's page. He brought them to me, and I tied one on each man.

This was one of the craziest stunts I'd ever seen here. And I wasn't sure about my position on the barrel being so safe anymore. Was that the idea? Would the queen be happy if one of them hit me with the lance or knocked me off the barrel?

Both men, blindfolded, took their positions. I climbed back up on the barrel and yelled out as I tossed up the last yellow rings.

THIRTEEN

Did anyone else think this was insane? I was screaming inside, but outside I was standing on the barrel like one of the lunatics. Had years of being here, considering the king and queen's commands valid, turned my entire brain to mashed potatoes?

The horses thundered toward me as I threw the rings in the air. The crowd cheered and stomped; a hail of chicken bones flew into the arena. Apparently, this was excitement at its best.

I felt frozen there, watching Chase and Sir Reginald gallop toward me as they lowered their lances. There was no way either one of them knew where the rings were. Sir Reginald's ring fell on the floor and rolled through the sawdust. He didn't slow his horse. He obviously wasn't cheating by looking around his blindfold or he planned on hitting me.

The lance would break, I kept telling

myself. Except that I wasn't wearing armor, so it would break off inside me. I had to get off the barrel and run out of the arena. But I didn't move.

Looking back on it later, I realized it was one of those fight-or-flight moments. There was no way I could fight two men on horses with lances. Flight should've been the obvious answer, but my legs refused to move. I was scared brainless.

At the last moment, as though the fairy of reason had suddenly swooped down on us, Chase threw down his lance and ripped off his blindfold. He got to me an instant before Sir Reginald and lifted me up on the back of his horse.

I thought we'd both be lanced, but Chase sidestepped Sir Reginald, and the Black Knight passed by us, ending up with his lance in one of the wooden beams on the other side of the arena. The impact threw him from his horse, and he hit the floor with a resounding clang.

The audience loved it. The roar of voices was deafening. I could still hear my heart pounding despite the noise. Chase's armor was cool against my face as I closed my eyes and leaned against him. "Thanks."

"Don't mention it. I don't know what we were thinking."

The king and queen were on their feet, demanding the match be replayed. Sir Reginald's squire tried to help him to his feet, but the knight pushed him aside. He staggered to the microphone in the middle of the arena and pushed Lord Dunstable out of the way. "My honor must be avenged," he yelled, his face unflatteringly red. "I will have vengeance."

Before anyone could say anything, Sir Reginald grabbed his chest and slumped to the arena floor. The crowd applauded and stomped their feet. Lord Dunstable called for a paramedic, but he could hardly be heard over the noise.

Chase jumped from his horse, not an easy feat in armor off a horse probably seventeen hands high. He threw his armor off as he ran toward Sir Reginald. I thought, *That's why Chase is the bailiff of Renaissance Faire Village. He's good in an emergency.* He administered CPR on Sir Reginald until the paramedics got there and took the fallen knight away.

"You were awesome!" I kissed him. "You saved the damsel *and* your opponent."

"Maybe." He glanced up at Harry and Livy. "They don't look too happy."

"Who cares? Let's get out of here."

Before we could leave the arena, King

Harry called for silence. "We must award our stalwart bailiff and knight the highest medal possible for his bravery tonight. Step forward, Sir Knight."

Chase glanced at me, then shrugged and walked toward the end of the arena. The Princess Isabel bestowed her favor by giving him a circle headpiece made of what was supposed to be silver but was really aluminum. She kissed him on each cheek, then launched herself against him, throwing her arms around him and latching on to his mouth like a lamprey.

The crowd roared and whistled as the kiss went on. I tapped my foot in the sawdust, looked at my nails, and glanced around the arena. How long was this going to take? It seemed to be going beyond the bounds of showing favor in a public place. But then the Princess Isabel showed her favor all over the place.

She finally had to breathe, and when she moved, Chase put one arm around her waist and held the other in the air. The king and queen shouted "Huzzah," and the word was repeated by everyone present. Except me. All that favor had left me a little cold and a lot angry.

I started out of the castle after picking up Chase's armor and leading his horse into the stable at the side of the arena. I didn't put the armor away, just left it lying there. He could put it away if he wanted to.

He was so busy with everyone talking to him, surrounding him, patting him on the back. I knew he'd done a good thing, and he deserved praise for it. I would've felt better about it if it wasn't for Princess Isabel standing so close to him.

I kicked a few empty drink cups after I emerged into the evening twilight outside the castle. I wanted a shower and some time alone. I hardly recognized myself in there. It wasn't like me to be jealous of a boyfriend.

It wasn't real, I told myself, and that was the problem. I was jealous anyway. That didn't bode well for my summer relationship. It never lasted more than the summer. At the end of August, I'd go back to school, and Chase would stay here. When I came back next summer, there would be someone else. That's the way it was supposed to work.

True, I rationalized; I had wanted to be with Chase for a long time. It had never seemed to work out, until this summer. But that was the only thing that made it different. I went on to list all the things I didn't like about Chase. It was a short list. Really, it was only that he didn't seem ambitious.

Otherwise, he was as close to perfect as I could imagine.

I started to walk past Wicked Weaves on my way back to my hut when I noticed a light on inside. I went around back and found Mary on the steps working on her basket. I didn't say anything, just sat down beside her. I watched her hands flying through the motions of coiling the sweetgrass and building on the foundation, row upon row.

It was hypnotic watching her hands move deftly through the sweetgrass and the palm strips. There were pine needles in the basket, too. There was only the faintest smell of pine. She coiled and stitched, her fingers never missing the perfect stitch, the basket taking shape before my eyes.

"You know," she began without looking up, "when we harvested sweetgrass when I was a child, we always gave thanks to God for it. People stopped doing that. Life changed as time passed. Today there isn't much sweetgrass left anymore. I think that might be why. My mama said when you don't appreciate things, they go away. I think that was what happened to me. I didn't say thank you for everything God had given me when I was home."

I put my arm around her thin shoulders

and leaned my head against the colored scarf that covered her head. "When my parents died, I thought I'd killed them because they were out looking for me. Tony and I were twelve at the time. I thought it was fun to stay out late. I knew they worried about me, but I didn't care. They left Tony at home with my grandmother and came out to look for me. A man was driving drunk and hit and killed both of them almost right in front of my house."

Mary's hands stopped moving. She looked at me in the dim light coming from inside the shop where the door was left open. "Child, you can't take that on yourself. God called them back to him. That had nothing to do with you."

"I know that most of the time. But sometimes, especially when I see how Tony is, I blame myself because he didn't have them when he was growing up."

"You didn't, either. But you grew up all right. Why do you think that is?"

"Because my guilt always pushed me forward. It never forgets or lets me rest with what I've done."

She shook her head and put her arm around me to hug me close. She smelled like talcum powder and sweetgrass. It was a lovely combination. "You can't blame yourself for what happened."

"You can't blame yourself because there's no more sweetgrass."

"Jessie, you're a smart girl. I don't know if you'll ever be a basket weaver, but you'll live a good life." Mary hugged me tight again. "And I thank you for being here this summer. Summer is a crazy time, you know. It gets so hot, people can't think straight."

"Did you find Jah and talk to him?"

"I did. It didn't change nothin'. He's gonna believe what he wants to believe. Young people are that way. And they're harder on their elders than they should be, because they can't understand what happened and why things happened."

"Do you think he could've had anything to do with Joshua's death?"

"No. He's a good boy. Only confused. He's been told one thing for so long and then come to find out it wasn't that way at all. He'll be fine, you wait and see. And he didn't kill his daddy."

"You back here, Mary?" a voice called out from the side of the shop.

"We're back here, Ham," she answered. "Come back and sit a spell. I've got some sweet tea and some good tomatoes. I think we could make us a little to eat. I ain't ate all day."

Ham came around the side of the building and smiled at me in the dim light. "I remember you." He reached out to shake my hand. "You might'a saved my life."

"What are you talking about?" Mary looked back and forth between us. I told her what had happened as she gathered her basket weaving materials together to go inside. "So someone has it in for Ham, too?"

"It appears that way." He put his hand to the bandage on his head. "I don't know anyone who thinks that ill of me. Or of Joshua, for that matter, though I admit I haven't seen him for a lotta years."

"Even so, who would do such a thing?" Mary asked.

"What about Abraham?" I tossed into the conversation.

"No way." Ham held the door for Mary. "He's not made like that."

"He *wasn't* made like that," I disagreed. "But with Jah finding out the truth about who his parents are and Joshua leaving the village to tell Mary that her son is still alive, who knows what someone might do?"

Mary and Ham refused to consider the idea that the killer could be Abraham. I sat with them for hours while they talked about their childhood together. We drank sweet tea and ate cheese biscuits and tomatoes while they thought about the past and avoided what was happening now.

Finally, I just couldn't take it anymore. "You guys have to consider that *something* is wrong here. Unless Joshua was behind the privies and saw a drug deal go down, the two of you could be in danger, too. And since Ham has already been attacked, I'd say my theory about Abraham is right."

Mary laughed. "Jessie, you don't know this man the way we do. He might be capable of some bad things, but not murder. And not Joshua. The two of them were close as the sweetgrass and black rush in my baskets. There's not a chance that he hurt his brother."

"Okay. Let's say someone else killed Joshua. We can't forget Ham was attacked, too. Who else in the Village would do something like that? What other connection do Ham and Joshua have?"

Ham sipped his tea, washing down the last of his cheese biscuit. "Girl has a point, Mary. Something's wrong. I don't know what it is. I don't think Abraham hurt me or Joshua, but we better consider the possibility that you could be next. That's why I came right over tonight. I think you should come stay with me, at least for a while."

"I'm not running again." Mary shook her

head. "I ran from our home but I promised myself that I'd never run again. And why would someone want to hurt me?"

I shrugged and swallowed a bite of cheese biscuit. "Why would someone want to hurt Joshua and Ham? Except for Abraham, there's only one other person who's been here and is involved with the four of you."

Mary shoved her chair out over the hardwood floor with a distinct grinding sound. She looked so angry, I wasn't sure if it was her teeth or her chair making that noise. "I won't hear none of that in my kitchen. Jessie, don't you even think my boy could hurt his father."

"He didn't *know* he was his father until recently," I argued. "He couldn't have had many feelings for him. Maybe he was angry. Jah seemed pretty angry with you."

Ham looked at her. "You didn't tell me Jah was mad about what happened."

"I think it's a normal reaction to being lied to and cheated of your real parents." Mary turned to me, her face vivid in the pale overhead light. "As for him not knowing Joshua, he was with him every day of his life. He knew him almost as well as he knew Abraham and his wife."

The conversation died out after that. Mary and Ham seemed to be lost in their individual memories. I thanked Mary for the sweet tea and biscuits, then left the shop. I took the basket I was working on with me. It was going to be a long, lonely night thinking about Chase and Princess Isabel.

It was quiet and dark in the Village. No wonder people stayed in their houses before streetlights. The Village had some lamps, but they were more for accent and giving the place a period feel than any real help getting around. The alleys going between businesses and houses were completely black. At least when the moon was out, you could make out shapes and forms.

A long, low howl came from outside the Village wall. At least I hoped it was from outside the wall. I reminded myself that was how stories of vampires and werewolves got started. It was all because of streetlights. People thought all kinds of crazy things in the dark. I shivered in the hot night air and wished I was in my little hut with the door closed.

There was cheerful, yellow light pouring out of the Peasant's Pub where all the residents hung out in the evening. It was unusual for them to be open this late; it was already after midnight. But the cheerful light eased those dark fears that are common to all humans, and I decided to stop in for a tankard of ale.

A handful of diehard souls were gathered around the wooden bar that Hephaestus, the owner of Peasant's Pub, claimed came from a real seventeenth-century pub in England. He was a tall, broad-shouldered man with a big chest that was almost hidden by his huge gray brown beard.

"Come on in, Jessie!" he yelled when he saw me. "First tankard's on the house for that exhibit at the castle tonight."

The other people, mostly fools, knaves, and varlets, all of whom I knew, cheered and agreed with him. I knew I was with my people as I sat down at the bar. "Thanks, guys. Is it just me, or does this place get weirder and weirder?"

They all laughed, then pretty much ignored me. I was hot for all of five seconds. Oh well. I guess that was better than not being hot at all.

"What's up with you and Chase this year?" Hephaestus habitually wiped his questionably clean rag across the surface of the bar.

"What do you mean?" I tried not to sound defensive. "We've been friends for years."

A couple of fools laughed. Hephaestus laughed with them. "Come on, honey. We all know you have a summertime thing here.

We're taking bets on it being Chase. We're all friends at the Village. Are you shacking up with the bailiff this summer?"

This was the height of boredom. Taking bets on my relatively dull life was like racing cockroaches. "That's none of your business."

"We could ask Chase," one of the varlets said, "*if* we could find him. He looked like he wanted to stay lost with the princess when they left the castle together after the feast."

I slogged down my ale, then got up and walked out of the pub. I was wrong. Fools, varlets, and knaves don't make the best company. I needed to be alone, even if a werewolf tore my throat out before I got back to my hut.

Humming a song I couldn't remember the words to, I kept walking past the dark alleys and shuttered businesses that lined the street. I clutched my basket in my hand. It wasn't much as far as a weapon if someone or something jumped out of the dark at me. Of course, it was enough to kill Joshua. But then he was too drunk to care.

It occurred to me that whoever attacked Ham might've had the same plans for him. Did it look like I was involved in whatever was going on? I hoped not. I was only an observer. But it made me nervous thinking about it after I'd had that drink at the pub. What if Abraham or Jah, whichever of them was responsible, thought I was drunk and an easy target? Was there some way to let them know besides walking in a straight line that I wouldn't be as easy to kill as Joshua?

My hut finally came into view. It was a welcome sight. The key was in my hand when a large form stepped out of the shadows toward me. I dropped into what I hoped looked like a karate stance I'd seen in a movie. "I'm not drunk! You might be able to kill me, but I'll take a piece of you with me."

"Easy, killer!" Chase laughed. "I think you must be drunk, if you think anyone is going to be scared by that pose."

I relaxed, thankful it was only him. Then I got mad. "Go home, Chase. Except for me telling you this, I'm not speaking to you."

"You're jealous of me kissing Isabel!"

"I am not."

"Yes you are. Admit it."

I had already put the key in the lock, but I couldn't let him leave thinking I cared about what he did with the princess. "I'm not jealous. I don't care what you do or who you do it with. I don't have any hold on you.

You're free to go your own way, just like I am."

"That's right. That's who you are, Jessie; the summertime girl. You love 'em over the summer then go on your way before fall. Everyone knows that."

"I don't want any involvements to impede my life." As I said it, I thought about what it sounded like and rushed to correct it. "I mean, I know what happens here isn't real."

"Just because it's Renaissance Faire Village doesn't mean the people who live here aren't real. They get angry and get their hearts broken just like they do in Columbia or anywhere else. You just think you can come here and play around and no one will know. Then you go back to the university and live your life without ever feeling anything."

I wanted to argue with him. I wanted to tell him it wasn't true, but I knew he was right. I didn't have romantic relationships at the university. I knew I was coming back here, and the summer with some knight or lord would be enough. And it wasn't real.

"I'm sorry." He leaned against the side of the hut, his face in the shadows.

"No. That's okay. You're right in some ways." I sighed. "I was jealous of Isabel. I don't know why."

He moved closer to me. "Maybe because *we're* real, Jessie. And what's happening between us is real."

Something inside of me wanted it to be real. I felt like the Grinch whose heart grew three sizes as he stood on Mt. Crumpit. I put my arms around Chase and closed my eyes as I laid my head on his chest. He pulled me closer, and the shadows didn't seem so bad with the two of us.

"My feelings for you are real," Chase whispered. "I hope you feel the same about me."

I was about to assure him that he was more than a summer fling for me when a loud scream pierced the streets of Renaissance Faire Village.

FOURTEEN

The screams were coming from Bawdy Betty's Bagels, which was located between my hut and the Peasant's Pub. Chase and I ran down there, the bells on my costume giving me away. He glanced at me, and I shrugged. There wasn't much I could do about the bells. I couldn't wait to get my new costume tomorrow. The troubadour outfit may have been lighter, but I'd be happy to have my linen back. At least it was quiet.

Bawdy Betty was doing the screaming. When she saw Chase, she ran up and threw herself into his arms. I wondered if I'd ever get used to women throwing themselves at him. It was annoying to be jealous, especially since Chase was aware of it.

"Did you see that?" She sobbed into his shirt. "There was someone skulking around down here. He was wearing one of those weird monk costumes. I was taking out the

232

trash, and there he was. It looked like he was trying to get through the Village without being seen. It was horrible. I don't think he had a face. All I could see was darkness inside the hood."

With that terrifying statement, Betty collapsed on Chase, one arm across her eyes as her knees went weak. I wanted to suggest that he drop her. I thought she'd get to her feet quickly enough. The woman was monopolizing my man.

"Call the paramedics." Chase looked back at me. "While you're at it, call the police. We have to get to the bottom of this monk thing before the Brotherhood turns ugly."

I reached for my cell phone, which wasn't there. Betty revived enough to tell us we could use the phone in her shop. "There's no need to call the paramedics. I'll be fine." She squeezed Chase's arms with her greedy little hands and gazed up into his face. "Although I may need someone to carry me inside. I don't know if I can walk."

I'd trained with the campus fire and rescue squad in my freshman year. I only mention it because what I did might seem extraordinary otherwise, but a fireman can lift a person twice his weight using the cradle.

And that's exactly what I did. Betty closed

her eyes and pretended to faint again. I grabbed one of her arms and hoisted her on my shoulders. She wasn't a lightweight, especially in her full-length gown and undergarments, but I managed. I took the back stairs into the bagel shop, glancing down when Chase didn't follow me. "I'll take care of her. You call the police."

Betty opened one heavily made-up eye as I took her to her bedroom. "What's this? This isn't right. Have you got a thing for me?"

"No. You said you couldn't walk. I'm helping you." I shifted her weight.

"I only said it to get some attention from that lovely boy." Betty shivered and smiled.

I dropped her on her bed, watching her bounce with some kind of fiendish delight. "You're old enough to be his mother, Betty. Why not pick on Roger Trent?"

"Not my type!" She looked up at me from the bed. "Is that how it is with you, sweetie? I'm sorry, I didn't realize you were set on the bailiff this year."

I took a deep breath, about to admit my darkest secret to Bawdy Betty. "Now you know." It was a relief to confide in someone. I felt much better as I went back downstairs.

Chase was still on the phone with the police department. I sat down on one of the tall stools at the bagel bar and watched him. I thought, *Mine, all mine,* a few times. The whole possessive thing was a little new to me, but I thought I could get used to it. Chase was a prize. I was amazed I'd never really understood before. I guess I was so busy comparing him to Tony that I didn't see they were nothing alike.

"Someone's on their way out." He hung up the phone. "Why are you looking at me like that?"

"Like what?"

"Like I'm a big steak on a stick, and you've got plenty of Worcestershire sauce."

"I don't know what you're talking about." I licked my lips.

"I'm not complaining. Although now might not be a good time."

"It takes them a good forty-five minutes to get here, even with a dead body." I studied his muscled legs in brown tights.

He thought about it, but not too long. "You're right. Let's go."

The police were pulling in as Chase and I ran back from the big swan swing. It was shaped like a swan with a large open space in the middle that could easily hold five or six kids, or one or two adults. It was scary and exciting being out in the open like that, even though it was the middle of the night.

I realized Chase had his tunic on backwards and we changed it quickly before anyone saw it. It was an easy thing to do because the tunic wasn't much more than a big T-shirt without sleeves.

Chase smiled and kissed me as he handed me one of the bells that had come off my costume. "We'll have to do that again sometime."

I agreed, then tried to get my love-hazy brain operating again. I didn't want to sound like a flake talking to the police. Someone's life could be at stake.

It wasn't Detective Almond but an officer who was looking around Bawdy Betty's yard with a flashlight when we got there. "Bailiff?" He looked up.

Chase shook his hand. "That's me. Thanks for coming out. We've got a problem out here."

We sat down in Betty's kitchen, and she made us all coffee while we discussed the situation with the officer. He nodded as he listened and ate a few bagels, then wiped his hands on a napkin. "Besides the assault you're attributing to this robed figure, do you have any *real* evidence that one of the monks has gone wacko?"

I glanced at Chase. Had either one of us

mentioned wacko monks? The Brotherhood wasn't going to take kindly to being herded up and questioned. Fortunately, we wouldn't have to do it. They could get together and try to intimidate the police with their late-night antics.

"Not really," Chase admitted. "But there's a man who isn't a resident of the Village who might be involved in what happened with the murder and the assault." He told the officer about Abraham.

"Can you describe him?" The officer took out a notebook and searched for a pen until Betty provided one with a large feather on it. Her smile was lascivious.

"He's tall, thin." I thought about it for a few seconds. "He's got a long, thin face. He's black, which may be why Betty thought the hooded figure didn't have a face at all. When I first saw him, he was wearing spats."

The officer raised his eyebrows and scratched his crew cut. "That's something you don't hear every day. Can you describe them?"

"You don't know what spats are?" I tried not to sound too amazed.

"I can't keep up with all the weird clothing you people wear out here." He looked at my costume. "Like what do you call what you're wearing? Are you the court jester or something?"

"I'm a troubadour, a singer who entertains royalty."

"Whatever. Describe the spats, please."

I described the shoes and Abraham's old suit. I'd lost confidence in the officer to take care of the problem. I didn't have a lot to begin with. He was so busy looking down Bawdy Betty's bodice that he hardly had time to write. I thought if we put a bagel down her bodice, Chase and I could leave, and he'd never notice.

"Is that all?" he asked when he'd finished writing.

"As far as we know," Chase answered. "Maybe you could station an officer down here for a few days. It's a long drive out here to catch someone."

The officer got to his feet and winked at Betty. "That's where you come in, Mr. Bailiff. You're a big, strong-looking boy. If you see this fella, take him into custody. Put him in your pretend jail, and then call us. We'll take care of the rest."

It was about what I'd expected. If Abraham had been tied to one of Betty's chairs, the officer might've questioned him. He wasn't going to expend any energy looking for someone who might or might not have committed a crime.

Chase thanked him for coming, and Betty gave him a bagel for the road. We left before Betty and the officer got sloppy by the car. There wasn't much else to do.

"We have to find some way to flush this guy out," Chase said as we walked toward the dungeon. There were no lights on in the Village by this time. Even the animals in the stables and Bo Peep's sheep were asleep.

"What do you have in mind?" I didn't comment on the fact that my hut was closer than the dungeon. Chase's bed was more comfortable. And since I'd decided he was mine, it didn't matter where we went.

"I don't know. I'll have to think about it. But if we don't find some way to get him out in the open, something else is bound to happen. He's not hanging around here for no reason. I don't like that he seemed to be headed toward your hut. Maybe you should consider moving."

"Okay. But there isn't anyplace available this summer."

He took my hand. "I know someplace that's available. Rent free, too, if you don't mind sharing."

It was what I was waiting for, at least since we'd talked that night. Funny how one day could change your perspective. Just yesterday, I'd been thinking I didn't want to be at the dungeon with him because it was too proprietary. Then tonight, it was all I wanted to do.

"I could handle that."

"Great!" He kissed my hand. "We'll move your stuff to the dungeon in the morning."

"I think I can wait until then."

"If not, there's always the swan swing, although I think I hurt my back over there. I might be getting too old to rescue damsels, subdue evil knights, and woo fair troubadours."

"Whatever," I blew off his excuses. "There's always aspirin."

The next morning Chase and I talked about what we could do to trap Abraham. Now that we knew the police wouldn't be any help, we had to find a way to take care of the problem.

"We could paint a mark on every monk we pass that you can only see with a black light and have handheld black lights to scan them," Chase suggested as we moved my stuff to the dungeon.

"That would work if we had handheld black lights and if the monks would let us paint their robes." I shuffled my suitcase from one hand to another. "I wonder why Abraham would see me as a threat. It's not like I know anything more than anyone else."

"I don't know. And he might not," Chase admitted. "But you'll be safer at the dungeon."

I laughed, feeling very alive and happy, even if an evil monk was after me. The morning sun was warm on my head, and my senses were filled with all the sights, sounds, and smells of Renaissance Faire Village. Someday, when I was old and content to be where I was, I wanted to live here year round. This place was more home to me than anywhere else in the world.

Thinking about home made me think about Tony. I tried calling him when we dropped off my stuff at the dungeon. His cell phone was dead, of course. If I didn't pay the bill, he didn't, either. I wondered how he and Tammy were doing in Las Vegas and if it was everything he'd hoped it would be. I hoped it was. It would be nice for Tony to be happy.

"I have to hold debtor's court in a few minutes." Chase smiled at me. "It'll be nice knowing you'll be here tonight. I hope this isn't rushing things for you."

I hugged him, and we kissed for a few minutes. I didn't want to think about how many fairies and other fair maidens he'd practiced that kiss on; he was too good at it for me to believe I was the first. But then, I considered myself to be a fair kisser, too. Together we made a pretty good team.

I didn't let myself think about the end of the summer. When it was done, it was done. It had been that way for me for many years. There was no reason to think it would change because Chase was involved.

"You're off to Wicked Weaves?"

"Yep. I've stopped injuring myself when I weave baskets. Maybe now I can learn the real fundamentals."

"Do you think Mary could be in danger like Ham said?" Chase raised that left brow at me.

"I don't know. I hope not. Maybe we can come up with something today. We need to get Abraham out in the open."

"What about Jah? You think they could be working together?"

"There's no way of knowing. Mary won't listen to anything bad about either one of them. It could be Jah and Abraham working together or each of them involved individually. The only thing I know for sure is that something's up."

We kissed once more before leaving the dungeon. I almost skipped back through the Village, saying good morning to Frenchy at his fudge shop and Kellie at her kite shop. The Three Chocolatiers were practicing their swordplay in front of their shop in full costume. Their large, plumed hats, capes, and thigh-high boots separated them from the rest of the crowd. They put on a good show and had excellent chocolates.

I waved to a few of my students who were exercising the camels and elephants, surprised they'd stayed with it for so long. Several young men were trying to take the sword from the stone as I approached Wicked Weaves.

Of course, it didn't come out. It was inserted into an electronic lock in the stone, but most boys from the ages of nine to sixty couldn't resist trying. A few girls tried, too, but mostly the females watched from the side with exasperated expressions on their faces.

Roger Trent stopped me before I could go into Wicked Weaves. "I'd like to talk to you alone for a minute."

I wasn't sure I wanted to be alone with him, but since I was thinking about apprenticing with him at some point, I thought I should learn to get over it. Maybe he'd have something to say that would make sense of everything that had happened. After all, he was a standard in the Village.

He knew everyone and everything.

He was an extraordinary glass blower. I was always stunned by his creations when I walked into his shop, the Glass Gryphon. He was a true artist. Tiny little dragons peeked out from behind glass trees while large glass birds and fairies dangled from the ceiling. The colors and forms were graceful and beautiful. He infused them with life, even down to the tiny details of their clothes and faces. Except for the burns I always noticed on his muscular forearms, I was eagerly anticipating learning the craft.

"I've been thinking a lot about what happened to Mary's husband," he said as we walked into his shop. "I don't think things are exactly as they appear."

I sat beside his worktable as he sat down to work on one of his creations. The fine piece of glass looked out of place in his big hands. "What kind of things?"

"I've heard the police say they found Joshua behind the privies and that he'd been moved."

"That's what I heard, too."

"What else have you heard, Jessie?"

I wasn't sure how to answer that question. I glanced into the side room off the main show area in his shop. There was a monk's robe hanging on the wall. My pulse jumped up.

There were many reasons Roger could have a monk's robe. Maybe he was part of the Brotherhood of monks. That was unlikely, since all the craftsmen were members of the Craft Guild, and I'd never heard of one crossing over to another group.

Maybe he just liked the way the robe looked. It was a popular costume for visitors. Maybe he had one of his own for when he wasn't wearing his leather jerkin and hose. It got chilly in the wintertime.

Or maybe Roger was involved in Joshua's murder, and he was pumping me for information, because he knew I'd talked to the police last night. If he was the one skulking around outside Bawdy Betty's, he'd know about that. And didn't someone mention that frequently one of the first people on the scene of a homicide is involved in it?

I knew I had to word my answer carefully. "I haven't heard a lot more than that, Roger. There was an attack on Ham. The police think it might be the same person."

He continued working with the glass figure. "Why would someone want to hurt Ham?"

"I don't know. Maybe they want to cover up what really happened to Joshua."

He looked up at that. "What do you mean?"

"I think there might be some question of how Joshua really died." I watched for his reaction.

"He was strangled, right?"

"Yes. But the police have to wonder how Mary could've killed him. I mean, she's a little bit of nothing to hold down a man Joshua's size and strangle him."

"I suppose that's true. Maybe she drugged him or something. Not saying Mary was involved, because I don't believe she could hurt anyone."

"I don't, either. I suppose the big question is, why would someone want to kill Joshua?"

He shrugged. "Maybe because he wasn't supposed to be here. We know his brother, Abraham, talked to Mary before we found Joshua's body. Maybe he was worried about what Joshua had to say."

It occurred to me that I was alone in the shop with the door closed and that Roger could be a killer. Did I want to confront him like this, or would it be better when I had Chase and several police officers behind me? I didn't want to become part of the investigation.

"Maybe." My best bet would be to pretend

I hadn't seen the monk's robe in the side room and get out of there. "I guess we may never know."

"You mean the police don't have any idea?"

"Not as far as I know. I like that color on the fairy." I pointed to one of his creations. "I wish I could find nail polish that color. Does it have a name?"

He laughed. "I'll be glad to find it for you."

"Okay. Thanks." I played with my hair and looked as vacant and stupid as I could. Maybe it wasn't a feat of bravery to get out of there alive, but I didn't intend to lose my life over this.

"All right. I'll talk to you later, Jessie. If you hear anything else, I'd appreciate it if you let me know. I like to keep up with what's going on, even if I'm not part of it anymore."

I couldn't resist asking, "Why did you leave the police department, Roger?"

"It's a long story. Nothing for you to worry your pretty head about, sweetie. We'll just say there was an unfortunate accident. It was best for me to leave."

I ran out of the Glass Gryphon. Roger might've shot someone and gotten away with it. Was strangulation too far a leap from that? I slammed the door behind me going into Wicked Weaves. Mary looked up from where she was displaying baskets. "What's wrong with you?"

"I think Roger might be the killer."

She laughed. "You think Roger killed Joshua? Yesterday, you thought it was Jah or Abraham. Make up your mind, child. They *all* didn't kill him."

I thought it was best not to tell her what I knew about Roger. It might only endanger her life further. I looked out the front window, but there was no sign of him following me. Apparently, I'd been able to pull off the dumb-girl persona.

I had to call Detective Almond again. He had to come out and investigate Roger before he could get rid of the monk's robe.

As if in answer, a police car pulled up beside Wicked Weaves. I ran outside to welcome them and point them in the right direction.

It was Detective Almond this time. He nodded to me as I reached him. "Miz Morton. Is Miz Shift in the shop?"

"Yes!" I was delighted he was taking an interest. "I have some news for you. I think we may have solved the case."

"That's funny, because that's why we're here," he said. "I'm here to pick up Miz

Shift and take her back to the office for further questioning."

FIFTEEN

I was sure I hadn't heard him correctly. He didn't say he was taking Mary in. "You don't understand. I have a *real* suspect. You should be questioning him instead of her."

He kept walking. I followed him into Wicked Weaves, pleading my case. "Mary may seem like a good suspect. Granted, she knew Joshua, and he was strangled with her basket weaving. Well, really *my* basket weaving. On the surface, that looks suspicious. But surely we've gone beyond the surface of what's happened here."

He stopped walking and stared at me. "What are you talking about?"

I took a deep breath. Patience was never my strong suit. "I'm talking about Roger Trent, the glass blower. He has a monk's costume in his storage closet. I'm sure your officer must've mentioned that someone has been skulking around the Village in a monk's robe."

"That doesn't surprise me, young woman. There was a man on stilts dressed like a tree out there. I've seen everything from some boy wearing pink long johns to a woman half naked riding a horse. Don't expect me to take exception to someone in a monk's robe."

"You know Ham the blacksmith was attacked by someone wearing a monk's robe, right?"

"Again, how many people have monk costumes out here? If we take everyone in who dresses weird, we'll be questioning them all day." He smiled and shook his head. "Besides, what would his motive be? We know your friend, Miz Shift, was divorced and hadn't seen her husband in years. We have information now that suggests she was involved in him being so drunk he couldn't stop her from strangling him to death. Leave the police work to the professionals. You go on and do whatever it is you do here."

I was glad I was wearing my linen skirts again. I couldn't imagine how he'd look at me if I were still dressed as a troubadour with all those bells. He started walking again, and Mary met him in the shop.

"Is there a problem, Detective?" she asked with her head held high.

"Ma'am, I'm gonna have to ask you to come with me. We have some questions that need answering. I hope it won't take long."

She nodded, then looked at me. "Jessie, I have that class of 4-H kids coming in to try their hand at basket weaving today. Will you teach that class for me?"

I seriously wished there was someone standing behind me whose name just happened to be Jessie, too. Unfortunately, I was alone in the shop with them. She couldn't mean what she was saying. I knew she wouldn't want me to teach something I was only moderately learning myself.

Detective Almond took Mary's elbow, and they started out the door together. "Wait!" I stopped them. They both looked back at me. "You'll need your shawl. I'll get it for you."

I wasn't sure what good it was going to do to prolong the inevitable. Detective Almond was intent on taking Mary with him. She didn't seem likely to run out the back door when he wasn't looking.

I brought her shawl to her and whispered, "Maybe I should just tell the kids you couldn't be here, and they can come back later."

"Don't be silly. You're a fine apprentice. You'll do good." She took the shawl from me and smiled. "Who knows? Maybe I'll be back in time to do it myself."

"But Mary —"

"Hush! Quit your weeping and wailing now. I got to go, and you have to take care of this place for me. You can do that, Jessie. I believe in you."

I watched them walk outside and get in the car. Part of me wanted to lock the shop doors and run away. I couldn't take her place. It was ridiculous.

But the instant the police car was gone, residents from the shops around Wicked Weaves poured in, wondering what was going on. "Was Mary arrested? Will the shop close? Will the baskets be at least half off?"

They were mostly stupid, nosy questions. I felt like grabbing a baseball bat and hitting each one of the questions back at them. Instead, I answered the best I could, and when I looked up, the twelve 4-H club members were standing in the shop, staring at me.

"I hope we're here at the right time." Their advisor was a tall, thin woman in an elaborate satin gown that looked like her prom dress.

"This is as good a time as any," I told her. "Take the kids into the backyard, and we'll get started."

I panicked for a minute as I watched their little bodies walk back out and get ready for an experience that could warp their brains forever. What did I know about basket weaving? My fingers were still sore from poking them with palm strips and black rush. Trying to be Mary wouldn't work. Trying to be me was even scarier.

Finally, I fell on a compromise between the two. I had worked as an educator for many years. I could teach, even if it wasn't exactly history. I picked up one of Mary's shawls and wrapped it around my shoulders, then stuck one of her new corncob pipes in my mouth. I walked outside to greet my class with renewed confidence.

"The first thing we have to do," I told them, passing out lengths of sweetgrass, "is cut all the sweetgrass to the same length."

One little girl's hand shot up. "Why do they call it sweetgrass?"

"Smell it. It has a very sweet smell. The slaves who created these baskets used simple words to describe what they saw and used in this country."

I explained the tradition of Gullah basket weaving the way Mary had explained it to me. "I have a bone for each of you." I passed out the smooth spoon handles. "You start your basket by tying a knot in the bottom, then work the grass around the knot in a circle. This basket weaving we do today will only be sweetgrass, but as you can see from these other baskets, there are many different types of materials that can be used."

It seemed to be going very well for me. The words flowed out as I guided my students and gave them a short history lesson on the Gullah people. Their little basket bottoms were showing promise when a voice from the door behind me stopped us.

"You cannot teach these children to weave in our tradition," Abraham declared with fiery intensity. "Where is Mary Shift?"

"She had to go away." I tried to stay calm. I wished there was some way to call Chase. I wished Detective Almond wasn't such an idiot. I wished I had a gun or a sword or some weapon to keep Abraham where he was. The best I could do was keep the 4-H club from knowing what was going on.

"And she left you here to teach these children?" The disdain in his voice was enough to slide the ground out from under my feet.

But I pulled Mary's shawl a little closer and held her pipe in my hand. "She left me here, sir. I'd appreciate it if you'd let us get on with the class. If you have a problem with me teaching this, you can complain to Mary when she gets back."

"I don't think he needs to do that." Ham came around him through the door. "I'll stay and help teach. Everything will be fine."

The two men glared at each other. I noticed Abraham wasn't wearing a monk's robe. But I knew he had one. He was still my best suspect for what had happened. He had plenty of motive, as far as I was concerned. If the police would open their ears, they might think so, too.

Ham came down and sat in the circle with us. I remembered Mary talking about the men from her home making baskets to catch fish. Abraham could've made that basket weave that killed Joshua as well as Mary or me. He probably knew what I was thinking, too. With a dour frown and a grunt, he left us there in the sunlight.

"I'm sorry that happened," Ham said. "Mary asked me to come in and help her this morning so she could tend to the shop in case you couldn't be here."

"Thanks." The shop bell rang as customers came in with the opening of Renaissance Faire Village for the day. I left him teaching the 4-H kids, divesting myself of the shawl and pipe that had given me courage.

There was a constant rush of customers that

prevented me from going back out to listen as Ham explained about basket weaving. I would've liked to have heard it from another source. Sometimes it paid to have more than one teacher. But it didn't work out that way.

Ham came into the shop as it was almost time for the first joust of the day, which meant most customers deserted the shops to watch the knights. He reminded me a lot of Mary in the way he held himself and the way he spoke.

"Thanks for rescuing us." I offered him some water.

"I'm sorry I was late. I was expecting to find my sister here. Is she with Jah?"

"No." I explained about Detective Almond. "He won't listen to me. He thinks Mary is the perfect suspect."

Ham shook his head. "I don't know how anyone can meet her and think she could kill anyone. Especially not Joshua. She always loved him, even when he let her go."

"I guess there's the whole thing with finding out he'd lied to her about Jah," I suggested. "What made the two of you end up here, anyway? It seems like a strange place for you."

"I suppose we have skills suited to another time." He shrugged. "It's been so long, I don't even remember how we decided to come here."

"You left home with her?"

"I did. I wasn't married. I didn't want her to be alone. Jah and Joshua meant everything to her. She never cried. I could see she wanted to fall on the ground and never get up again. But she kept going. When Joshua told us Jah had died, I thought she would die, too. The idea of him growing up in our home with our traditions was the only thing that had kept her going."

"And he'd lied to her so Abraham could raise their son." I hated it, but I had to agree that Detective Almond wanting to question Mary again about what had happened made some sense. "I think they might've caught on about the funnel."

"What are you talking about?"

"Mary bought a funnel from Merlin. I think it may have been used to force alcohol into Joshua. Then he was strangled."

Ham pondered the idea for a moment. "They'll never prove it. Mary didn't kill Joshua. You may be right about Abraham or even Jah himself. But my sister isn't capable of killing."

I agreed with him. I hadn't known Mary a long time, but I could feel she was a good person. How could anyone look at her life without realizing that? She was the wronged party. And it was possible someone had set her up to take the fall for Joshua's death.

"Do you think Abraham could've killed his brother?" I asked.

"I feel like I don't know anything about my home anymore. I've been gone for so long. I thought it was a magical place when I was growing up. It was full of stories and games. Then I found out Joshua had tricked Mary and had given Jah to Abraham. How could he tell her Jah was dead? Didn't he realize what she would go through?"

"Mary doesn't think it's possible because Joshua and Abraham were brothers."

"Brothers kill each other, too." Ham looked down at the wood floor. "How sad it is that we should have this conversation. I don't know why Abraham or anyone else would come after me, but we may all be in danger until this is over."

"I hope we can find the answer quickly. It's getting creepy being in the Village at night, not knowing what's going on."

We parted company when two customers dressed like archers entered the shop and began exclaiming over the baskets. Ham was right. We might all be in danger. I had to talk to Chase about setting a trap to catch the killer.

■ ■ ■ ■

"No, we can't set a trap for the killer." Chase's voice was loud, carrying easily over the top of the crowd at the Pleasant Pheasant.

I expected people to turn, look at us, and wonder what was going on. But this was Renaissance Faire Village. It was just as likely we were rehearsing a skit for the next day as discussing a real-life killer. "We could do this," I coaxed. "We could put our heads together and come up with a way to catch Roger or Abraham or whoever is behind all this."

"What would that be like?" Fred the Red Dragon, without his costume, asked. He used his bread trencher to sop up some gravy that he pushed around on his plate. "I mean, how would you trap someone if you didn't know who you were trying to trap?"

"I'm not sure." I was getting angry that Chase was ignoring my plan and I was discussing it with Fred. "I only know there has to be a way."

Arlene, wearing clothes instead of her Lady Godiva bodysuit, tossed her real blond hair and looked at me with her open mouth crammed full of grapes. "Police do it all the time. My daddy is a policeman in our hometown. We don't have much crime, but that's because we work smart. We don't mind trapping a speeder or a killer."

Have I mentioned how much I hate sitting across from Arlene when she's eating? The fact that I was listening to Arlene talk about something rational disturbed me even more. I covered my face with my hands; it blocked out the half-chewed grapes and gave the impression that I was upset. Both were good things. "We need a plan."

"We don't need a plan," Chase argued. "We're not the cops or the Scooby Gang. We need to sit tight and let the police handle it. We get enough little stuff going on here every day. None of us is capable of taking on a killer."

"And if you did," Sir Reginald announced his entrance by hitting his tankard of ale down on our table, "the police wouldn't be able to use it. The killer would be free before you got back to the Village. Chase is right. Stay out of it. You don't see Livy up in arms about it, and she was the first one there."

I didn't see Livy at all, which was unusual. When you saw Reggie, you saw Livy. I'd heard a rumor that they were breaking up, but I'd attributed that to what had happened at the King's Feast with him and

Chase. And since I knew Chase wasn't sleeping with Livy, I knew someone else had to be. I wondered vaguely if it was Harry.

"Exactly my point, Sir Knight." Chase held his tankard up to Reggie's, and they slammed them together, ale spilling everywhere. "It's good to see you on your feet again. I hope you're feeling better."

"Never better, Sir Bailiff." Reggie sketched him a decent bow. "My thanks for your efforts. I'm fortunate it was only indigestion and not a real heart attack."

All of us were covered in ale. Fred laughed and poured a little more ale from his tankard on his head. Arlene started giggling. I liked ale, don't get me wrong. But I didn't like having it showered on me.

I stood up and started for the door. Chase caught up with me as I stepped outside. The air was cool, and it wasn't so loud. I hadn't realized when I was inside, but I'd been nursing a headache for the last hour.

"Hey! Wait up! Where are you off to?"

I curled my lip at him. It's a thing I've been able to do since I was a little kid. It used to scare the pants off of Tony. "I'm going to change clothes and take a shower. It's been a long day, and Mary still isn't home. I hate what's going on. This isn't supposed to happen during my summer here."

"It wouldn't be any better in the winter," Chase concluded.

"I wouldn't be here." I started walking across the King's Highway. A troop of dancers was practicing some new moves, and there was music coming from the Dutchman's Stage. The visitors were gone for the day, but everything was always in preparation for the new day when they'd return.

"That's a little self-centered." Chase started walking with me past Daisy the sword smith's ringing blows. "This would be a bad thing whether you were here or not."

"You don't understand. I only get three months every year. I want those months to be perfect. That doesn't seem so wrong to me."

He laughed. "You could stay here all the time, if you wanted. It's your decision every year to go back to academia at the end of the summer."

"I can't be like you or Roger or Livy. I enjoy being here, but it's not the real world."

"Where *is* the real world, Jessie? You can't say college is the real world. It's about as far away from corporate America as Renaissance Faire Village. I think you just want it all."

"Is that a crime?"

"Not exactly. At least not one punishable by the stocks or the court. But maybe you should decide what you really want and go after it instead of playing around with everything."

That last part had hurt my feelings. It was probably true, but I didn't want to hear it from him. I was sorry I'd moved in with him and given up my stupid hut. Maybe it wasn't much, but it was mine. If Chase and I broke up, I'd have to leave the Village unless I could find another place to stay. A belly dancer had already taken my hut.

"I'm sorry you feel like that about me." I wasn't good at holding back, even if it meant cutting my summer short. "I wouldn't refer to what I do as playing around. I'm working on a dissertation for my Ph.D. I know you're a lawyer, but you don't really practice, and you don't care if you make anything of yourself. I care."

I could tell by the look on his face that he was angry now, too. Maybe it was for the best. Maybe we were getting too close. Maybe I was stupid enough to let Chase walk out of my life.

At that moment, I wasn't sure. He turned to the left and kept walking up the King's Highway toward the castle as I went into the dungeon. It was a bad moment for us.

Possibly only the first one. I didn't know.

It occurred to me that keeping Chase at arm's length was more about protecting myself than what he was or wasn't doing. My own argument about him wasting his life was wearing thin. What more did I want from him? Or was it that he was *so* good, *so* real, it scared me. I always knew where I stood with the Alexes and Robins of the world.

I went inside the dungeon with a painful bout of retrospection adding to my headache. I didn't want to think about why Chase was good for me or why we should be together, maybe for longer than the summer. I certainly didn't want to consider the ins and outs of my psychological profile.

The shower water was tepid and less than full force, but it felt good after the long, hot day. I was worried about Mary, afraid I'd see her next in the newspaper announcing that she'd been arrested for Joshua's murder.

And where was Chase, the knight in shining armor, while the police put the thumbscrews to Mary? He should've been helping her instead of irritating me. I was well on my way to building a righteous anger against him by the time I'd finished washing my hair. He was a lawyer. Maybe not the right kind, but he could've found someone to help her.

I got out of the shower, working myself into a lather over Mary's unnecessary incarceration. It became all Chase's fault as I pulled on a short green dress I'd saved for nights after work when we could dress normally. Hardly anyone did it. It kind of spoiled the mood, but I was hot enough without wearing a heavy costume. I turned around to find my sandals and found Chase lying on the bed watching me with his hands behind his head.

"How long have you been here?"

"For a while." He grinned at me. "Are you really mad at me because I don't have a corporate job?"

"No. I'm mad at you because you could've helped Mary after I called to tell you Detective Almond took her."

He raised his left brow. "You turn around really fast, Jessie. When did this offense get lodged against me?"

"I guess I was thinking about why it was important for you to have an outside job. People can depend on you. You can have a real life."

"You mean it wasn't enough for me to call a defense lawyer to be there with Mary today?"

"What did you say?" I had to stop dead, since what I was about to say no longer applied. I hated it when that happened.

"You heard me. So you'll have to find something else to be mad at me about."

He just lay there, looking at me. It was a smug kind of look. I hated that my anger was evaporating, and all I had left was how much I cared about him, how hot he was, and that he'd helped Mary when she needed him.

"I can do that." I sat carefully on the edge of the bed. "What have you done for world peace lately?"

"Are you sure you want to talk about that right now?" He patted the side of the bed next to him and smiled.

I was about to tell him there was no way. I really was. At least I think I would've. But at that moment there was shouting from the street, and a voice called out for the bailiff.

SIXTEEN

The shouting in the night was going to have to stop. It was playing havoc with what little love life I'd managed to have between bouts of depression and trying to figure out how to find Joshua's killer. Overall, it was a weirder summer than usual.

I started to tell Chase that being the bailiff of Renaissance Faire Village was just slightly more significant than being the dog catcher in Columbia. But how could I say that after telling him he had no sense of responsibility? I had to be consistent in my criticism.

He looked out the window above the stocks and gathering place for the popular court trials that happened during the day. "What's going on down there?"

"Aha! I see you are at home, Sir Bailiff! Methinks you should come down."

I knew that voice. It was Robin Hood himself. And that wasn't just his persona at the Village. He'd had his name changed from Toby Gates the first year I was here. He was legally Robin Hood. He took his responsibilities to the name very seriously. He was completely crazy. I found that out the second summer I'd spent here when he and I were lovers.

I didn't plan to mention that to Chase. He probably already knew, and it was tacky to talk about past men or women in your life.

Mostly Robin hung out in the five acres of woods dubbed Sherwood Forest located off the Village Square between Frenchy's Fudge and Harriet's Hat House. Whenever something went missing in the Village, it was assumed Robin and his merry band of outlaws were responsible. They were just doing what they were supposed to do, robbing from the merchants to give to themselves.

Toby — *Robin* — and I had long discussions about the ethics involved with this practice. There were no orphans or poor villagers here, only students and residents who made decent money during the good seasons. They weren't rich. The occasional missing toaster oven or clock radio probably didn't break any of them. It was just annoying.

Chase glanced back at me. "This might only take a minute."

"Or it might take an hour or three." I sighed over the lost time I'd spent angry at him.

"We'll be back by midnight," he promised. "I think I should go down, or no one is going to get any peace and quiet tonight."

Peace and quiet wasn't what I'd had in mind when I saw Chase lying on the bed. But none of that was going to happen, either, with Robin yelling at the window. I put on my sandals, and Chase and I went downstairs to see what was wrong.

Robin put his green gloved hands on his hips and tilted back his head for one of his loud laughs. It was one of his least endearing qualities. He was still in good shape, if his tight leather jerkin and green hose were anything to judge by.

He and his Merry Men worked out in the woods every day for the visitors, building their tree forts and chopping wood. It was a rugged existence, considering the Village and civilization lay just outside the trees. But every year, a hundred or more strapping lads tried to become Merry Men.

"I see our bailiff has a fair visitor." Robin laughed again, and the handful of men he'd brought with him laughed, too. Alex was one of them. "No wonder you were so slow to come to our calls."

"Yeah, whatever, Robin. Let's cut to it and tell me what's so important you have to shout down the dungeon at this time of night."

Robin looked at Chase like he couldn't believe his ears. "This is your vocation, Sir Bailiff. If we cannot turn to you in times of travail, who will we turn to?"

Chase folded his arms across his chest. "I'm warning you. If you don't get to the point, I'm going to put you in the stocks for disturbing the peace."

All five of Robin's Merry Men raised their handmade bows and arrows, pointing them directly at Chase. This was out of line. Robin and his men had crossed some kind of invisible crazy barrier while they ran free in the woods.

I stepped in front of Chase. "Are you going to shoot me, too? Have you guys hung out in Sherwood Forest stealing toaster ovens for so long that you've lost all sense of reality?"

Robin laughed again. I swore I would shoot him with an arrow myself if he didn't cut it out. "The maid has a point, my Merry Men."

I was pleasantly surprised that he agreed with me. "That's right. You guys put down the bows. You look ridiculous. And if you've got something to say, spit it out. If not, we're going back inside."

"You still have fire and spunk, Maid Jessica," Robin commented. "We come on important business. The bailiff asked us to keep an eye on the goings-on in the Village. We have done that and found an interesting visitor we believe he might want to speak to."

At Robin's words, two more of his men came out of the shadows holding someone dressed in a dark monk's robe between them. I took back most of the bad things I was thinking about Robin and his men. They'd caught the skulking monk.

The young man on the left threw back the cloaked figure's hood. The dim light gleamed on Jah's young face. "You have no right to hold me. This isn't a court of law or a real jail. There's nothing real here at all. I demand you release me. I plan to sue all of you as soon as I leave the Village."

As far as speeches that were supposed to convince someone to let them go, this was one of the worst. If the Merry Men really meant to hurt him, he'd given them a good reason to continue.

But they didn't plan on doing anything more than holding him for Chase to question; he was safe in that respect. Seeing him in the dark robe made me wonder. He was angry about what had happened with his parents and Abraham. He was verbally abusive to Mary. It wasn't much of a stretch to imagine he could be angry with Ham for helping his mother, but there was no proof of him doing anything wrong, as Chase liked to remind me.

"I appreciate your help, Robin," Chase said. "No one else has been able to find this man."

"You hear that, lads?" Robin lifted his fist high. "Huzzah!"

The Merry Men followed his lead and soon the square was filled with loud *huzzahs.* Since that was what Chase was trying to avoid in the first place, he quieted the group. "Where did you find him?"

"Alex and Barry found him sneaking into the Village from a hole in the outer fence behind the apothecary. He was lucky *we* found him instead of the monks. The penalty for dressing up as one of the Brotherhood is steep."

Jah struggled with his captors for a moment but couldn't get free. "You people are all insane! Did you hear what I said? I'm a U.S. citizen. You have no right to hold me."

Chase walked up to him, standing a head taller and twice as broad as the younger man. "We have *every* right to hold you. You're trespassing on private property if you're here after hours or you've sneaked in through the fence. That means you didn't pay for a ticket. That's like shoplifting."

A little concern began to show on Jah's face. "You still have to turn me over to the police or someone who has half a brain around here."

"That would be me." Chase grinned. "I'm really the constable for this Village, deputized by the Horry County sheriff himself. And I'm not talking about the Sheriff of Nottingham."

Robin dropped to his knees. "The sheriff! That man plagues me! Wherever I go, there's a price on my head. Prince John will never be happy until he can take the throne from good King Richard." Everyone paused as he delivered his soliloquy.

"You can't really be the law around here." Jah broke the silence. "I demand a lawyer. I demand a phone call."

"You seem to have Village justice confused with outsider justice," Chase replied. "Although the two *could* be combined if you know anything about who killed Joshua Shift and attacked Ham the blacksmith."

"What are you talking about? I admit I snuck in the Village. I'll be glad to pay for a ticket. I don't know anything about killing or attacking *anyone*. You're talking about my father and my uncle. I want justice for both of them."

"You seemed pretty harsh when you spoke to your mother," I added. "And Alex here saw a man in a monk's robe attack Ham in his smithy."

"I admit I've been on edge, and I admit to searching the Village for information about what happened to my father. But that doesn't mean I killed anyone! Besides, half the people I've seen here are wearing monk's robes," Jah argued. "How can you tell one from the other?"

He had a good point about the robes and a good reason for sneaking around the Village. "You don't understand how it works around here," I explained. "There are some visitors who wear monk's robes while they're here, but those are different than the one you have on. That one belongs to the Brotherhood."

"An important distinction," said a voice from the shadows. Four robed monks stepped out of the darkness that surrounded the dungeon. "We're glad to see *someone* here has noticed that difference."

"I don't think this is one of your brothers," Chase told him. "He's an outsider who happened to find one of your robes. I'm sure he'll be glad to return it."

Carl stepped closer into the circle we had all become. "The Brotherhood of the Sheaf doesn't allow for transgressions against it. This man has now become our prisoner."

Two of the monks moved to take Jah's arms away from the Merry Men. It was becoming an ugly scene from some kind of weird Renaissance book.

"Hold on. No one is anyone's prisoner," Chase told them. "I know you only want to take him back to the bakery and make him eat bread or bake bread or whatever you usually do as a punishment for borrowing one of your robes, but I think this time we're going to have to do it my way."

Carl didn't seem happy with that idea. "This is our concern, Bailiff."

"Sorry. This man was caught trespassing, which is a graver crime than borrowing a robe." Chase didn't back down from the monks.

I wasn't sure if the monks would step back. It looked like a standoff to me. But Carl suddenly relented. "All right. But we'll have our robe back."

"Sorry. I can't do that, either. I've been in touch with the police, and they want me to collect all the robes in the Village to have them tested. It's possible whoever killed Joshua Shift was wearing one of them."

Carl's face was comical. "You can't take our robes. What would we wear?"

"I don't know. Not your robes for a while."

"For how long?" Brother John asked from beside Jah.

Chase shrugged. "It could be a while. I don't know what kind of tests they need to do. All the robes might have to be processed in Columbia."

There were some murmured discussions between the monks before Carl turned to Chase and said, "Do we have to? This is really a hardship for us. Isn't there a hardship law?"

"Not that I've ever heard of," Chase answered. "If you have them ready for me in the morning, I'll take them in. If not, Detective Almond will come for them."

Disgruntled groaning and complaining followed, but Carl assured him the robes would be at the dungeon in the morning. "That doesn't mean we can let this transgression go." He turned and stared at Jah.

Robin came up and clapped one hand on Carl's shoulder and one on Chase's shoulder. "I have an idea. Let's sport for the lad's fate. I'm sure the bailiff will find that idea agreeable."

"We're monks," Carl said. "We don't sport."

"You throw darts," Robin reminded him. "I never said what *kind* of sport, Brother Monk."

"This is getting way out of hand," Chase said. "You can't have a dart contest to see who gets this kid. He belongs to the court right now for trespassing."

"I can see Robin's point." Carl warmed up to the idea. "It's not so much what happens to him now as what happens to him after you finish with him. If we win, the boy goes with us to the bakery."

"And if we win, the boy stays with us as a lackey in the forest for three days."

Jah tried to speak but was almost too outraged to be coherent. "You can't make me do anything! I refuse to be part of this."

Chase shook his head. "I think I've already made that clear. You can do your penance with one of these two established groups, or I can call the police and they can take you in for trespassing. It's up to you."

I came up with one of my really crazy, off-the-cuff ideas. "I'd like a part of that dart action."

Chase sounded skeptical. "What are you talking about?"

"I want to try my hand at making him do

penance. I want to be part of the sport."

"Are you representing the Craft Guild?" Carl moved closer to me.

"Not exactly. I'd be representing Wicked Weaves. If I win, he spends three days working at the shop."

"What if you lose?" Robin slanted me a sideways stare.

"I didn't hear anyone else put up what they want to lose," I remarked. "What are you putting up if you lose?"

He considered the question. "The men of Sherwood Forest put up one toaster oven if they lose the event."

There were catcalls from the rest of the Merry Men. No one could best them in a sporting event.

"And what of you, Brother Carl?" I moved a step back from him. He was standing in my personal space.

"The Brotherhood of the Sheaf will wager five loaves of bread that we can throw darts better than anyone in this Village."

"And what of you, Maid Jessica of Wicked Weaves?" Robin sneered, his bow falling over his shoulder.

"I wager my first basket. The first one that's usable, anyway."

The other monks agreed amid complaints that the toaster oven Robin offered was no doubt stolen. Monks and Merry Men argued and complained, but in the end, the wager was set.

"Are you sure you want to go through with this?" Chase asked as we all walked to Peter's Pub.

"Sure. Why not? What have I got to lose?" I walked beside him, behind all the others. "I may never finish a usable basket. And I have a better than average shot at winning."

"Why's that?"

"Because I have a secret weapon. I was dart champion for two years in college. I think I can take these guys."

"Really? Are you sure? There might be some under-the-table wagering going on." Chase kept his voice low. "I'm sure you're going to be the underdog. I could make some money."

"You can put your money on me, Sir Bailiff. Believe me, when I was in college, no one could beat me. There are several dozen plaques and trophies with my name on them in my old sorority."

He grinned. "That sounds like fifty bucks on Jessie. I'm glad you told me. I know now not to try to beat you at darts to get you to go home with me."

I laughed and kissed him. "You had me when you patted the bed."

Robin and Carl yelled from inside the pub, "If we're playing darts, let's do it sometime tonight."

Peter's Pub was mostly deserted. Only a few Craft or Artist Guild residents still lingered over wine and ale. The pirates were probably still out drinking, but they'd be at the Lady of the Lake Tavern. Peter's was more respectable.

Robin, Brother John, and I sat down at a table with some tankards of ale. The contest was set that each of us would throw three darts at the board fifty paces away and total the score. The two high scores would then throw against each other until the victor was clear.

The monks urged on their contestant as the Merry Men cheered their leader through the first few tankards and the first three darts. After that, the enthusiasm waned as everyone else was drinking their fair share around us.

Robin set his fifth empty tankard down on the wooden table after he threw his three darts. "What ho! I could drink and sport like this all night!"

Brother John belched, then threw his darts. All three missed the target completely. One of the wood carvers sitting close to the board yelled as a dart grazed his table. The other brothers complained and mourned their immediate loss to the Merry Men. He was a poor choice to represent the Brotherhood.

The monks pulled him away, trying to insert another contestant, but Chase made sure the rules of the contest were observed. It was down to Robin and me. The Merry Men began laughing and cheering again. Certainly their leader could best a mere wench.

Alas for them, I was no mere wench. I set my tankard down on the table, clearheaded, and picked up the three darts. Robin was barely able to put his tankard on the table. He looked at me with his head cocked to one side, which made his pointy green hat fall off. "Methinks there may be some magic going on here. Maid Jessica seems overconfident."

"You have the wrong guild." I threw my three darts. They all hit dead center. "I'm with the Craft Guild. No magic involved except for the magic of practice."

Robin moved, and his bow fell on the floor beside him. He tried to get it but fell down with it. His men rushed forward, and everyone waited quietly to see if he'd get back up again. "I'm all right," he said at last. "There was no rule about where we had to be to throw the darts. Right here will do fine for me. Bring me the next tankard."

I saw some money being passed back and forth while Peter brought two more tankards and Robin took the darts. I hoped Chase was making some money. Maybe he'd like to spend it on me. I'd been eyeing a new shawl like Mary's.

I was surprised that Jah stayed quiet beside Chase through the whole thing. He looked like he'd given up. Carl had taken his robe, and he was left in jeans and a black T-shirt. He didn't look angry anymore. It was probably more than he could take in at one time. The Village affects some people that way. It would do him good to spend a few days with his mother. She could teach him a thing or two.

I looked at Robin, who could barely hold his head up. I knew I was about to win a lot of bread and a stolen toaster oven. I wasn't sure what I'd do with all the bread, but the toaster oven would come in handy for breakfast pastry.

"A toast." Robin's shaky hand held up his tankard. "You are as iron-stomached as you are beautiful, Maid Jessica. You would be welcome in Sherwood anytime. Right, lads?"

There were a few minor huzzahs to his remark. I acknowledged his compliment.

"Thank you, Robin. You are as gracious in defeat as I'm sure you would've been in victory."

With that and loud encouragement from his Merry Men, Robin threw his darts. Only one made the target. Robin dropped his tankard and slumped to the floor under the table.

"It gives whole new meaning to drinking someone under the table," Chase said. He held up one of my arms. "The winner! Wicked Weaves of the Craft Guild will take this man's penance. Three days with the basket weaver. Do you consent?" he asked Jah.

Jah shook his head. "I guess I don't have any choice."

"That's true." Chase gathered his money from the Merry Men and the monks. "Good night, gentlemen. We'll expect to see five loaves of bread, a toaster oven, and all of the robes at the dungeon by morning."

Jah walked out with Chase and me. "I guess this makes me some kind of servant for the next few days."

"More like a lackey," I answered. "Do you know how to weave baskets?"

"Of course I do. I'm in college, but I grew up in Mount Pleasant. Everyone learns how to weave. Not all of us do it our whole lives."

"How about murder?" I kept my voice as breezy as if I were asking him if he could change the oil in my car. "Do you think you could murder someone?"

"If you're referring to my father, I didn't kill him. I might've had more reason than most people, but I have some sense of propriety, not to mention the rest of my life to fulfill. I only came here to see my mother. I couldn't remember what she looked like. When I found out she wasn't dead but instead living here in this traveling circus, I was ashamed but still curious."

Chase sniffed. "This circus doesn't travel. We're here in this spot all the time. It's probably a lot like the area you came from."

Jah laughed, the sound brittle in the cool night air. "This is nothing like where I grew up. You people are all insane. Why would anyone want to live here?"

"I could think of a few reasons." Chase smiled at me.

"How did you steal the monk's robe?" I asked Jah.

"I found it, actually. That first night I sneaked in through the hole in the wall. It was there along with this." He pulled a funnel-shaped object from the pocket of the robe.

Seventeen

The next morning we found five loaves of sourdough bread, a toaster oven, and twenty-five monks' robes piled on the front steps of the dungeon.

Jah was still in the cozy cell Chase had set up for him. He didn't reply when I said good morning. His good-looking, dark face stared mutinously in the other direction.

Apparently he was angry about the whole situation. Too bad. I thought it would be cathartic for him to spend some time with his mother. To categorize her as being part of a circus was just wrong. He'd be impressed by her, if the police had released her.

"I wonder what they decided to wear." I looked at all my winnings, ignoring Jah. The toaster oven wasn't in the best shape, but it might still work. The bread was more than I could use in a few days, so Chase and I kept one loaf and gave the other four away.

The snake charmer and the Village idiot were my first choices. The charmer's snake was too pathetic to ever get many tips. And the idiot was too, well, idiotic. Most people ignored him sitting on the ground banging pots and pans together.

Chase walked with Jah and me over to Wicked Weaves with a stop for breakfast at Fabulous Funnels. They were the best funnel cakes in the Village. I liked mine with strawberries and powdered sugar. Jah refused to eat his, so Chase ate it instead.

The Village was busy, considering it was still early. The Green Man was practicing the new routine of picture taking with visitors held between her branches. It was impressive and scary. The fairies were holding a gathering. I didn't realize how many of them there were until I saw them all together. They met around the fountain in front of Da Vinci's Drawings. Sam Da Vinci was outside drawing the multitude of fairies, or whatever it is that fairies come in. They were a pretty sight; all multicolored and gauzy in the sunlight. All of them giggled and called Chase's name as we walked by. I ignored them. Fairies could be pesky and problematic. There was no sense in borrowing any more problems than I had already.

Mary was back. I rushed up to her and hugged her. "I'm so glad they let you go."

"Me, too." She looked at Jah. "What's going on?"

Jah finally found his voice. "I'll tell you what's going on. These people have pressed me into servitude despite my telling them I wouldn't do it. They locked me up overnight. When this is over, I'm going to find a lawyer and close this place down."

Mary looked as though she was considering what he said. "So you found out you're not above the rest of us."

He lifted his chin a notch higher. "I'll always be above this rabble."

"Maybe," I added. "But for the next three days, he's going to work here at Wicked Weaves. He was trespassing and had the choice of doing this or going to jail. For some reason, he chose this."

"I don't want him here if he doesn't want to be here," she said.

Great. Now she was going to be difficult. I wasn't in the mood for it. I mean, where was the gratitude? "Too bad. He's already been assigned here. I'm going with Chase to the police station. I'll be back as soon as I can."

Chase stared hard at Jah. "You better be here when we get back."

"You have my driver's license and bank card. Where else would I be?" Jah stared back but not as effectively as Chase.

"So now that everyone is happy, we'll see you all later." I smiled and waved as we walked out of the shop. "Yeah. This is going over real well."

Chase shrugged. "Give it some time. It'll work out. Like you said, Mary's a great woman. Jah will come around."

"I just don't know if you can expect that in three days."

Detective Almond pulled up next to us at the main gate. He stepped out of his car, and an officer, who looked like he was in drag, got out after him. "I think I've finally come up with a plan to solve this problem." Detective Almond looked at the man beside him. "This is Officer Tom Grigg. He'll be stationed here at the Village until we catch this culprit. We even put him in costume so he'd fit right in."

I couldn't look at Officer Grigg without laughing. He'd only fit in if this was Rocky Horror Picture Show Village. He didn't look the least bit historical. His costume must've come from prostitutes the police had busted. I didn't know what the makeup was all about. And I didn't know how to say it without making Officer Grigg feel ridiculous.

"I'm glad you're here, Detective." Chase bypassed the subject by giving him the monks' robes we'd put into large trash bags. "I bagged this one by itself. It was found in a hole in the Village wall along with this." Chase produced the cardboard funnel Jah had pulled from his pocket.

Detective Almond examined the funnel in the plastic bag. "It's not exactly forensic evidence, but I guess it's better than nothing. We might be able to use these things for clues, but we're gonna need a confession."

"We'll get one with me here, sir," Officer Grigg promised.

I ignored the way the sun brought out the heavy red rouge on his face and the red lipstick. "In the meantime, this must count for something."

"No doubt." Detective Almond looked up from the funnel. "The doc found some pieces of cardboard wedged in the decedent's teeth. I can see where there are tooth marks on this thing. That's the only thing that's kept Miz Shift out of jail. That leather funnel she had didn't test right. I guess this is what we were looking for."

"We should bring in the boy who found this," Officer Grigg said.

"Let's give this some time, Grigg," his boss said. "We've been running around like a rooster after some hens. Let's see if you can get us some real answers. The three of you keep your eyes and ears open. You'll have Grigg if you need any help. You two," he pointed to Chase and me, "know this place better than either one of us ever will. There's a killer here somewhere, folks. Let's not make the mistake of thinking he or she might not strike again."

Officer Grigg nodded and pulled uncomfortably on his corset. His fishnet stockings were tight on his hairy legs. "Don't worry, sir. We'll find out what's going on."

Chase nodded in agreement. I could tell he was on the verge of laughing, too. "Yeah. We'll keep an eye on everything. But let us know if anything comes back from the robes or the funnel that might help. I haven't slept very well since the murder thinking about the killer still walking around the Village."

"I'll do that, son. You all be careful out here." Detective Almond hitched up his pants and got back in his car.

Officer Grigg looked at Chase. "I understand you're what passes for the law here." He looked at the tall gates where the young maidens of the Village had begun gathering to throw rose petals at visitors as they came in. They were giggling and simpering at Chase as well. It almost made me wish I'd fallen for a less hunky guy. Almost, anyway.

The town crier was laughing at Grigg as he tried to read the news of the day. Grigg looked even funnier with rose petals in his dark hair. Something had to be done if he was going to blend in.

"I'll take Officer Grigg to costumes." Chase raised his voice over the sound of the musical quartet beginning their daily round of song.

"I'll keep an eye on Jah," I promised. "I hope we're doing the right thing not telling Detective Almond about him."

"I think we both agree the only thing he's guilty of is trespassing."

"But what if we're wrong?"

"It's not like the police have been able to figure this out any better than us."

I agreed with him and glanced at Grigg, who was watching the organ grinder with his monkey. "Make sure you clean his face. There was lipstick and rouge during the Renaissance, and men wore it as well as women. But most people don't know that."

Chase laughed. "Don't worry, Jessie. I'll take care of the details. I was just thinking that we lost Tom, Tom the Piper's Son a couple of days ago. Officer Grigg could fit right in there."

"That's a little too symbolic, isn't it?"

"Around here?" Chase looked at the giant chasing Jack, the Green Man out for a stroll, and a knight attending a young lady in robes. "I think he'll be exactly what we're looking for."

I left him to take care of the problem. Officer Grigg was already looking lost and bewildered. Not everyone could handle stepping back through time.

I was glad to head back to Wicked Weaves. My weaving was right on the verge of competency. If I could get in a few more sessions with Mary, I was sure I could produce a basket. It might not sell for four hundred dollars, but it would be enough for my purposes. I'd planned to have something substantial to go with each one of my craft papers.

I turned to walk back to the shop when I was accosted by the Tornado Twins. They were a brother act that usually confined themselves to one of the play stages. Between acts they walked around the Village drumming up an audience for the next performance.

Both of them were kind of cute and sexy. The only problem was they didn't mind honking horns or throwing cream pies at the worst possible moments. I'd dated Diego for a few days one summer. When he wasn't greeting me with a hand buzzer or telling the worst jokes in the world, his brother, Lorenzo, was dropping water bombs on us or throwing cream pies. They were both completely obnoxious.

"Good morning, Jessie." Diego swept his large, blue-feathered hat off his head as he bowed. "You're looking very fair and desirable today."

Lorenzo consulted the plate-sized watch on his wrist. "And it's early in the morning to be able to say that." He held out his watch for me to consult.

"I'm not that stupid." I brushed by them. The watch squirted water, of course.

"Jessie!" Diego turned and ran up to me, grabbing one of my arms as Lorenzo took the other. "Why don't you write about *us?* You could be our apprentice for a summer."

"A summer of love." Lorenzo kissed my hand. "You would *never* forget us."

"Or forgive us!" Diego pinched my butt as Lorenzo honked his little horn.

I slapped at both of them until they moved away from me. "You guys need to find someone who appreciates you."

"Don't you mean *two* someones who appreciate both of us?" Diego laughed and was right back at my side.

I kicked at Lorenzo as he used a stick to lift up the hem of my skirt. "No. I don't think you'll be that lucky. If you can find one woman between you, you'll be doing good."

At that moment, there was the sound of trumpets as the queen strolled through the Village with her entire court. Livy was resplendent in blue velvet that morning. Her crown glittered in the sun as she slowly inclined her head to visitors who addressed her as she walked by.

I felt a tug at the side of my skirt and slapped at the hand, thinking it was Lorenzo or Diego. Instead, it was the queen's royal page. He yelped and gave me an angry look. "The queen requests your presence at the castle this afternoon at three p.m.," the page said. "I suggest you be there."

I bowed to the page, who was a high school student from Brooklyn dressed in livery that matched Livy's costume. "I thank you, Sir Page. I will attend the queen at her command."

Lorenzo picked that moment to stick his whole hand under my skirt. I reacted instinctively, lashing out with my right fist. I hit him squarely on the jaw, and he collapsed on the ground at my feet.

All the fairies, damsels, maidens, ladies-in-waiting, and even the queen herself began applauding. It was something they all wished they'd done.

Lorenzo laughed. "The view is even better down here."

Wicked Weaves was busy when I got back. Mary scolded me for leaving her with so many customers. Jah sat in one corner, ignoring the rest of the world. I guess we could make him stay there for three days, but we couldn't make him like it.

I was a little put out that Mary didn't seem to be grateful for everything I'd tried to do for her. Here I was, bringing her and her son together, single-handedly trying to solve the murder of her husband and run the basket shop for her. What else could I do?

"How did the class go yesterday?" she asked me after the rush of shoppers had passed.

"It went fine. Ham showed up and was a big help. I think everyone had a good time and learned something." It sounded good to me.

She sighed and began straightening baskets, ignoring Jah the way he was ignoring her. This was never going to work. How could they reunite as mother and son in three days if they didn't interact? As usual, I was going to have to take care of this problem, too.

"I'd really like to get started on a new basket," I told her. "I think I'm past the stage of sticking my finger with bulrush and bleeding all over everything. I think I'm ready to produce something."

"All right. Let's give it a try." Mary picked up her corncob pipe and looked at it strangely for a moment. I wondered if she could tell that I'd had it in my mouth. She pulled on her pink shawl that matched the scarf covering her head, and we moved to the back steps.

I was ready. I cut my sweetgrass to even lengths, tied the knot in the bottom of what would be the base of the basket and then began to work the sweetgrass together. I could feel Jah hovering over me as I began to coil and sew the first row.

"What am I supposed to do?" he asked finally. "You won me, remember? I was supposed to do something, not sit around being bored to death."

Mary nodded. "So you *do* have a tongue. Likely you have hands and feet, too. The shop could use a sweep, and those shelves need to have the cobwebs swept down."

297

Jah didn't move. "She's weaving baskets, but I have to sweep the shop? She weaves like she has too many fingers. Her knot is sloppy, and her technique is bad. Why doesn't she sweep the shop, and I'll make baskets?"

This would've suited my purpose fine. I was prepared to go inside and sweep, leaving the two of them alone on the stairs. I could always work on my basket.

"It appears to me that she was here first." Mary spoke without looking up from the bone that moved quickly around the coils of new grass. "Jessie's a fine assistant, and she's learning a craft. You sweep the shop. We'll see what else we can find for you to do when you're done."

I sat back down and picked up some pine needles to thread with my sweetgrass. It wasn't a good beginning for the mother-child reunion. "It would be all right if he worked with you."

She huffed at me. "Maybe for you. Not for me. He can't just come in and tell me how to run my shop. He may be my son, but he has a lot to learn."

I heard a customer come into the shop and left Mary working on her basket. It was actually a man and woman dressed like Robin Hood and Maid Marion. It was probably one of the most popular costumes for visitors. "Can I help you, my lord and my lady?"

"We're looking for a basket," Marion told me. "It can't be more than a foot high."

"I think I see something for you, my lady." I led them to the smaller baskets. "These baskets are made right here by our expert basket weaver."

"Who doesn't mind selling out her own people," Jah said quite clearly.

"Ignore him, good sir and lady. He is only a simpleton who cleans this shop." I glared at him but apparently not hard enough.

"My people were making baskets when your people were still gathering eggs in their skirts," he growled. "None of you deserve to touch these works."

Robin and Marion looked unsure and were about to leave when Mary came in through the back door. "Don't pay him no mind. The boy is all mouth and no brain. I made these baskets to sell. My ancestors did what they had to do with theirs. I do what I want with mine."

Jah opened his mouth to speak again, his hands still on the broom. Before he could say anything, Mary grabbed him by one ear and took him out the back door like a naughty child. It was amazing to see her, barely reaching his shoulder, yet she was in command.

I smiled at Robin and Marion again. "Have you decided, my lady?"

Marion bought three small baskets. Even though they were small, they were nicely priced. Of course, the price could never really equal the work that went into each piece, but I thought Mary made a fair living.

I crept toward the back door to find Jah sitting on the ground with the beginning of a basket in his lap. He and Mary weren't saying anything to each other, but I thought that would change.

I watched his long fingers weave the sweetgrass around the bottom knot, sewing with the bone as he went. He fed the new grass into the coil with a uniformity only time and experience could achieve. I couldn't tell yet what kind of basket he was creating, but I knew he was already a master of the craft.

I wanted to throw myself at his feet and ask him to teach me everything he knew until my hands moved with that same dexterity between the sweetgrass and the black rush. I knew better; the peace between Mary and her son was fragile. They'd have to find a way to get back what was lost between them before I could declare him my weaving idol.

Wicked Weaves' front door opened again. It was Chase with Officer Grigg. "What do you think?"

I looked at Grigg. Chase had found a red hat and tunic with green breeches and matching boots for Grigg. He looked every inch the piper's son from the rhyme. The only thing missing was a real pig, but I was sure Chase would find a way to supply that. "He looks great! Where are you going to put him?"

"He'll be stationed near Mother Goose, but he'll be free to wander the Village."

"Queen Olivia sent her page to summon me to court this afternoon. Maybe you'd like to come with me?" I smiled up at Chase but was rudely interrupted by Grigg.

"Is that the woman who found the body?"

"Yes. But I doubt if that's what she wants to talk about." The piper's son was going to have to learn his place in the hierarchy of the Village. Merchants were under royalty, but piper's sons, especially those who stole pigs, were on the lower rung.

"I'll walk over there with you," Chase volunteered.

"So will I."

We both stared at Grigg, then took turns

trying to talk him out of going with us. I'd had a more leisurely pace in mind while traveling to the castle; one that would take us by the dungeon for a while. But that wasn't going to happen if Grigg came along.

Grigg brandished his badge, which was stapled into the underside of his shirt. "If there's any intelligence to be had about this crime, I want to be there to gather it."

Chase finally gave up and shrugged. "Fine. Come along then. But don't forget Village protocol; you have to walk ten paces behind us."

Grigg nodded and tucked away his badge. There was nothing more to say.

Grigg kept his respective distance behind us as we walked past the privies, Peasant's Pub, and Bawdy Betty's. "Good move," I told Chase. "At least he's not all up in our faces."

"Yeah. Better than nothing," Chase agreed. "I didn't know he still had his badge."

I giggled. "I wasn't sure for a minute what he was going to pull out."

Chase laughed with me and put his arm around my shoulders. It was hot and humid as it can only be on the southern coast. The fairies gave me dirty looks as we strolled down the King's Highway. Adora at Cupid's

Arrow, a Renaissance boutique for lovers, smiled and waved a little. Beth Daniels from Stylish Frocks raced past us toward the castle with an arm full of dresses no doubt destined for Livy's closet. The pirate ship was in full sail across Mirror Lake, which was only a few acres wide. But it made a gorgeous sight with the white sails blossoming against the clear blue sky and the turrets of the castle.

The master-at-arms greeted us at the gate. "I heard she'd sent for you. Go on in. You're late already."

"I did the best I could," I argued. "I work for a living, you know."

He shrugged brawny shoulders beneath leather padding. Gus Fletcher was a professional wrestler before he came to work at the Village. "Don't matter to me. Explain it to *her*."

One of Livy's ladies-in-waiting took us through the main entrance to the private quarters after taking a look at Grigg's badge. The castle was divided into public and private sectors along with the King's Feast and joust area. The biggest difference between the two areas was that the elaborate wall hangings and other ornamentation in the public sector were cheap fakes. In the private sector, Livy and Harry had the expensive Renaissance decorations, they thought were still faux.

Livy turned on me the minute I walked into her domain. "You took your own time about getting here, Jessie. I suppose my life being in danger because of what I know about that man's death means nothing to you."

EIGHTEEN

I tried to calm Livy down, but even when she's not using the royal *we,* she's still pretty high maintenance. That day she was worse than usual, wringing her hands and pacing the floor. "Really, Livy, why would anyone want to kill you?"

Her white face was blotchy from crying, and her red hair was a mess. "Because of what I know. I should've told the police, but I didn't think anything of it until today."

"What happened today?" Chase asked politely.

"The killer, aka Roger Trent, tried to get rid of me. He knew what I saw and must've been afraid I'd talk."

Chase and I exchanged meaningful glances. I didn't know what he was thinking, but I remembered the monk's robe I saw hanging in Roger's shop. "Slow down and start at the beginning," I encouraged. "We don't know what you saw, so we don't know what you're talking about."

She stared at Officer Grigg. "Who is this man, and why have you brought him into our presence?"

"I'm a police officer, ma'am." Grigg stepped forward. "I'm here to solve this crime and set the Village to rights."

Sensing a new and untried audience, Livy managed to swoon languidly on the brown brocade sofa behind her. "It's all so terrible. I don't know where to start."

"How about at the beginning," Chase suggested. "I assume that was the day we found Joshua Shift next to Wicked Weaves."

"That's right." Livy's lady-in-waiting fetched her a glass of water. "I was taking one of my usual strolls through the Village. I was wearing my new gown; it's quite beautiful, really. The little seed pearls make all the difference."

Chase rolled his eyes. "Sometime today would be nice."

"You have become quite rude, Sir Bailiff. Methinks it may be your close association with Mistress Jessica. It has not gone beneath our notice."

"In just a minute, I'm walking out, and if someone wants to kill you, they have my blessing." Chase got to his feet.

Livy looked at Officer Grigg imploringly.

"You see what we have to endure here, sir. Perhaps you can be of assistance to us."

Grigg all but prostrated himself at Livy's silk-slipper-clad feet. "I'll do everything in my power to keep you safe."

This was almost too much for me to watch. If it wasn't for my curiosity about what Livy thought she saw the day Joshua was killed, I would've left. Instead, I took a deep breath and tried to be patient. "Tell us what you saw, please, Livy. We all want to help."

"As I was saying, we were strolling through the Village when we saw Roger Trent slipping away from behind Wicked Weaves. He looked right at us, then put his head down and crossed the street to his glass shop."

"Why was this mysterious?" Chase wondered.

"He was right where we found the body a few minutes later. If we wouldn't have walked up the alley, we wouldn't have seen anything. But Roger knows we saw him there and that we've realized he killed that poor man."

"Just because he was there doesn't mean anything," I argued with her. "His shop is right across the street. He was probably walking around."

"We might have believed that except

today, someone followed us back to the castle. We barely made it inside before he pounced on us."

"What made you think it was Roger?" Chase played with one of Livy's snuff boxes that were on the table beside him.

"What about this?" She held up a blue polishing cloth. "This is the same kind of cloth Roger uses after he makes something."

I had to admit she was right. When I was watching him at his shop, he had a dozen of them on his worktable. "But this really doesn't prove anything. He walks around the Village. One of the cloths could've gotten lost."

"Jessie's right," Chase agreed. "We have to have more proof before we accuse anyone of trying to hurt you. Especially since we have no proof he killed Joshua."

Livy cried prettily into her lace hankie. "Do I have to die before someone takes action?" She completely forgot the royal *we*. She had to be upset.

"No!" Grigg jumped to his feet with surprising agility. "I'll go and talk to this man. If he's the killer, I'll know right away. I have instincts about this kind of thing. They trained me to spot liars and other criminals."

"Oh brother," Chase groaned. "Has it occurred to you, Grigg, that if you accuse Roger of something before we have any proof, we may never know what happened?"

"Something needs to be done," Grigg reiterated. "We'll find a way, Your Majesty."

Livy held out her hand and let him kiss it. "We rely on you, Sir Officer. Our life is in your hands."

Some people can handle the melodrama of day-to-day life in the Village, and some people can't. I was afraid Grigg was one of the latter.

We left Livy in her sitting room and went back outside where the pirates were attacking the Lady of the Lake Tavern. They had a nice crowd of spectators for the fake cannon fire and smoke. The noise was deafening as the tavern surrendered to the band of thieves and blackguards.

"This place is really something." Grigg looked more like a twelve-year-old first-time visitor than a hardened police officer. "I don't know why I've never been here before. It's great!"

"Let's get back to this thing about Roger," Chase said. "I don't think he's involved in this. He's an ex-cop himself. If he was up there by Wicked Weaves that day, I'm sure there was a good explanation."

"For one thing, his glass shop is right

there where they found the body," I agreed with him. "For another, what would his motive be? I can see Abraham, even Jah. But Roger? How would he be involved in this?"

"Maybe we should ask him," Grigg said. "I can tell if he's lying."

Chase rolled his eyes as we walked past the swan swing and frog catapult. "Even if that's true, unless you plan on arresting him, it won't be much help. If there are any clues he left behind, he'll just cover them up."

Grigg stared at him. "Besides being a play sheriff here, Mr. Manhattan, what experience do you base this on?"

"Gut instinct," Chase replied. "I know this place. We need to figure out what happened before we accuse anyone else of anything. I think Detective Almond said the same thing."

It was good, rational thinking, but he'd already lost Grigg's interest. "Look at that! Is that really a sword in a stone, just like the myth? I have to try that."

We stood off to one side as Grigg tried his hand at the sword. "He's never going to find anything, Jessie," Chase said. "We have to do it ourselves."

"I think you should let me talk to Mary first and see what she has to say." I was thinking back to how well Roger seemed to know her and how he'd stood around with her while we were waiting for Detective Almond to take us away that first day. "Then we can break into his shop and steal his monk's robe to have it tested."

"And I thought Grigg had some dumb ideas."

"No. Really. I told you I saw that monk's robe. Maybe Roger is involved in what happened. Maybe he and Mary are involved somehow, and he was threatened by Joshua showing up after all these years. Maybe he got rid of his competition."

"That's crazy." Chase heaved a large sigh and went to grab Grigg to get him away from the sword.

"I almost had it," Grigg complained. "That's the way it works, you know. Whoever can pull the sword from the stone is king."

"Not here," Chase assured him. "Only Arthur has the remote control gizmo that releases the sword. No one else can do it. You can come back at ten, noon, or four to watch him do it. This isn't real, Grigg. All of it is playacting. That's what makes it so fun and so hard to tell what's fake."

Grigg seemed to digest this information. "I still think I should talk to the glass blower. If he was thinking about hurting the queen because she saw him, he'd know we're all on to him, so there wouldn't be any point."

Chase put his hand on Grigg's shoulder. "Why don't we have a tankard of ale at the Peasant's Pub and talk it over. Jessie has to get back to work. Maybe you and I can decide what to do next."

Grigg went for that. I kissed Chase goodbye and walked back to Wicked Weaves. I was surprised and pleased to find Jah and Mary selling baskets together. I listened in fascination as they described to customers how the baskets were made and their history on the South Carolina coast. The plan had worked. The two were bonding. I might still become a master basket weaver by the end of the summer.

I needed some time alone with Mary. After uniting them, I was going to have to split them up, at least for a while. I didn't want her to have to answer to my questions about Roger in front of her son.

When the customers had left with their baskets, the three of us went back outside to weave. Jah seemed suddenly very content with his lot. I wasn't sure I trusted that facade. He'd been too angry, too rebellious, to give in so quickly. I wondered what his game was and again reminded myself that he had motive and opportunity to kill his father. It sounded awful, but I knew it had happened in other families.

"Jessie, you're stitching needs to be neater," Mary said to me. "Pull those coils in tighter. The basket will unravel before it goes home."

I looked at my stitching, and it looked the same to me. Still, I tried to pull it tighter as I used my bone to weave the sweetgrass coils. "So you learn to do this when you're a child where you're from?"

Mary nodded. "That's right. Any five-year-old can make a basket."

I felt there was an implied *better than you* in what she'd said. I ignored it. If it wasn't constructive criticism, it was useless to me. "I can see that Jah has done this for a long time."

"Actually it's been years since I even thought about it," he retorted. "I never thought I'd do this as an adult."

"There's great pride and heritage in what we do," Mary said. "I'm not ashamed of making these baskets and selling them."

"But haven't you ever yearned to do something more, be something more?" Jah stopped weaving to look at his mother. "I could help you go to school or learn to do some other work."

Mary laughed. "I don't want to do anything else. I've watched the people you're talking about. They scurry around like sand crabs on the beach. I wouldn't want to be one of them."

"There's pride in doing things other than manual labor, too, Mother," Jah shot back.

The front door to the shop opened, the little bell chiming. "I'll get that," I offered.

"No. I'll get it. You need the practice." Jah threw me what passed for a smile. It was really more like a tight grimace that moved his mouth but not his face.

This seemed to be as good a time as any to ask Mary about Roger. "Livy told me she saw Roger coming from behind Wicked Weaves the day Joshua was killed."

She didn't look up. "So?"

"So, I was wondering where he was. I didn't see him back here when I came down the steps."

"Maybe he was already gone."

"But from where?" I recalled that she'd been missing, too. "Is there something going on between you and Roger?"

"I think that's none of your business." Smoke puffed frantically from her pipe. "This thing with Joshua is over. We don't need to keep talking about it."

I told her about the monk's robes and the funnel being tested by the police. "This isn't over at all. You could still go to prison. You're the top suspect right now. You had motive and opportunity, as they say on TV. They can keep coming out here and taking you back to the office as long as they want to."

She looked up finally with a mutinous expression on her dark face. "I'm not afraid of them. I didn't kill Joshua." She took two more stitches in her basket. "But Joshua and I stopped being husband and wife a long time ago. Roger has always been there for me. All these years we kept our relationship a secret. I don't see why that has to change now."

"You're doing it with *Roger?*" I could hardly say the words. I couldn't believe I missed their relationship. But suddenly, all those meaningful glances and small, almost unnoticeable touches made sense.

"Shh!" She glanced toward the open door. "I don't want to have this conversation with my son. He only just lost his daddy. He doesn't need to think about this."

I supposed this was good news. Mary and Roger might be each other's alibi. Even though Joshua was killed before I'd noticed Mary was missing and Olivia saw Roger

315

come out of the alley, maybe they were together during the night when the murder happened. I mentioned it to Mary.

She quickly shook her head. "I thought of that when I was talking to the police. Roger was with me earlier and again before you all found Joshua in the alley. But when they say Joshua was killed, I was alone. I don't know about Roger."

Which put us back to square one. Except now, Roger could be a real suspect. He had a motive to get rid of Joshua. He wouldn't want the other man coming in and taking his wife back after all these years. There was the matter of the monk's robe in his shop as well. I knew Mary wouldn't want to think her lover could be responsible for her husband's death, but it seemed possible to me.

There was arguing coming from inside Wicked Weaves. I offered to handle whatever the problem was for Mary. She accepted with a grunt. I knew it was okay when she didn't get up.

I went in the back door, not thinking about sneaking in exactly, but the two men facing each other over a table of sweetgrass baskets didn't hear me. I hid behind the door that led up to Mary's apartment. Maybe I'd hear something useful as Jah and his adopted father, Abraham, argued.

"I don't understand why you're here," Abraham said. "You should leave this place."

"Are you afraid for me to spend time with my birth mother?" Jah asked him. I was glad to hear Jah sounded as angry with Abraham as he did everyone else.

"I'm not afraid of anything. But you're wasting your time here. You start school in the fall again. You should be concentrating on that."

I wished I could see the look on Jah's face, but I had to be content with hearing the tone in his voice. "You're afraid I might like her, even grow to love her again."

"Don't be ridiculous! I just don't want you to be brought down by her."

"Is that what happened to my real father?" Jah asked. "Were you afraid I'd be brought down by him, too?"

Abraham's voice was full of outrage. "I've given you everything, yet you must come here to speak to the woman who abandoned you. I've been your father most of your life, yet you cling to some stupid idea about your birth father. They did *not* want you. That's why I raised you. You should be content with that."

"You didn't answer me about my birth father. Did you kill him?"

"Yes." Mary's voice entered the conversation, and I realized that I'd hidden well enough to fool her, too. "Tell him the truth for once, Abraham. You've lied to him all of his life. Tell him the truth now."

"I don't know what you're talking about, old woman. Go back to your weaving. Leave my son alone."

"Did he tell you the story of how his son, who was sick and weak, died while I was caring for him? Did he tell you how he demanded I leave my home and then forced my husband to lie to me about your death? He wanted to raise you as his own, but you'll never be his."

"Is this true?" Jah asked.

"You don't need to ask such questions," Abraham reprimanded. "She left you, and your birth father could not care for you. If I hadn't taken you in, you would have died. Where were they when you were sick or scared? I am your father. You will do as I say and leave this place."

"What about Joshua?" Mary pursued the subject. "Did you kill Joshua because he wouldn't go home when you told him? All this time, I've told everyone you could never hurt your brother. Now I'm not so sure. You stand here and defile his memory to his son. I think you could do anything."

There was silence where I imagined they were all staring at each other, waiting for Abraham to answer the charges brought against him. I wished I could sneak around and watch, but I was afraid if I moved, it would change the dynamics, and the question wouldn't be answered.

"You've both lost your minds," Abraham said finally. "I won't answer to either of you. Jah, go home. Get ready for school. Obey me now, or you will no longer be my son."

Jah's voice, when it answered, was full of tears. "No, Father. I won't leave yet."

"So be it." The front door opened and closed again, the chiming bell belying the strained silence in the shop.

Could there be any further doubt that Abraham had killed Joshua? I didn't think so. I had no way to prove it unless the police lab found some DNA that would speak for itself. I didn't wait. I sneaked back outside and was sitting down, weaving, when Mary and Jah came back out.

Neither one of them said anything. We all sat in the shade of the small plum tree and worked on our baskets. The day clouded over and threatened rain as customers came and went in the shop. I was waiting for some kind of declaration of Abraham's guilt between Jah and Mary, but it never came.

At six p.m., we closed the shop. Mary asked if Jah could stay with her for the next two nights that he was sentenced to be in the Village.

"I don't think Chase would care," I told her. "I'm glad it's worked out for you two to be together."

She looked at me with narrowed dark eyes, sharp and bright in her brown face. "You heard everything, didn't you?"

"I did. I guess we don't have to wonder who killed Joshua anymore."

"Don't be a fool. Abraham was angry, but he didn't kill his brother."

"How can you say that? I heard him. He didn't *deny* killing him."

"His pride was hurt. That's all. I've known this man all of my life. What he did with Jah was wrong. What Joshua and I did was wrong. That doesn't make any of us killers. You'll have to look somewhere else, Jessie."

I didn't think the police would agree with her. Of course, until we could prove it, nothing mattered anyway. We needed a confession from Abraham. That didn't seem to be forthcoming.

"Your basket looks good," Mary complimented as she locked the front door. "You've come a long way. I'm glad you are here this summer. You brought Jah back into my life."

I wasn't sure how much of a blessing that would turn out to be, but at least she had her son. If we could make some connection between Abraham and Joshua's death, that would be something.

Chase was waiting outside the shop for me. We started walking up the King's Highway together, watching the other shops closing around us. Little dust devils whirled across the cobblestones as heavy, dark clouds settled in for the evening. I told him about Jah's confrontation with Abraham and said, "I think we can safely say we have the killer." He didn't seem to be as impressed by it as I was.

He put his arm around me as we started running when the first raindrops fell. "There's a long way between saying that and proving it, Jessie. Got any ideas on how we do that?"

NINETEEN

"The killer has to be staying here some-where." That was my brilliant deduction as we brooded about it over supper and ale. Tonight was dinner at Baron's Beer and Brats. Apparently, the baron had made a few too many brats and offered them to the residents.

"That's true," Chase agreed. "It probably wouldn't be that hard to track him down. He either has to be hiding in one of the closed shops or staying with someone."

The rain beat a steady rhythm on the roof. The eatery was full of hungry Village residents looking for whatever establishment was doling out free food that night. Everyone seemed subdued. There was none of the usual loud banter between tables.

Debby, my student, came to sit with us accompanied by Fred the Red Dragon. It seemed they had discovered each other this summer.

"You guys look down," she said. "Is something up?"

"Yeah. You guys breaking up?" Fred snickered.

"There's nothing down or up," I assured them. "We were just talking."

"Talking leads to trouble." Fred tore into his brat as he philosophized. "Take my word for it; men and women weren't meant to talk."

Debby stared at him. "What does that mean?"

"Nothing, baby." He rubbed her back, then winked at Chase.

I hadn't finished eating, but I was ready to go. The fun had gone out of communal eating for me. Chase had just started on his third brat and wasn't responsive to my nonverbal eye commands. I sat back and let everything wash over me.

Roger walked in exactly on a crack of lightning that filled the dark doorway. It was ominous. Of course, I thought Roger was a little ominous on his own without the storm. He stood there for a few minutes dripping water without trying to wipe his face then focused on us and stalked across the room to our table.

"What the hell do you mean, accusing me of murder?" He glared directly at me, water drops dripping from his nose and chin.

"I didn't accuse you of anything." I looked at my companions for backup.

"Officer Grigg seemed to have a different story," Roger said. "He said you and Livy think I killed Joshua Shift. Did you say that to Detective Almond?"

I looked around again. Debby and Fred only had eyes for each other and whatever they were doing under the table. Chase had his mouth full of brat and was valiantly trying to clear it. There was only Roger, who was dripping water on the table, and me.

"I never said you killed anyone." It was relatively true. I said it was possible, and knowing what I knew about him and Mary, it seemed even more possible. Except that Abraham was still my top suspect. His motives were much stronger than Roger's.

"I don't appreciate people gossiping about me, Jessie. I'm an ex-cop. I know how it goes. Officer Grigg gave me the low-down on your investigation into me. All I can say is, watch out. It's a two-way street. You and Chase were right there, too. You could be involved."

Was he threatening me? I got to my feet, prepared to do battle. "Look, Roger —"

But before I could tell him he didn't scare me, Chase had finished his brat and stood up beside me. "We were speculating on everyone in the Village. It's nothing personal. You should know that, being an ex-cop and all."

I knew Roger liked Chase. I could see his features soften as they talked. "You know I think you do a good job here, Chase," Roger said. "But some people are troublemakers. This murder investigation is bad enough. Let's not get at each other's throats over it."

Chase reached out his hand to shake Roger's. The two men nodded, and the air seemed to clear. Roger grunted and frowned at me, then walked back out into the rain. The door closed behind him, and I took a deep breath.

"Wow! He sounded pretty guilty to me," Fred said aloud what I was thinking. "You know how it's always those guys who know so much and tell everybody they didn't do it that end up being the ones who did it?"

Debby giggled, and Chase shook his head. I wasn't sure exactly what Fred was getting at, but I felt the same way. If I hadn't heard Jah and Abraham arguing in the shop, Roger would be my suspect.

"I think we should go if we're going to explore that *other* possibility." Chase gave me a meaningful look.

"What other possibility?" I was totally

confused and wondered how many tankards Chase had consumed. Or was it the brats? I got to my feet and took his hand. If nothing else, he shouldn't be wandering around by himself. Besides, I was ready to leave. The world had become strange. Maybe it was the rain. We stood in the alcove just outside Baron's for a moment.

"So, what were you talking about?" I asked Chase.

"I think I've come up with where we might find Abraham. He seems to show up at Wicked Weaves a lot. And if your theory is correct, he could've been watching for Joshua and Jah to put in an appearance. He needed to be close to her shop. The Three Chocolatiers have that outbuilding they sometimes use for extra staff. It'd be a good command post."

Chase was right. It was the only empty place around Wicked Weaves. If Abraham was hiding out there, he could keep a close eye on Mary. "Is that the possibility you were talking about?"

He kissed me as the rain changed direction, and we started getting wet. "You got it, baby."

I laughed. "Well, what are we waiting for?"

We ran through the shuttered Village together. The rain was heavy but warm with all the sweetness of summer. The few trees along the King's Highway bent and swayed with the storm. There was a clap of thunder followed by a burst of lightning that made me recall the statistics for being hit by it.

The lightning didn't make me nervous, but the revelation it brought with it when I looked up into Chase's handsome face made me cringe. I was pretty sure I was in love with him. I hadn't asked for it; I didn't want it. I wasn't looking for it. But there it was. It was like the lightning was Cupid's arrow striking my heart.

It sounded stupid and romantic. Nothing like me at all. But I realized Chase had always been there waiting for this moment. I tried to ignore it, but a big, sloppy grin spread over my face and almost made me blurt out what I was feeling. I didn't know if Chase was ready for that yet.

We ran under the shelter of the Three Chocolatiers' porch, pushing wet hair out of our faces. I was glad I'd changed out of my heavy linen into shorts and a tank top. Linen was terrible when it was wet. I smiled at Chase but didn't make eye contact, scared he'd see some of what I was feeling. I couldn't help wondering what he was feeling, if anything different.

"There it is." He pointed to the shed.

"There's no light on. If Abraham is staying there, he may be caught out in the rain somewhere in the Village. Now could be a great time to take a look."

I was a little disappointed that Chase's thoughts were of sneaking into the shed. I guess I wanted him to be thinking of me. I realized he might not feel that flash of insight that was still tingling through me. "What are we waiting for?" I asked. "Let's go."

We raced across the wet courtyard. I'd stayed in this particular shed/residence before, actually. It was small but not as tiny as the little hut I'd been assigned this year. It was cozy, really, and more than one person fit in the bed.

I mentally slapped myself for picturing Chase and me in that bed. *Pull yourself together. You can't go around daydreaming all over the place.*

The door was locked, but Chase had one of the master keys. He opened the door slowly, like we could sneak into a one-room shed without being noticed. If Abraham was inside, he'd know we were there.

Someone jumped up in the dark room and yelled, "Who's there?" but it wasn't Abraham. I hit the light switch at the doorway. I knew that voice.

My brother Tony was there, wearing only a pair of jeans, his tan chest bare along with his feet. I glanced at the bed, but there was no sign of Tammy. "You scared the crap out of me," he complained, putting down a spatula that he apparently was going to use on us.

"What are you doing here?" I asked. "I thought you were in Vegas."

"Yeah. Well, that didn't work out. At least not for me. Tammy seemed to like it."

"You can't just stay here, Tony," Chase told him. "You'll have to reregister as a resident and be assigned a place."

I thought about the great upstairs loft he'd given up to have his try at Vegas. It was above Sir Latte's Beanery, right across the street from Wicked Weaves. "This may be a wash, but I have another idea where we could find Abraham."

"Okay." Chase glanced back at Tony, who had slumped down on the bed. "Take care of it if you want to be back on the payroll. I won't say anything for a couple of days."

"Yeah, like that's something special."

I felt like kicking my brother, but I could see he was too busy doing it for me. He didn't need my help. "Are you broke?"

"I had to ask Bo Peep for her leftover cinnamon roll for supper tonight. What do you think?"

"They might still have some brats at Baron's." I gave him five dollars. "If not, this might get you something."

"Thanks, Sis. I know it was stupid for me to leave. I thought I could do something right for once. I thought I could get out of here and do something worthwhile. I guess I was wrong, huh?"

I hugged him. "Let me buy you breakfast in the morning, and we'll talk. I love you."

He kissed my cheek. "Love you, too. Nice catch." He nodded at Chase, who waited by the door. "The bailiff is a good choice. About as close as either one of us will be to normal."

His comment bothered me, especially since it came right on the heels of my revelation about feeling the *L* word for Chase. I hadn't realized I wasn't normal until Tony told me. Then I started worrying about all of my so-called relationships. What if Tony was right? What if I was clinging to Chase because I couldn't find what I wanted in my own life?

"So what's this new idea about finding Abraham?" Chase asked when we were outside.

I told him about Tony's loft. "Maybe he moved in there after Tony left. What are the chances Village housing would notice?"

"Not many." He glanced at the shed. "I'm sorry if I came off too rough about Tony registering again. But they come to me if something like that shows up. I'm supposed to know everything that goes on around here."

"That's okay. I was surprised to see him. I'd hoped he'd managed to escape this place."

"Why do you keep coming back if you don't like it here? Lots of people do worse stuff for a living than live in a Renaissance Faire Village and Market Place."

"I don't really have anything against it unless you're using it to hide out from the rest of the world. That's what Tony does. I thought that's what you did, too."

He kissed my forehead. "Must be too much sun. Come on. Let's check out the Beanery. Maybe we can make Jonathan as angry as we made Roger."

Chase and I left Tony at the shed and started walking past Fabulous Funnel Cakes. The Beanery was on the other side, conveniently next to the Glass Gryphon. It had stopped raining as hard, but a light mist had settled over the Village. It looked surreal, like a gauzy, romantic painting. A few lights flickered in the windows of the shops we passed. The rain must've knocked out the streetlamps. The King's Highway was dark.

From the distance I could hear the animal sounds from the end of the street. Elephants trumpeted, and camels snorted. Sheep and horses added to the symphony. The smell from the rain hitting the dry pens was a little ripe, but it added an interesting note to the evening.

Chase was right about there not being a better place to live than this. Yes, it was commercial, but it had almost as much charm as a real Renaissance village. I guess I was scared of winding up here with nowhere else to go. I didn't want that for me or Tony. As unique and charming as it was, many of the people here were hiding out.

"You can stay down here if you want to," Chase said when we reached the bottom of the steep stairs that led to the loft over the Beanery.

"That's okay." I started up. "I don't want to miss anything."

He came up behind me, our combined weight making the wet stairs sway a little. "I think this needs to be repaired." He put his hand on part of the banister, and it broke away, crashing to the cobblestones beneath it. "It definitely needs to be repaired."

"I don't think Tony stayed here a lot, even when he was officially living here. There's always been a fairy or a flower maiden ready to take him in for the night."

I waited at the top of the stairway on a narrow landing beside the door. The rain was starting again. A few large, fat drops fell into my face.

"I think this whole thing needs to be replaced," Chase said when he reached me. "That bothers you about the fairies, doesn't it?"

"Not really. Not the way you mean. He's my brother, not my boyfriend. I just want what's best for him."

"Fairies don't mean that much to anyone. I'm sure Tony is safe. You worry a lot about him, don't you?"

I watched him put the master key in the lock. "He's all the family I have. I guess I feel a little more maternal about him than I should. He needs someone to worry about him. I guess that's why I do it."

He shrugged. "He's a big boy, Jessie. He can take care of himself. I don't think he needs you to save him from his mistakes. In fact, he may make more of them because he knows you're always there to bail him out."

"What do you mean? I don't bail him out exactly. And he makes plenty of mistakes."

"Okay. I'm sorry I brought it up. I was just saying you might be doing more harm than good."

"You don't understand what it's like to be alone without anyone else who cares about you. I'm there for Tony, and he's there for me."

Chase paused before he opened the door. "I know you're there for him. I'm not sure he feels the same way about you. When was the last time he bailed you out of a jam or did anything besides worry about himself?"

That was taking things too far. But my brother was my responsibility, not his, and I didn't expect him to understand. "I'm not worried about it. Tony would be there if I really needed him. You don't know him like I do."

"You're right about that. He doesn't develop personal friendships with anyone. Except the fairies, and I think they shore up his backbone like you do."

"Not everyone our age has had a long-term relationship with one partner." I tapped my fingers on the banister until I realized I might push the whole thing down. "Have you?"

"Not yet. But that doesn't mean I wouldn't commit to the right person." He looked at me and asked, "Would you?"

I let loose with an entire barrage of excuses as to why I wouldn't. He stood and listened as the rain fell harder, soaking through what was left of our dry clothes. If Abraham *was* hiding in the loft, he had to wonder what was keeping us.

"I think that must be every excuse known to men or women," Chase said. "But what's the real excuse, Jessie?"

I felt drained and exhausted. I hoped I could make it back down the stairs without falling. It was hard denying what I felt for Chase, especially since he kept looking at me with those big, dark eyes. I wanted to tell him that everything had changed for me, but I was too afraid. I couldn't have told him what I was afraid of. I wasn't even sure myself. Was I ready for the personal commitment he was looking for?

"Until this year, I've never met anyone I thought I could commit to for more than a summer," I ground out. "Maybe now things will be different."

I couldn't see the look on his face, even in the shadows. I was breathing fast, my heart pounding in my chest. I'd given everything away, and there was no response from him. I was terrified he didn't feel the same way about me. Maybe Chase was the one man I could really love, and he might never care for me the same way.

"Door's open," he said finally. "He must know we're out here. I guess we'll go in."

We walked around the dark loft. There were only two rooms and there was no sign that anyone was staying there.

I didn't know what to say. All my thoughts were jumbled. Why couldn't he have waited until the end of the summer for this discussion? Everything seemed wrong and stilted with him now. I didn't see how we'd go on together for the next few weeks.

"I don't think anyone's been here," he said finally. "If Abraham was hiding up here, he didn't leave anything behind."

"Yeah." I searched for other words, but they wouldn't come. I'd given him my heart on a platter, and he'd sent it back to the kitchen. I guessed this was why I'd always kept myself apart from making this kind of commitment. "I guess we might as well call it a night and start over again tomorrow."

"That makes sense."

I couldn't make out his face in the dark loft. I could hear the edge in his voice. I wanted to shine my flashlight on him to see if the nuances I heard matched the reality in his eyes. I stood there, looking down at the floor, wondering what I should do next. I supposed I'd have to move out of the dungeon. Maybe housing would let me stay in the shed where Tony was. I didn't want to go up and down these stairs every day.

"Jessie, if you've met someone else . . ."

"What are you talking about?" Had he lost his mind? "Who else would I have met?"

"You said you met someone this summer you could finally care about."

I grabbed his arm and shook it. "I was talking about *you,* you big idiot! I was saying I could commit to *you.*"

"Really? For how long?"

"I don't know. Does it have to have a time frame, Chase? Can't we take it a day at a time? I'm willing to commit to that."

He slid his arms around me, and we kissed. Our faces were wet from the rain. We were standing beside the bed in the loft. It was dry and warm. One thing seemed to lead to another, and we were suddenly on the bed with our wet clothes on the floor.

"I wish I could do more than one day at a time," I promised feverishly against his wide, smooth chest.

"I won't ask for something you can't give." He kissed me, and I didn't argue with him. Outside the window that overlooked the street, lightning flickered in the dark sky and thunder rumbled around us. Words weren't necessary for what we felt, and any awkwardness melted away as we pressed closer to each other.

I wanted to tell him more than ever how I felt, but I knew it might be wrong. I didn't know how he felt about me yet. Then I forgot to think about anything but being there with him. He had the gentlest touch of any man I'd ever known. I suspected Chase had a soft heart and someday would make some woman a wonderful husband.

A sound penetrated the foggy darkness of my brain. Chase must've heard it, too. Both of us held still, listening.

"Did you hear that?" His question was barely out when the door to the loft opened.

TWENTY

A bright flashlight beam shone on us from the doorway. "What's going on in here?"

I pulled on my tank top standing behind Chase as he scrambled into his shorts. I hadn't been caught in a situation like this since I was a sophomore in high school making out in my grandmother's basement with Tommy Weller.

It was different now. I wasn't a kid anymore, and I had nothing to feel guilty about or defend. But it felt the same with the flashlight shining on us.

"Is that you, Chase?" Officer Grigg lowered the flashlight. "The power is off all over the Village."

"It's me. And yes, the power goes off here after storms." Chase pulled his shirt down over his shoulders and glanced back at me. "Are you okay?"

"I'll survive." I stuffed my feet into my sandals. I didn't want to think about what happened to my underwear.

"Are you two investigating up here?" Grigg obviously was farsighted and stupid at the same time. If I'd seen us getting dressed like the house was on fire, I'd know what was going on.

"Yeah. We thought we'd look around up here, since we knew it was empty. Have you seen anything unusual?" Chase asked him.

"Not much. It's been quiet. Probably because of the rain. I had a conversation with that Trent guy earlier. He doesn't have an alibi for his whereabouts at the approximate time of Mr. Shift's death."

"That's interesting." I took up the slack for Chase, who was looking for one of his shoes. "He confronted us at the pub and was angry that I'd mentioned his name."

"He's suspicious, that's for sure," Grigg agreed. "I've checked out the whole Village and can't find any place that Abraham fella could be staying. He's like a ghost."

"He's here somewhere." Chase finally found his shoe under the bed. "We're just not looking in the right places."

"I'm going over to check out the forest area," Grigg said. "If you'd like to come with me, that would suit me. This place is bigger than it looks on the outside."

"I don't think Abraham would hide out in Sherwood Forest for long," Chase said. "Robin Hood is tough on trespassers."

"I've heard that name before. Wasn't there an actor named Robin Hood back in the fifties?"

"Actually it was a real person who lived during the real Renaissance," I explained. "This Robin Hood is our personal Robin Hood."

"What's his real name?" Grigg asked.

"Robin Hood." I shrugged. "He had it changed."

"This is a weird place. I wouldn't like to live here all the time. I don't know how people put up with all the craziness."

"It's not that crazy when you understand how it works." Chase straightened the mattress that was falling off the side of the bed. "I'll come with you to the forest. It's the only way you won't end up hog-tied on my steps in the morning. I'm not kidding about Robin and his men disliking trespassers."

Grigg laughed. "I worked the bad streets of Atlanta before coming here. I'm not worried about a bunch of sissies in tights. But I'd be glad of the company."

"Okay." Chase looked at me. "Are you okay with that, Jessie?"

"You know, I'm kind of tired. I think I'll

just go back to the dungeon and get some sleep."

"This shouldn't take long," he whispered near my ear so Grigg wouldn't hear. "I'll be back to wake you up."

I shivered, not from the damp clothes, and kissed him. "I'll be waiting."

The rain had completely moved off to the south where I could still see forked lightning in the dark sky. The mist and haze cocooned the Village around us as we left the Beanery and skirted across the Village Square together. At this time of night, with the mist swirling around the cobblestone streets, anything seemed possible. All the fairytale creatures might be asleep in their beds, but this was the time you could really feel the magic spell the Village wove.

It was my favorite time. I didn't mind the crowds since they were the lifeblood of the Village. But when it was quiet and kind of spooky like this, it seemed more real than ever. It was easy to forget that past the walls that surrounded us were tall hotels on Ocean Boulevard and Ripley's Believe It or Not. Myrtle Beach was certainly the most commercialized beach from here to Coney Island, but in the Village, it was quiet and otherworldly.

"Are you okay to go back from here by yourself in the dark?" Chase asked when we reached the big fountain in the middle of the square. The four large fish squirted water from their mouths in the fountain, the splashing water even louder in the cool night air.

"I'll be fine." I was touched by his concern, but the dungeon wasn't that far away, and I'd walked these streets at night a few hundred times alone since I'd been coming here.

"I'll see you as soon as I can," he promised with a kiss.

"Okay. If not, I'll bring a knife down to cut both of you free in the morning."

Chase laughed. "It's been at least two years since that happened to me. Robin wouldn't do that now."

We said our temporary good-byes and walked in opposite directions. As Chase and Grigg disappeared into the mist down Squire's Lane, I heard Grigg say, "You two have a thing going on, don't you?"

I didn't hear Chase's reply, but I was amazed at the man's ability to state the obvious. If it took him that long with us, what possible chance did we have of catching the killer?

I was walking between the Hands of Time

clock shop and DaVinci's Drawings, when I saw a man in a hooded robe walking quickly between the privies that separated the two shops.

The first thing I thought was one of the monks had kept his robe anyway. But I'd counted the robes, and Chase had counted the monks. We had twenty-five robes and the same number monks.

Then I thought about Roger. Of course, there could be other robes, like the one Jah had found in the hole in the wall. It could be Abraham as well. Either way, it might be a good idea to follow and see what was going on.

With the lights out and the mist covering the ground, it was easy to go from place to place, keeping the solitary hooded figure in my line of sight. I leapfrogged from the privies to Da Vinci's, then hid behind the Little Mermaid Fountain and the Lovely Washer Women's Well. The figure continued up between Fabulous Funnels and the Beanery, glancing back occasionally.

If I hadn't known the area so well, I might've gotten lost. The only illumination came from shop windows where someone had left a lantern or candle burning. It would be easy to get turned around in the square or behind the privies and buildings.

The robed figure seemed to glide over the foggy cobblestones as it headed toward the glass shop. It had to be Roger. What had he been up to? He seemed to be headed back home. Had he followed me, Chase, and Grigg from the Beanery toward the forest to find out what we were doing?

A hand snaked out from behind a statue of William Shakespeare where the bard sat and quoted his verse from ten until four each day. I almost screamed as it took me by surprise. Thank goodness my hand reached my mouth before it could come out. I would've sounded like some bimbo in a cheap movie.

"Shh!" I recognized Brother Carl's voice, if not his outfit.

The dim light from a lantern in a window behind me picked out what the monks must've chosen as replacement garments until their robes were returned. The black and silver domino was eye-catching and evil looking at the same time. "What are you doing out here, and where did you get that costume?"

"I think we're doing the same thing," he replied, "following whoever that is in one of our robes. Let's not talk about the costume. It was the only thing Portia had enough of so we all looked the same. The thing's a menace to bake in. Keeps getting in the way."

I held back my laughter, only indulging in a small smile I didn't think he could see. "I think it might be Roger." I explained about the robe I'd seen.

"The glass blower?" Carl's voice was full of surprise. "I guess anything's possible."

"Were you planning on taking the robe from him?"

"No. Someone's trying to make the Brotherhood look bad. We won't stand for that. Whoever is behind these late-night visits has to be stopped and identified as not being one of us."

I agreed with him, and we had an unspoken decision between us to help each other at least until we knew what was going on. The monks never helped anyone outside the group, but I supposed even they could be goaded into a partnership.

Carl and I stayed together until we reached the Glass Gryphon. We split up to survey each side of the street to make sure the hooded figure hadn't gone somewhere else.

I wasn't sure what I was going to do at that point. I didn't see anyone besides Carl on the street. Should I burst into the glass shop and confront Roger? If he was guilty, he'd still be wearing the robe. He could also have a gun and shoot me. I could think of ten different places he could hide my body. Chase wouldn't miss me for a while. By that time, I could be inside a privy or buried outside the wall.

If Carl and I were together, it would be better. It seemed like it would be harder to shoot both of us. Whoever wasn't shot could attack Roger and take the gun away. I liked that plan better. If we didn't do something out of the ordinary, we might never know what was happening in the Village. This seemed as good a time as any to confront Roger.

Carl came back to the side of the glass shop. "I didn't see anyone else. It has to be Trent. Should we go get Chase?"

"No. It would take too long. He's in the forest with Tom, Tom the Piper's Son."

"Oh. I thought you and Chase were a couple."

"We are. He's helping Tom with something that has to do with Robin." I didn't want to give away Grigg's secret identity. "We'll have to take care of this ourselves, Carl. Are you ready?"

"Let's do it, Jessie."

He produced a key from his pocket as I was debating how best to open the back door to the glass shop. "How did you get that?" I recognized the master key Chase carried, the same key Tony had. Did everyone have one except me?

"The monks have been around since the birth of this Village. We have many secrets."

I didn't push him for a better answer, but I planned to tell Chase about it. I stepped aside to let Carl open the door. The lock opened silently, but the heavy wooden door squeaked as it slipped back.

We stopped moving, huddled together in the doorway despite Carl's sense of righteousness that had allowed him to possess a master key. Nothing happened. It was possible Roger was asleep upstairs.

"Where did you see the monk's robe?" Carl whispered.

"I'll show you." I took the lead, and he followed me into the workroom and show area in the front of the shop. All of the tools I'd hoped to use in the future as an apprentice glass blower were laid out alongside Roger's elegant creations. The best I could hope for was that another glass blower would come to the Village. After this summer, it was doubtful Roger would let me apprentice with him.

I carefully maneuvered past the showcases and opened the closet door where I'd seen the monk's robe. Carl shined his flashlight into the storage space, but there was no sign of any robe. "It was here yesterday."

"I don't see it now," Carl said. "We better get out of here. Residents can be expelled from the Village permanently for breaking and entering."

It was the wrong time to mention that rule, but I agreed. We had violated enough rules for one night. The robe was gone. I hoped Roger was still out roaming the Village in it.

At that moment, the lights came back on. Apparently, Roger had left his lights on when the power went off. The bright lights were blinding after being in the darkness. Carl dropped his flashlight as he ran for the back door.

"Who's down there?" Roger demanded from the stairs.

Lucky for Carl, who was already outside. Not so lucky for me.

I spun around, deciding the front door was my best avenue of escape since the stairway led down closer to the back door. I thought Roger was still on the stairs as I bolted past the showcases toward the front of the shop.

Roger was spry for an older man. He managed to get down the stairs and between me and the front door before I could reach that destination. I wished I had Carl's domino costume. At least I could've pretended to be someone else.

"What are you doing in here, Jessie?" Roger held a large shotgun in his grip. It was aimed directly at me while he scanned the room around us.

It occurred to me that I could lie, tell him I wanted to see him about something. I just couldn't think of what I wanted to see him about. I opened my mouth, and something came out, but it was only gibberish.

"Are you alone?" He finally focused back on me, content that he didn't see anyone else.

"I guess." I wished it wasn't true. At least if Carl were there, we could make something up together. Or Carl's staunch Brotherhood code would make him look worse than I looked at that moment.

"Did you come to steal from me while the lights were off?" Roger shook his head. "I can't believe it. You've always seemed a little scatterbrained, but I thought you were honest."

I latched on to the least of the charges. "Scatterbrained? What made you think that? I'm not at all unsure of what to do. I'm very organized and thorough in everything. I don't think anyone has ever called me that before."

"Where's Chase?"

"The last time I saw him he was headed for Sherwood Forest. I was on my way home, and I ended up here. It's strange what darkness can do to your sense of direction. I guess your back door was open. And here I am."

Would he buy it? I looked at his face and not below his chin where he was shirtless. I wasn't sure if he was wearing his usual tights or not. I tried my best to only look in his eyes.

"There's been some strange stuff going on this summer." Trent gestured with the shotgun. "I think we better go find Chase and then have a little talk with Officer Grigg."

"I didn't touch anything, Roger," I protested. "Look around. I was lost."

"I know I locked the back door, Jessie." Roger gestured with the gun again. "I think you have some explaining to do. I've been here twenty years, and nothing like this has ever happened to me. I've never had to press charges with the bailiff, but I guess there's a first time for everything."

"Roger, you're making a mistake."

"Start walking toward the dungeon. If

Chase isn't there, we'll wait for him."

I wasn't sure if the shotgun was real or not, but I didn't want to find out the hard way. We started walking with me in the lead, feeling the cold stare of the shotgun's eye in the middle of my back. It was terrible.

I opened the back door, hoping I would think of something to get out of this spot. Mary stood in the doorway, hand raised to knock. I put my arms around her and wouldn't let go. "You have to help me," I blubbered. "He's gone crazy. He's going to kill me."

She patted my back and looked around me at Roger. "What's going on?"

"I found her in here after the lights came on. She was planning to steal something."

"This girl may not be much of a basket weaver, but she's honest. She wasn't going to steal anything, were you, Jessie?"

"No!" I slowly made my way around Mary so that she was between me and Roger. I knew it was cowardly, but I wasn't good with guns. Knives, hatchets, axes, and swords aren't too bad. Even a knight's lance, I can handle. Guns made me want to cry.

"See?" Mary pushed the gun to one side. "She wasn't stealing anything."

"Then what was she doing?" Roger demanded. "And not that lame thing about wandering into the wrong place because it was dark."

I could see I was going to have to come clean. "I thought you might be Joshua's killer," I muttered.

"What's that?"

I repeated it louder for him. "I'm sorry. I saw the monk's robe hanging in your closet. Livy said she saw you coming from behind Wicked Weaves right before she found the body. I knew you and Mary had a thing going on."

"A *thing*?" Roger's left eye squinted his disapproval.

Mary laughed. "When you put it that way, I think he could be the killer, too."

"What are you saying?" He put the shotgun down. "Mary, you know I didn't kill Joshua. As much as I love you, I wouldn't kill a man for you. Now, it's not that I haven't killed before, but it was in the line of duty when I was a cop. I wouldn't randomly kill anyone, and especially not for personal gain."

Mary put her arms around him and kissed him. "I know. I was funning you."

I looked away while they kissed again. I didn't understand what she saw in him, but I could see their relationship was real. They probably had never married because she was technically still Joshua's wife. Of course, that could be seen as another motive for Roger to kill Joshua.

"As for you," Roger suddenly remembered I was still standing there, "you need to mind your own business. If you weren't in here where you didn't belong, snooping around —"

"I wasn't snooping around when I saw the monk's robe," I defended. "I was in here talking to you."

Mary looked at him the same way she looked at me when I was messing up a basket. "So? Why do you have a monk's robe, and where is it?"

"I can have a robe if I want to. The nights get cold here over the winter. It keeps me warm and stays in character."

"And where is it?" I asked. "I followed you across the Village while you were wearing it tonight."

"I wasn't out in it tonight." He shook his head and glanced at Mary. "I've been in all evening keeping an eye on things. I'll get the robe, and you can check it out. It would be wet from being outside."

He went upstairs, and Mary grabbed my ear the way she had Jah's. "What are you about, sniffing around this thing that could

354

get you hurt? Child, you are too curious and worried about other people. You have to get over it."

I couldn't answer. It felt like she had my ear in a vise. She let go as Roger started down the stairs. "See here," he held out the robe, "it's dry as a bone. And before you go thinking I dried it, look around. I only have the fence to dry my clothes."

I didn't have to touch the robe (thank goodness) to tell that it was dry. It wasn't the robe I'd seen earlier with Carl. Whoever was wearing that robe was still out there. "I'm sorry. It was a logical assumption. Even Mary thought so."

"Don't be dragging me into this." She looked away.

"I think next time you need to ask, Jessie," Roger said.

"I don't think you get it. If I'd asked you if you'd killed Joshua, what would you say?"

He shrugged. "No. I didn't kill Joshua."

"Now, what do you think the real killer would say if I asked him or her if they killed Joshua?"

"I get your point." He grunted. "But I didn't kill anyone. Livy saw me leaving Mary's apartment that day. That's all."

It made me feel squirmy inside realizing that what I'd feared was true. Roger may not have killed Joshua, but he was sleeping with Mary. *Yuck!*

TWENTY-ONE

"So now we don't think Roger killed Joshua." Chase and I talked about the events of the night before over bowls of Cheerios the next morning.

"I'm not a professional," I said, "but I believe him. It was a total surprise when I accused him. He told me everything. Even the part about the monk's robe made sense. We're back to Abraham or Jah being the killer."

Grigg joined us, taking off his red stocking hat as he ducked into Fabulous Funnels. He ordered two powdered sugar funnel cakes then sat down at our table. "Hey! Where'd you get the Cheerios? I thought modern foods were off limits."

"Did you think they had funnel cakes and pizza during the Renaissance?" I hated to burst his historical bubble, but beyond the basics, the Village couldn't exist totally during the 1600s.

He shrugged. "I wasn't ever much good at history. I can see why you all want to live here. Last night in Sherwood Forest was a blast. All the dancing and the girls. Right Chase?"

"Yeah," Chase mumbled between mouthfuls of cereal. "It was a blast."

"What dancing girls?" I wasn't jealous. I knew Chase wouldn't do something so obvious. I was just interested.

"The Merry Men went out and got some dancing girls," Grigg stumbled to explain. "They were all like belly dancers with colored costumes and scarves and bells and stuff."

"Robin convinced some of the girls from the Caravan Stage to come over and perform," Chase explained a little better, if not in great detail. "I think it was some kind of cultural exchange."

"Yeah," I agreed. "It's always a cultural blast around here."

"I had a word with Detective Almond this morning." Grigg returned from grabbing his plate of funnel cakes from the counter.

"Why not talk to the Sheriff of Nottingham? He'd probably do you as much good." I played with the rest of my cereal, not as hungry for the hard-to-find food as I'd thought.

"Is there a *real* Sheriff of Nottingham?" Grigg's eyes got big. "Can we go visit him?"

"He wanders around the Village when he isn't doing the falconry act over at the Hawk Stage," Chase told him. "He's the one with the really big, leather gloves."

Grigg seemed to consider the idea as he started eating his funnel cakes. It only took a moment before he was covered in powdered sugar. "Well, Detective Almond said they're almost positive the pieces of cardboard they found in the dead man's teeth match the cardboard funnel you gave him. There were traces of whiskey in the cardboard fibers, too."

"I guess that was the real funnel then." I looked at Chase. "Maybe that was the real robe, too."

"Nothing on that yet," Grigg said. "It takes a while to get most forensic tests back. We're lucky the ME for Horry County is experienced enough to do some of the tests himself, or we wouldn't know about the cardboard yet, either."

I sat back in my chair and tried to zone out of all the yawning and stretching going on as the residents of Renaissance Faire Village woke up. Everyone was talking about the power outage and damage done to their shops.

"So someone, probably dressed like a monk, used a funnel to get Joshua drunk. Joshua didn't just sit still while that was going on," I tried to get us back on track. "He must've been unconscious already. I mean, why go to all that trouble? Whoever the person in the monk's robe was could've just strangled him while he was unconscious."

"That's true," Chase agreed. "Maybe we should consider finding the hole in the wall Jah found and retrace what may have been the killer's path."

Grigg nodded in agreement, his mouth too full of funnel cake to speak.

I was about to agree with the idea when Mary came into the eatery, glancing around like she knew I'd be there. Those laserlike dark eyes found me, and she made a beeline for our table.

"Jessie, there you are! Child, I've been looking for you everywhere. You have this bad habit of disappearing when I need you most."

"I was hoping you wouldn't need me so you and Jah could spend some quality time together."

"That detective is questioning my son about his father's death. Seems someone said he found an old funnel they say was used on Joshua. If it's not me they're after, it's a member of my family."

Chase and Grigg looked at me. "I didn't tell anybody."

"Never mind how he found out," Mary said. "I'm expecting a group that wants to learn basket weaving again this morning. I'll need help with the shop. Are you almost finished here?"

"I guess so." I didn't enlighten her about the new plan to find the killer. I turned to Chase and Grigg as she bustled out of Fabulous Funnels. "I guess you'll have to go without me. Let me know if you find anything."

Chase walked me out of the shop. "You seem kind of out of it after last night. Are you okay?"

"You mean, did I take Grigg's story about the dancing girls to heart?"

"I guess." He smiled and slid his arms around me. "You know I wouldn't bother with that stuff, right?"

"At least not right now." I nodded and kissed him. "Every Merry Man would beat a path to my door to tell me about it. You know there's nothing secret here. Remember when Mother Goose's assistant Carol got pregnant last summer? I knew before Carol's boyfriend."

"You're right," he agreed. "News travels

fast across the cobblestones. I watched Grigg with the caravan girls. All I did was eat supper with Robin."

"Did he give you another toaster oven since the one he coughed up for the contest didn't work?"

"You know Robin." He grinned. "You'll have to beat him at something else if you want a working model."

"I'm sure you're right." I hugged him. "I guess I'd better go over to Wicked Weaves. I wonder who told Detective Almond that Jah found the funnel?"

"It could be anyone present that night. I'm surprised. What happens in the Village usually stays in the Village. I get to hear it, but it's unusual for someone to call the police."

"Don't you mean the sheriff?" I mocked Grigg.

"I'll see you later." He kissed me quickly. "Unless something big turns up. I'll come and tell you if that happens."

I hummed a little song as I walked across the street to Wicked Weaves. It was possible we were all missing the idea that whoever really killed Joshua could have called the police to throw off the investigation. It seemed unlikely to me that Abraham would sacrifice his adopted son unless he was sure he'd be exonerated.

Mary was on the back steps finishing a basket. It was tall and thin, almost like something you'd put a wine bottle in. I asked her what it was for, and she looked at it from all sides. "I was thinking about a bottle of milk maybe or a flower holder. What do you think?"

"I like it." I sat beside her and showed her the progress I was making on my basket. "I'm not sure what mine is for, either."

She looked at it critically and nodded. "You're doing a good job, Jessie. I think it would be good for a loaf of bread. You could bake one and give it to someone in this basket. Or it could just cool in here."

Her words gave a whole new world to my creation. I'd never baked a loaf of bread, but that didn't mean it wasn't possible. "Mary, I hope you know I didn't say anything to the police about Jah finding that funnel."

"But you and your bailiff friend gave them the funnel and the robe Jah found."

"That's true. But we didn't mention Jah." I worked on the next coil in my basket, securing the sweetgrass with my stitches. "We keep going around in circles looking for Joshua's killer, just like making a basket."

"Maybe you aren't meant to find him. The

Lord works in ways we don't understand."

"Maybe you could help. Joshua's death seems to be centered around you."

Her eyebrows went up, disappearing into the yellow scarf around her head. "Are you accusing me again?"

"No. I'm saying that Joshua was your husband. He and Abraham showed up here at about the same time. Now Joshua is dead, and Jah's here, too. All these years you haven't seen them. Don't you think it's a little strange it should all happen now?"

She laughed and patted my leg. "You know, child, life is that way. Things go along just dandy for a long time, then all of a sudden, things happen. Life is never the same again. It's like a hurricane that comes through and destroys so much of what we know and love. We get back up and rebuild, but things are never like they were. It turns quickly when it turns, Jessie. Life isn't different than the weather or the tides."

The front door opened to the shop, and Mary left to tend to the customers who entered. I thought about what she'd said. Maybe she was right, but she was involved with Joshua's death, even if she hadn't asked to be. If Joshua hadn't come there to tell her about Jah, he might still be alive.

"Morning," Ham greeted me, coming

around the corner of the shop. "It's a beautiful morning after all that fury last night."

"I know. It's like everything was cleared away so it could be nice today."

"What are you making?" He looked at my basket.

"Mary said she thinks it's for fresh bread. I'm not sure."

"Looks like it could hold bread to me. Are you going to put a handle on it?"

"Maybe. Right now I'm happy to be able to sew the coils in place. I might just keep doing that."

He grinned. "It's hard starting something new. Mary and I had a hard time getting things set up after we left home. Finally it worked for us, and we were here. Been here ever since. It's a good life."

"I like it here, too," I agreed with a smile.

"Is she inside?"

"Yeah. She's waiting for the group of basket makers. I guess you're helping her since Jah is gone for the day."

"Looks like. I like egg baskets best. I like the shape of them. You keep practicing. Things will get easier for you, too."

I liked Ham. He was like a male version of Mary, only his face wasn't as harsh, and his eyes crinkled at the corners when he smiled. I could see the faraway look in his gaze as he talked about their home. It must've been hard for them. It was a good thing they had each other to fall back on.

By the time the group of basket weavers arrived, I was on the tenth row of my basket. Not a sign of blood anywhere on the coils. I looped the top quarter of the strand around the tip coil and through the lower one. I finished the sides of the basket with my single stitch accompanied by my bone. Would it have a handle? I'd decided to leave that for tomorrow.

I watched the group of basket weavers with Mary and Ham behind Wicked Weaves. The day that had started out sunny had turned overcast and a little cool for summer weather at the beach. That meant fewer people in the Village and a little rest for the residents. I noticed a few shopkeepers standing on ladders, repairing roof tiles that had blown off in the storm.

I was enjoying the quiet. The Three Chocolatiers were practicing their swordplay in the road by the Lady Fountain. I called it that because there was a lovely Renaissance lady sitting on the top with water cascading from under her dress. Obviously, the artist was a man. No woman would ever create something like that. I liked it anyway.

Bo Peep was exercising her sheep, her beribboned crook guiding them through their paces. They were actually quite talented, taking commands to sit and stay. Their wool was beginning to grow back despite the heat of summer. Bo Peep always had them sheared in the spring.

Arthur was making a big show of pulling the sword from the stone for a group of appreciative young ladies who giggled and applauded as he accomplished the feat. Bawdy Betty laughed from her space, the smell of bagels cooking telling me what she was doing as she watched.

Roger waved to me from the Glass Gryphon. I guessed we'd be friends after all. It hadn't started out looking that way this year, but maybe there'd still be room in his apprentice program for me. Even though he was probably the most unattractive man I had ever met, I was glad he and Mary had found each other. It reminded me of Hephaestus and Aphrodite. Not that Mary was so beautiful as clever and wise. They made a good pair.

Thinking of making a good pair made me think about Chase. It was something I did routinely anyway. It had always been hard *not* to think about him, even when I was dating other guys in the Village. We'd always been friends, mostly because I didn't think any other spot was available for me in his life.

But now that I had accomplished the impossible, and I was staying at the dungeon with him, I wasn't sure where I was going. I knew summer would be all too short. After that, I'd go back to my job in the real world, and this time with Chase would fade like the summer I'd spent with Alex. And David. And Jeff. I wasn't sure I wanted it to be that way, but what were the odds it would be any different?

Sighing, already thinking about the summer slowly vanishing into history, I started on another basket. I decided ahead of time that this one would be for Chase. He could remember me when he looked at it.

I studied a basket Mary had shown me the first day I'd met her. She'd said it was a keepsake basket that could be for a man's cufflinks or a woman's trinkets. I decided it would be for Chase's trinkets, whatever those were. I knew he collected swords; they were all over the dungeon. He also collected knives. Both of those were too big for my basket. He'd just have to learn to collect something small. Or maybe he could put his pocket change into it.

It made me melancholy as I started the

process of creating a basket again. I found Mary's stash of sweetgrass, growing more expensive every day as it grew in fewer and fewer places along the coast. I cut some strands to the same length and began to weave them together, picturing Chase's handsome face in my mind as I worked.

I could hear Mary's singsong voice as she told her stories of growing up in the Gullah community. I was sure basket weavers came from across the state to hear her stories as much as to learn her almost forgotten craft.

I was sitting on the floor in the shop, almost in a trance, when the front door burst open. The little bell that signaled a customer's arrival went crazy then jumped down on the floor.

"Where's my mother?" Jah demanded.

"She's in back."

He didn't say another word, just stalked through the shop and out the back door. I heard Mary stop talking, her lesson voice replaced by Ham's. I watched Jah and Mary hurry down the street together and wondered where they were going.

I retrieved the bell to see if I could fix it when the door sprang open again, and Chase entered the shop. "I think I've found something."

"Something like what?" The image of the

sad Chase, sitting alone in his room above the dungeon, looking at the trinket basket I'd made him years before, was lost in the reality of him being there with me.

"Can you leave? I told Grigg to stay put so you could see it, too."

I glanced through the back door. Ham was still in the backyard with the dozen or so basket weavers. "I don't know. Jah just got back from his conversation with the police. He grabbed Mary, and they took off down the street."

"Grigg already called Detective Almond. If you don't come soon, you won't get to see it before they close off the area."

"Maybe I could put the Closed sign up for a few minutes." I didn't want to miss the find that Chase was eager for me to see. "Ham probably won't notice."

I put the little bell on the windowsill and turned the Open sign. I glanced through the back doorway again. There was no change. If someone asked, I'd say there was an emergency. I wasn't sure what kind of emergency, but I'd deal with that later if I got caught.

Chase hurried me through the sparse crowd, along the smooth cobblestones. Arlene waved from her horse, back in her skin suit again. I saw her and Tony exchange a meaningful glance as he emerged from Brewster's. There might be something going on there. It wouldn't be the first time for them.

"What is it we're going to see?" I asked Chase, hoping it was worth running my feet off. Cobblestones aren't all that easy to walk on.

"It'll spoil the surprise if I tell you." He smiled at me, and I decided not to argue. The summer was passing quickly, and it wouldn't be long before it would only be a memory, like Rome or Parnassus. Chase and I might never be together again.

I grabbed his hand and smiled back at him. We hurried past Galileo, who was showing a group of middle school students how to read star charts. I could hear the sound of canon fire from the lake and knew it was time for the pirates to attack the tavern again.

"We found the open place in the wall, which I'll have to have rebricked before Livy or Harry find out about it. It was where Jah found the monk's robe and the funnel. Grigg and I came through it just like the killer might've done. The hole is behind Merlin's Apothecary."

"I can see we're headed that way," I said breathlessly. "Are you sure it's the same hole in the wall and there aren't any more?" There had been holes in the wall for as long as I'd been coming here. Someone always got caught sneaking in that way.

"We checked the entire perimeter," he said. "It was the only place we could find."

"I'm surprised Nurse Wanda didn't see it and have someone walled in there."

"It's not a big hole. It would be easy to sneak in without being seen." Chase slowed his frantic rush as we reached Cupid's Arrow. "I'm hoping this is one time the police don't beat us here."

We skirted the edge of the wall behind the shops and privies. I could see Grigg standing guard over the hole in the wall. No one seemed to notice him or the broken wall. Most people were too busy watching the pirates.

"No sign of Detective Almond yet," Grigg reported. "I didn't think there would be. It's a long ride from the office to here."

"Stand here by the wall and see what the first thing is that catches your eye." Chase had me put my back against the wall and face the back of the shops.

"Can't you just tell me what I'm looking for?" I scanned the buildings, tiny yards and alleys. There was a pile of neatly stacked cement blocks partially covered with a blue tarp. "I don't know what I'm looking for. Nothing back here looks that important."

"Looks can be deceiving," Grigg qualified. "You all taught me that with the sword in the stone trick. Look for the unexpected. That's what you do here, isn't it?"

I was getting impatient. Was this a new game show or something? If they didn't tell me what they found, Detective Almond would be out here before I saw it.

"Doesn't the blue tarp remind you of something?" Chase grinned. "We looked straight across from here and saw it."

"Saw *what?*"

"The tent! There's a tent between the wall and the pile of blocks." Grigg rocked back and forth on his heels. "Guess what's inside?"

"Come on, guys. Let's get on with it."

"Evidence that someone has been staying there. There's a battery-powered lantern, some food, a sleeping bag." Chase started walking toward the tarp as he spoke. "The rain probably drove him out last night. That might've been why you saw him out walking."

"Even more impressive," Grigg continued, producing a man's worn leather wallet. "The wallet belongs to Abraham Shift."

TWENTY-TWO

"You know, history always repeats itself." I was sitting at the table inside the Peasant's Pub with Chase and Grigg.

Detective Almond had come and looked around the Village with a team of officers. There was no sign of Abraham in any of the empty buildings. Almond concluded that Abraham was probably gone for good because of the pressure he'd put on him through his investigation.

I wasn't sure I agreed with that, but I didn't have a better answer for his disappearance. It seemed odd to me that he'd leave and not take his wallet with him. That made me believe he was still in the Village somewhere.

Chase argued that it was possible Abraham had lost his wallet without realizing it. Detective Almond ignored him as he bagged the wallet and the funnel. He had his men dust the tarp and lantern for fingerprints.

Grigg was congratulated on his role in the investigation. He accepted his boss's praises, then abruptly quit his job rather than return to the office and his other duties. I wasn't sure who was more surprised, me or Detective Almond.

"I don't know what that means," Chase said. "It looks to me like we still have a killer in the Village."

"The police have an APB out on Mr. Shift," Grigg said. "He won't get far."

Chase shook his head. "You don't seem to get it. He's probably still here. Just because you guys didn't find him doesn't mean he's not better at hiding than you are at seeking."

"Not if Detective Almond and the other officers couldn't find him." Grigg stuck to his beliefs. "They're specially trained. Nothing misses their eyes."

"You've seen this place. It would be impossible to look in every crack and crevice," Chase argued. "Abraham didn't leave without his wallet and clothes. He's here somewhere."

"Which brings me back to my original statement." I looked at my two companions. "What caused the murder in the first place?"

"Probably Abraham trying to continue manipulating Mary and Jah." Chase said exactly what I was thinking.

"And right now, he thinks he has them where he wants them. But what if history repeated itself, and something else happened to change their lives? What if he was forced to do something else to gain control?"

"Like what?" Grigg slurped his coffee.

"Like get Jah out of here, away from Mary's influence."

"I'm not following this whole history logic thing," Chase said. "Just tell me what you think we should do."

"I think we should put him on the offensive again. What does this Village do best?"

"All these questions are giving me a headache," Grigg complained.

"That would be debatable," Chase replied. "What do you think it does best, Jessie?"

"Gossip. You said it yourself. Everyone knows everything going on here. All we have to do is get it out that Mary and Jah are leaving but not going back to their home. That should force Abraham's hand. He wants Jah to go home with him. He'll have to do something to keep it from happening and we'll catch him."

"Where are they going?" Grigg asked.

"It doesn't matter," I answered. "It's just

pretend."

"Even if it's pretend, we still need one single answer," Chase reminded me. "Like Mary and Jah are going to Pennsylvania to get jobs in a basket factory."

"That wouldn't happen," I disagreed. "No one would believe that."

"That's why I asked where they were going." Grigg finished off his hamburger and sat back in his chair.

"It would have to be something more like they were going to teach basket weaving at a museum in Virginia."

"How is that better than working at a basket factory?" Chase asked.

"I can't believe you don't see the difference," I argued. "Mary is an accomplished basket weaver, a master craftsman. She wouldn't go make baskets at a factory."

"Okay. Fine." Chase threw up his hands. "They're working at a museum in Virginia. Does that suit you?"

"I think that's fine. You tell all the worst gossips you know, and I'll do the same."

"Where exactly will that take us?"

"It will flush Abraham out. He'll have to do something unless he wants to lose his son."

"So, he'll try and kill Mary, right?" Grigg seemed to get it, even though I wasn't crazy about his follow through.

"I guess so." I considered the idea that Mary's life could be in danger. There wouldn't be a way to know when Abraham might strike. Maybe I was wrong, and there was a better plan.

We talked about it for another twenty minutes while Grigg munched down two hot dogs. I wondered how he was going to feed himself on his meager Village salary. We broke up without being sure what to do next. Grigg was intent on getting a job in the Village. Chase had to sit in on a meeting with Livy and Harry after security guards reported the hole in the wall to them. I kissed him good-bye and walked back to Wicked Weaves.

The Closed sign was still up in the window like I'd left it. There was no sign of Mary or Jah. Ham was in the shop, putting away basket materials. I surprised him when I came in the back door. He jumped, and I laughed. "Sorry!"

"That's okay." He glanced behind me. "Where did Mary and Jah go?"

"I'm not sure." I thought I might as well start the process right here. We were going to have to do something to get Abraham back out in the open. My plan was as good as anything else. "Jah said something about him and Mary leaving the Village."

"Really? Did he say where they were going?"

"No. But I'm sure they'll let you know. You're Mary's brother."

"That's true." He nodded. "Did the police find anything? They came tearing through here like the building was on fire."

"I don't think they found anything, at least nothing that really matters." I told him about Abraham's stuff near Merlin's Apothecary. "I don't think he left without his wallet. I don't know where he is now, but none of us are safe until we find him. Who knows what he might do next?"

Ham left a note for Mary and said he had to get back to the smithy. "If you hear anything, you let me know."

I promised I would and closed the shop door behind us. It seemed a shame all of this should happen just as I got really good at basket weaving. I told Ham that as we walked down the King's Highway toward the jousting field.

"Don't worry. It's not something you'll lose. I went years without picking up a piece of sweetgrass. The weaving came right back to me. It's either in you or it's not."

"How did you end up shoeing horses and working in a smithy?"

"I'm not sure. Back then, there wasn't as much money in making baskets. Mary and I had to make ends meet. We did the best we could."

"It had to be hard for you." I thought about his encounter with Abraham. "I hate to ask you to go through it again, but did you notice anything about the man who attacked you that might be helpful in finding him?"

Ham invited me into the smithy and sat down away from the forge that gleamed red in the cast iron. "I've tried to think on it, but I had my back turned and couldn't see anything. It was over so quickly. Next thing I knew, I saw you, and my head hurt."

"It's too bad. You know Abraham as well as Mary. What's he like? Is there some way we could play into one of his weaknesses?"

"Abraham is a man who likes to get his way." Ham nodded sagely. "Like with Jah. My sister never had a chance taking that boy away from home. Abraham knew all along what he had planned. He wanted to replace his dead boy with my nephew. And for a while, it worked, didn't it?"

I heard a strange scratching sound coming from the side of the smithy. I looked that way, wondering what it was.

"Rats," Ham guessed what I was thinking.

"We got a big problem with 'em down here by the stables. They love that feed."

I shuddered and moved closer to the open door. "Anyway, I hope we can find Abraham. I'd like to feel safe walking around at night."

He put on his heavy black apron and gloves, then opened the forge to build heat back into the fire. "I hope so, too. He's a bad man who's due some comeuppance."

"I agree. I'll talk to you later. Take care."

I could hear the ringing of his heavy hammer on the horse shoes as I walked away from the smithy. I hated not to tell him the plan, especially since I could see he was distressed by learning Mary and Jah were leaving the Village. It wouldn't matter, I assured myself as I strolled toward the dungeon. We'd have Abraham soon enough. But in the meantime, if we were going to spread this rumor, we needed an additional plan for keeping Mary safe.

Chase was still gone an hour later when I left the dungeon. I couldn't wait any longer and left him a note on the bed. I'd thought about Mary. She had to know what was going on. I'd take first watch after that. Grigg and Chase and whoever else we could recruit could step up later.

I was hoping for an immediate reaction from Abraham. Historically, as things came back around to certain stress points, there were quick reactions. In this case, I realized I was hoping he'd go after Mary. But my plan allowed for that. I'd be there to intervene.

I stopped off at the shed beside the Three Chocolatiers. As I thought, Tony was still sitting around feeling sorry for himself. He hadn't been out all day. Even worse, he was in his underwear. Not something I'd planned to see again in my lifetime.

"I have something for you to do," I told him. I figured two was better than one in this case. No one else seemed to be available. Tony was going to help me keep Mary safe.

"Does it pay?"

"Yeah. I'll buy you supper and not tell Chase you're still here. Did you talk to anyone about getting your job back?"

"No. What's the point? I'm not sure if anyone even noticed I was gone."

I sighed. I hated him when he got in these moods. "Well, I noticed. And I know you're back. Get up. Take a shower. Get dressed. I'll talk to Livy about rehiring you."

His face, a strange caricature of my own, seemed to lighten up a little. "Really? You'd do that? What exactly do I have to do? I'm not robbing any banks unless I get half of everything."

"Ha-ha. That was a great laugh." I kicked his foot off of the bottom of the recliner. "Get dressed. Let's go. This offer has a short shelf life."

To my surprise, he actually did what I said. Twenty minutes later, we were headed down to Wicked Weaves. I was nervous the whole way down that I'd find Mary dead when I got there. The guilt was going to be an incredible burden. I could've gone down without Tony and had him meet me, if I'd trusted him to be there.

But she was standing by the front of the shop, cleaning the window. "There you are!" She saw my reflection in the glass. "I was wondering where you'd gone off to."

"I walked Ham back to the smithy, then went to get my brother. We were about to have some dinner. Would you like to come with us?"

Mary used her laser eyes to scan Tony's face. "He's a good-looking boy. Doesn't look much like you except around the eyes. Lazy though, huh?"

Tony wasn't crazy about that remark. "Who said I was lazy?"

She laughed. "Why don't you two have

dinner with me and my boy? I never eat none of that stuff they sell here. They don't know what real food is."

I decided to take her up on her offer. That way I could keep an eye on Jah at the same time. Tony wanted to go to the pub. He didn't understand the nature of the help I needed from him. That was okay. It only took a pointed look to let him know we were staying for supper if he wanted me to talk to Livy for him.

Jah was inside, in the little kitchen, cooking something that smelled like dirty tennis shoes. He shook Tony's hand, and the two of them fell into a friendly rapport talking about college basketball.

Mary handed me a knife and some sweet potatoes. "Slice these up round ways, and we'll fry them. It's not the healthy way to eat them, but they taste better."

After I started slicing, which Mary watched with a close eye, she began frying up some meat she called fatback. I'd heard the term before but had never actually seen it, much less eaten it. I wasn't even sure which part of the pig or cow it came from.

Jah started singing a song I'd heard Mary humming before. The words were Gullah, which meant I understood some of them, but others were a mystery. I didn't care. I sang with them, almost slicing my finger with the sweet potato knife. Tony looked at me like I was crazy, but I was having a good time.

The little kitchen was hot and steamy when we got done cooking. Like all of our ancestors who'd settled in this area, we took our plates outside where it was cool. There was music and laughter coming from the Peasant's Pub. I could see the look in Tony's eyes; he wanted to be there. I frowned at him and the look went away. It was great having that small amount of temporary power.

I ate almost everything on my plate. The collards tasted like they smelled, no matter how much vinegar I poured on them. The sweet potatoes were good. I hid the fatback in the grass behind the tree. I washed it down with sweet tea as the shadows began to settle around us.

I was getting a little nervous as it got dark. I was only supposed to be first watch. Where were Chase and Grigg? I wished for a cell phone, but nothing appeared. Tony and I were going to have to stay there until someone else showed up.

"I thought I smelled supper," Ham said, joining us.

"There's plenty left if you want some,"

Mary told him. "You'll have to get it though. I'm too comfortable to get up right now, and my belly is too full." She lit up her pipe as Jah and Tony lay back in the thick grass, talking about sports.

"I got something I need to talk about," Ham told her. "Come in with me for a minute. Help me slice up this watermelon."

He helped Mary get to her feet. There was a large age difference noticeable between them at that moment. He smiled down at her and opened the door into the kitchen. I watched them walk inside, the door swinging closed behind them.

I wished I'd brought some weaving with me. I remembered that I'd left the new basket I'd just started in the front of the shop. I didn't want Mary and Ham to think I was spying on them, so I walked around to get it from the front door.

The voices coming from the kitchen were low but insistent. I was drawn to the doorway without realizing it.

"Your girl told me about your plan," Ham said. "Where are you going now?"

"I'm not going anywhere. I don't know what Jessie told you." Mary smiled. "She's a good girl but kind of crazy."

She reached for the watermelon on the cabinet, and Ham put his hand over hers.

"Just because you have your boy now don't mean you don't need me."

"I didn't say it did. What's wrong with you tonight? You're acting kind of crazy yourself."

Ham paced what there was of a kitchen floor between the table and the back door. "I stayed with you. We stay together, no matter what, remember?"

"I told you, I'm not going anywhere. Jah is still at school. He'll visit when he can."

"I wish I could believe you."

Mary put her arms around her little brother. "You know I won't leave you. We've been through a lot together. There's nothing I wouldn't do for you."

I left at that point, sneaking back out the front door and around the back with Jah and Tony. I couldn't find my weaving, but it was too dark to see outside anyway.

There was fear and something else that scared me in Ham's eyes. He seemed obsessed about staying with his sister. I liked to be with Tony, but I'd never looked at him that way.

"There you are!" Chase's voice brought me to my feet. I ran and threw myself against him. "I guess we should be apart more often. What's wrong?"

"I don't know. Probably nothing. Have

you been spreading the word around the Village?"

"I wasn't sure we'd agreed on that plan. Wasn't there some question of Mary's safety?"

"What are you talking about?" Jah demanded. "Is my mother in danger?"

"Take it easy, guy." Grigg got between him and Chase. "Nobody is in any danger right now."

"It was a plan to trap your adopted father," I explained. "Detective Almond couldn't find him. We knew he was still here, because we found some of his stuff."

"Abraham would never hurt my father," Jah defended. "You need to look for another suspect."

"All of the pieces fit," Grigg argued. "Sometimes there's no understanding what makes a man go bad."

I glanced at the back door. Were Mary and Ham still arguing? I wished she'd come out so we could discuss this with her, too. After all, it was her life on the line if the plan worked.

Chase, Grigg, and Jah were arguing about the plan and about Abraham. Tony got up to confront me. "This is why you wanted me here? You thought I could take a bullet or something for your basket weaving friend?"

I barely heard him. That closed door bothered me. The look in Ham's eyes when I was spying on them in the kitchen bothered me, too. It didn't seem possible he could be involved in what happened to Joshua. Except that he wanted Mary to stay there with him. Joshua might've changed all that.

"Are you going to answer me or stare at that door all night?" Tony asked.

Ignoring him, I ran to the door and shoved it open. I called for Mary. There was no answer. There was no sign of either one of them.

"Is the watermelon in here?" Grigg asked. "I'd like a nice piece of that."

The watermelon was still on the counter, uncut. "I think someone took Mary."

He looked around. "She went mighty peaceably. No sign of a struggle."

"What's taking so long?" Chase joined us. "I have my pocketknife if we need it to cut the watermelon."

"Something's wrong," I told him. "Mary's gone. She was arguing with Ham. I can't explain it, but I think he might be the killer."

"So now my uncle killed my father?" Jah sounded as imperious as I'd expected. "Why don't you stop picking on my family?"

"Wasn't Ham attacked by the killer?" Tony raised an interesting point.

Grigg nodded. "I took that report myself. He was attacked by a hooded figure."

"We can't stand here and do nothing. If I'm right, Ham's taken her somewhere." I started walking toward the front door.

"What if you're wrong?" Chase called out after me.

"There's always vegetable justice." I shrugged. "We have to find Mary. I think he may have taken her to the smithy."

I ran out into the night, hoping I was wrong. What's a little embarrassment compared to finding out your brother is a killer? I could hear all the men coming up behind me: Grigg falling down the front stairs, Tony swearing as he ran into the Lady Fountain, Chase right beside me, and Jah sprinting like he ran five miles every day.

It seemed like a long way to the smithy. We met Roger coming back from Kellie's Kites. I didn't have the breath to tell him what was going on. I'm not sure when I'd run that far before, but it couldn't have been since high school.

Chase explained in a few words what we were doing. Roger joined us with an expression of anger on his broad face. Jah suddenly began to outdistance me, heading for the smithy, where lights still glowed from the open door.

Twenty-Three

Ham was standing at the forge, hitting a red-hot horseshoe with his hammer. He looked like he'd been there all night instead of only a few minutes. There was no sign of Mary.

"What's all the fuss?" He looked up at us.

Grigg and Roger were barely able to breathe, leaning against the doorway. Chase, Tony, and Jah were in better shape. I was somewhere in the middle. I could stand on my own, but talking was like wheezing.

"Where's Mary?" I demanded in a squeaky voice.

"I don't know." He smiled at Jah. "I left her in the kitchen when I remembered I'd left this waiting here for me. You know, the shoes need to be hot, but they can't be too hot."

"You see?" Jah stared at me. "This was stupid. I'm going back."

"Where is she then?" Roger was finally

able to move. "We didn't see her on the way here. She didn't just disappear."

"You know Mary." Ham nodded to me. "There's times when she just has to get off on her own. I don't hold her back."

"I'm sorry, Uncle," Jah apologized. "These people won't bother you anymore."

He gestured for all of us to leave, but Grigg was the only one who stepped outside. Roger wasn't taking no for an answer. Chase seemed uncertain, but he didn't move. Tony shrugged and followed Grigg outside.

The heat in the smithy was sweltering. My face turned as red as the coals in the forge. Ham kept banging at the horseshoe, apologizing, but explaining it had to be done.

"Stop doing that!" I didn't know exactly what I was listening for, but I knew I couldn't hear it with all that racket. He didn't stop, and I yelled it at him, "Stop hitting that horseshoe!"

"She's lost it," Tony said from the doorway. "Let's all head back to the pub."

"No!" I grabbed Chase's arm. "We can't leave without her. Make him stop."

I could tell Chase was divided. He didn't know what to think. But to his credit, he came down on my side of the fence. "Ham, would you mind stopping for just a minute?

Then we can all go home."

"I'd like to help you out, son, but this horseshoe is almost ruined. If I don't finish it now, it won't be usable. You know how Livy feels about waste."

Chase put his hand on Ham's shoulder. "Just for a minute. If it goes bad, I'll take the responsibility for it."

I didn't know if Ham was going to agree. There was a moment when he looked at Chase with the hammer in his hand and made me cringe. It would only take one hit from that instrument to cause terrible damage. How was I going to live with that guilt, especially if I was wrong?

But Ham put the hammer down on the forge and stepped back. He smiled at Chase, then took off running out the back of the smithy.

"What the hell?" Tony couldn't believe it.

"Where are we going now?" Grigg demanded before he took off after him.

Chase ran with him, but Jah stayed with me. "I don't believe this. He'd never hurt my mother."

"Listen." I stood still and tried to hear that scratching sound I'd heard earlier. With everyone silent, I heard it again. It sounded like it was coming from behind the storage panels. I ran to the first one and tried to open it. I looked up, and Tony was coming toward me with a crowbar.

"This is crazy," Jah complained. "This isn't happening. Nothing is behind there."

He was right about the first panel. There was only some old gloves and blacksmith aprons stored there. The second panel came off easily, and there was nothing behind it.

"You see?" Jah scoffed. "You ran my uncle away for nothing."

"Then why did he run?" Tony took the crowbar to the third panel.

The area behind the panels was a tight fit for the man who tumbled out as we removed the piece of wood. Abraham sprawled on the floor, covered in sawdust. He was alive but barely conscious. His fingernails were bloody from trying to escape from the storage area.

"Call 911," I yelled at Jah. He stood there, not moving. He looked unable to grasp what he saw. I hit him hard in the arm. "Call 911! Get some paramedics here right now!"

But instead of doing what I told him to do, he started tearing at the storage panels like a madman, finally understanding that his mother was probably behind one of them. The only hope I had at that moment was that Abraham was still alive. Ham didn't have time to do much to his sister.

Tony used the crowbar again and again to empty out the storage areas behind the panels, but there was no sign of Mary. Jah started screaming and fell on the floor.

She had to be here. I looked at the big pile of straw someone had almost tried to hide Ham in. He'd used that as a ruse before. Maybe he'd tried the same thing with her. He didn't have much time to hide her. He knew we'd come when we missed her.

I fell on the straw and started brushing it away. It only took a moment to see her face. She was roughly bound and gagged. Jah ran up to help me untie her and get her off the floor while Tony went to find a phone.

By the time we'd helped Mary out of the straw, Chase, Grigg, and Roger were back with Ham between them.

Ham was crying, sobbing hysterically. He was barely walking, held up by the three men. "I never meant to hurt you, Mary. I didn't want you to go back with Joshua and ruin both our lives. I didn't think about the police accusing you of killing Joshua. You know I'd never hurt you."

I sat down in the sawdust next to Jah, who was cradling his unconscious mother in his lap. The plan had worked after all . . . it had just worked on the wrong person.

■ ■ ■ ■

Mary and Abraham were fine, and Renaissance Faire Village recovered from the bad press it received. Ham confessed to the murder of his brother-in-law. Joshua had visited him before he'd gone to see Mary. Joshua had told him he wanted to bring his wife home and had accused Ham of keeping her away so long. Ham had only wanted things to go on as they had for the past ten years when he made the decision to kill the other man. He insisted he wouldn't have killed Mary, only kept her away until Jah had left.

The police accepted Mary and Roger's statement that they had been together in her apartment above Wicked Weaves when Joshua was killed. It wasn't something I liked to think about, but it was a good alibi.

I sat with Mary on the back steps at Wicked Weaves the morning I left to go back to my normal life. She was humming and working on a fanning basket that was rich with multicolors of tawny bulrush and rusty pine needles. It was a work of art as unique and beautiful as any painting in any museum.

"You done good," she commented on the

ten baskets I was taking home with me. "I didn't think you'd do it at the beginning. You surprised me, Jessie. A good surprise. I'm going to miss you."

"I'll miss you, too." I started to hug her, but her dark face said that wasn't allowed. "I'll be back next summer. Maybe I'll have a few more baskets and you can sell them for me."

She made a noise from the back of her throat that I took to mean, *No way*. I laughed and told her I was only joking. "Is Jah back at school?"

"Yeah. He left yesterday. But he'll be back, too. He said to tell you good-bye."

"I don't think he liked me very much."

"People never like folks who show them the hard truth about their lives. Finding out about Ham was a hard truth. I'm not giving up on him, either. The doctor says he can be well again. I'll wait."

I stood up to go, hoping to see Chase again. We'd said our good-byes last night and again this morning. I wanted to see his face one more time, but it didn't seem to be in the cards. It was probably just as well. I already missed him more than I should have. This was going to be a hard summer to put behind me.

Mary and I said good-bye, and I picked

up my backpack to leave. Roger, who'd become chummier in the past few weeks, said good-bye and told me he'd put my apprenticeship application on top of the pile. "Thanks. I think I'd be good at glass blowing."

Mary made that sound again. "Except instead of bleeding all over, you'd be full of burns. I don't think you're cut out to do anything that involves fire, Jessie girl."

I ignored her. I knew in my heart I was meant to be a glass blower. I was right about being a basket weaver. When you're determined enough, not even a lot of pain can stop you.

Epilogue

It was the end of October. The weather was getting colder, which meant I was scrambling for sweaters. After the warmth of the summer, the autumn winds were too chilly.

Debby was in my second-year history class. We'd been sharing lunches as well as reminiscing about the summer at Renaissance Faire Village. She was texting Fred the Red Dragon, ignoring my sage advice about leaving him behind.

I was going to meet her with a thermos of soup in my hand as I walked across the campus of USC-C. I was having trouble with my advice about Chase. I thought about him a thousand times a day. Myrtle Beach wasn't that far away. I could've driven down any weekend, but I held myself back. It would get better on its own.

There was a hint of rain in the air and piles of brown leaves on the ground. I walked across them, listening to them crunch under my feet. If I'd been a poet, I would've likened them to the brown crunchy thing my heart had become. I missed Chase. I wanted to be with him again. I wanted to forget my stupid rule about leaving the summer behind me. For the first time in five years, I wanted to wallow in my misery for the man I loved.

I heard someone call my name and turned, smiling. What I saw took my breath away and destroyed my thermos as it crashed on the sidewalk.

"How about lunch?" Chase was dressed in a black suit with a striped tie and a crisp white shirt. He was leaning against his shiny BMW as he opened the passenger door for me.

"What took you so long?"

YE VILLAGE CRIER

Greeting and salutations!

It is fall again and time for another Renaissance Faire Village newsletter! I had a great time learning to weave baskets with the help of master basket weaver Mary Shift. I created several of my own, wrought from sweetgrass, a plant that grows wild on the Southeast shore. It was a painful process, but I mastered it.

Basket weaving is the creation of any container made from vegetable fibers and formed into whatever shape you choose. It dates back at least 12,000 years, earlier than any pottery ever found. All of our ancestors, no matter where they were from, had basket weaving in common. They were used as tools of life: to carry eggs, fish, flowers, and bread. Baskets were even used as burial vessels.

Basket weavers like Mary Shift still gather many of their own materials. Supplies in some cases have grown short as development has displaced many native habitats. There are five types of basketry: coiled, as I learned this summer, uses primarily rushes and grasses; plaiting uses wider, flatter materials like palm or yucca; twining uses roots and tree bark to create baskets; wicker and splint, probably the best known, use reed, cane, and willow.

Basket weaving has never been duplicated. While many crafts can be made with machines today, baskets are still handmade. Most basket weaving techniques date back hundreds, if not thousands, of years and are still done much like they were by our ancestors.

My next apprenticeship at Renaissance Faire Village will be with Master Craftsman Roger Trent at his shop, the Glass Gryphon. Next summer, I'll learn to make glass art.

Jessie

LITTLE-KNOWN FACTS
OF THE RENAISSANCE

One question I am frequently asked by first-timers at Renaissance Faire Village: Why is there so much ale?

The answer to that lies in the Renaissance time itself. Most water was not filtered or purified, and many people bathed in it and let animals drink from it. What was left was used for the basest kind of sanitation. No one wanted to drink water and get sick.

So we at Renaissance Faire Village like to keep this tradition. Even the lowliest peasant could have small beer, a weak form of ale that probably tasted like warm dishwater. Full ale was only consumed at taverns and pubs with neighbors or on special occasions. Wine was only consumed by the wealthy lords and ladies.

Prosperous English peasants in the sixteenth century had a limited diet. They might eat two to three pounds of grain as bread or pottage, a few ounces of protein, and three pints of small beer per day.

The common grains to eat were rye, oats, and barley. There wasn't much wheat. Meats were expensive and usually only appeared at special feasts.

Eggs, cheese, and vegetables were common. The peasants used herbs, onions, leeks, and garlic to season their food. Cabbage, turnips, parsnips, peas, and beans were also staples of the kitchen.

Fruit was available but scarce and always cooked.

A pottage or pudding was common fare for both peasants and wealthy lords and ladies. It could be made with oatmeal, cracked barley, rye, or wheat. It would be cooked with milk, honey, currants, and spices, a little like our hot cereal today.

A peasant would have made this pottage his entire meal, maybe once or twice a day. For a lord or lady, this would have been a side dish, accompanied by meat.

The language of the Renaissance was colorful and different than our language is today. If you plan to visit a Renaissance faire, you might want to consider changing your language as many of the residents do.

If not, at least you will be able to understand them!

Yes — aye: "Aye, that is a juicy apple!"

No — Nay: "Nay, I do not want cheese."

You — thou or thee: "Thou art standing on my foot."

Listen — hark: "Hark! Methinks a cart is approaching."

Excuse me — I crave pardon: "I crave pardon for blundering onto your foot, sir."

Please — I pray you or pray: "I pray you be gentle with my turkey leg."

Wow or Cool! — marry! (A contraction of *by Saint Mary!*): "Marry! You handled that ax well, good sir!"

Good-bye — fare thee well: "Fare thee well, my lady!"

The knighting ceremony was held at the age of twenty-one for any young man who had been a good page or squire and was hosted by a lord for the position. Becoming a knight was an important matter, accompanied by a ceremony and vows for the young man and a party for the entire village.

A candidate for knighthood knelt all night in prayer before the ceremony to prove his worth. In the morning, following a religious ceremony, a knight's armor was buckled in place in front of whatever lords and ladies could be assembled. His sword was girded about his waist, and spurs were attached to his feet. He knelt to receive the pass upon his shoulder, which was dealt by his lord with the flat of his sword.

The ceremony was followed by jousts and other merriment to celebrate the occasion and test the new knight's skill and bravery. Afterward, the knight rode out in quest of adventure to slay some evildoer or rescue a damsel in distress. His family was blessed by his fortitude and waited breathlessly to hear tales of his shining good deeds.

YE OLDE RECIPE

BANBURY CAKES

These delicious little fruit-filled pastries were first mentioned in English text in 1586. They were originally sold in little baskets and wrapped in white cloths to keep them warm. The cakes have been made in Banbury since that time, inspiring poets to create sonnets for them. They are that good!

2 oz. butter, melted
4 oz. raisins
4 oz. currants
2 oz. mixed peel
4 oz. coarsely ground brown sugar
1 level teaspoon mixed spices
1 lb. puff pastry
Egg white
Caster sugar (powdered sugar)

Preheat oven to 425° F.
  Mix the melted butter, raisins, currants,

peel, sugar, and spices together in a bowl, combining well.

Roll out the pastry on a lightly floured surface and, using a saucer, cut into about 16 circles. Divide the fruit mixture evenly between them, then dampen the edges of the pastry circles and draw up into the center, sealing well. Turn over and, with the hands, gently form the cakes into ovals, then press down very gently with a rolling pin.

Make 3 diagonal cuts across the top of each cake, then brush with egg white and sprinkle with caster sugar. Place on lightly greased baking trays and bake for 15 to 20 minutes or until golden. Serve slightly warm.

MAKES ABOUT 16.